“*Steal Away* is one grand, good l
gifted writer draws you into the mysterious waters of betrayal and mercy. The characters feel like people you know—whose pains and joys you recognize within your own circle of friends. It’s a page-turner you won’t want to stop reading and never want to end. Happily, Hall’s protagonist, a newlywed female private investigator, promises to bring us many more fascinating cases—weaving faith and story with both beauty and grace.”—Jane Kirkpatrick, best-selling author of *A Name of Her Own*

“*Steal Away* is a fascinating puzzle. Linda Hall takes her readers through ever-deepening layers of story, doling out clues one tantalizing morsel at a time.”—DeAnna Julie Dodson, author of *In Honor Bound* and *To Grace Surrendered*

“What a clever, fun read! The characters are real, the story line original, and the emotional and spiritual complexities of life so true. Don’t miss *Steal Away*.”—Gayle Roper, author of *Autumn Dreams*, *Summer Shadows*, and *Spring Rain*

“Wow! With intriguing characters and mysteries within mysteries, *Steal Away* snared me on page one and wouldn’t let go till the end! Honest, forthright, and engaging.”—Lyn Cote, author of *Autumn’s Shadow*

“Linda Hall’s latest book captivates from the first page, and does not let go. Love, jealousy, greed, betrayal and redemption—a mystery within a mystery—*Steal Away* has it all!”—Lois Richer, author of *Tucker’s Bride* and *Inner Harbor*

“An intricate and masterfully woven tale of deceit and redemption! *Steal Away* kept me guessing, revealing its secrets at just the right moments. Highly recommended!”—Marlo Schalesky, author of *Cry Freedom* and *Freedom’s Shadow*

"From the very first line of *Steal Away,* I knew I wouldn't be able to put the book down until I'd turned the final page. Linda Hall brings a cast of memorable characters to life in this riveting story of choices, consequences, and second chances."—Carol Cox, author of *Aloha*

"I loved it! *Steal Away* is a finely crafted novel teeming with mystery and suspense—a great read."—Patricia Rushford, author of the Jennie McGrady and the Helen Bradley mystery series

STEAL AWAY

Teri Blake–Addison, P.I., Mystery Series
Book One

LINDA HALL

Multnomah Pulishers *Sisters, Oregon*

This is a work of fiction. The characters, incidents, and dialogues are products of the author's imagination and are not to be construed as real. Any resemblance to actual events or persons, living or dead, is entirely coincidental.

STEAL AWAY
published by Multnomah Publishers, Inc.

International Standard Book Number: 1-59052-072-6

Cover images by:
A & J Verkaik/Corbis
Darryl Torckler/Getty Images
Stock Newport/ImageState

Printed in the United States of America

For information:
MULTNOMAH PUBLISHERS, INC.
POST OFFICE BOX 1720
SISTERS, OREGON 97759

Library of Congress Cataloging-in-Publication Data
Hall, Linda, 1950–
Steal away / by Linda Hall.
p. cm.
ISBN 1-59052-072-6 (pbk.)
1. Absence and presumption of death--Fiction. 2. Private investigators--Maine--Fiction. 3. Spouses of clergy--Fiction. 4. Maine--Fiction. I. Title.
PS3558.A3698S74 2003
813' .54--dc21 2002156093

03 04 05 06 07 08 09—10 9 8 7 6 5 4 3 2 1

Dedicated to my sister, Janet Buffington

Acknowledgments

Thank you to the kind people on Grand Manan Island who showed my husband and me such hospitality on our trips there, and to Eric Allaby, Fundy Isles MLA for telling me all about Old Maid Rock, the hidden hazard at the bottom of the island which has tripped up many a boat.

There is no lighthouse built by a rich duke from Scotland anywhere on the island, but if there were, I envision it somewhere on the path between Southwest Head and Bradfords Pond.

Also, a special thanks to David Maier for sharing his expertise on handguns with me, showing me safe gun handling and taking me out to the range to actually shoot the handguns.

Thank you, Rod Morris, my editor at Multnomah, for teaching me to show and not tell.

And to Rik, thank you for supporting me through late night work sessions, for brainstorming with me, and for always being my first editor.

Prologue

It took her three days to dig the grave. Exhausting work, and made more so by the fact that it could be done only at night. She could not risk Audrey finding out. Better if she didn't know. Better if she lived the rest of her small life not knowing.

"She is gone. She's just gone," is what would be said to the child.

There was no coffin, no satin-lined casket, no memorial service broadcast on national television, no flowers; just a body wound in a new blanket and hidden behind the foundation stones at the back of the house. She had toyed with the idea of taking the body out to sea. There was a wooden dory pulled up on the shore below the cliff. At high tide she could heave it down to the water, place the body inside, and row out as far as she was able. But that presented its own set of problems. Could she manage to slide the body out of the boat without capsizing it? And what if the body, instead of sinking and burying itself in the layers of bottom mud, washed up on some distant shore, a product of these unpredictable tides and swirling currents? There would be fingerprints, hair and cloth fibers. There were things they could do now, things they could discover. DNA. She had no idea how these things worked, but she couldn't take the risk. There was Audrey to think about. No. Burial in the earth would be a comfort, she thought. No one deserves to die at sea.

The site she chose was a hundred feet up the hillside, protected by trees, and offered a view of the bay. She had walked the length of these, her woods, that bordered the craggy foggy cliffs, and all was sea swept and harsh, save for this one sheltered space. Flowers actually grew here in the summer, and the ground was pliable for digging.

Only once in all of those three nights had she thought she heard a scratching in the underbrush. She had turned, alarmed. But it was merely a deer who looked up at her.

"You will keep this a secret, will you not?" she said. The sound of her own voice startled her. These were the first words she had spoken aloud in many days. Even to Audrey.

The deer turned and bounded away.

At the end of each night's digging, her hands were blistered and raw, and sweat drizzled down her face despite the cold. When the hole was almost waist deep, the woman climbed out and shook off the dirt. But by now it had crusted in the folds of her skin, and she breathed it in through her nostrils with every breath and tasted it with every swallow. She wondered if she would ever forget that peculiar humid aroma of fresh earth.

Down at the cottage it was silent. Audrey would be asleep, her mouth opened, perhaps. She would be jerking a bit in dreams, calling out her unintelligible words. But Audrey was silent tonight, still, and the woman did not know if this boded ill or well.

She bent over the girl's bed, straightened the quilt around her, and with the corner of it swabbed a smear of drool that had settled on her chin.

"Dear sweet one, rest," she whispered. "Mama's here. Mama will always be here. Everything will be all right now." The girl whimpered, but did not waken. The woman closed the door soundlessly behind her.

It only remained to carry the body up the hill to the grave. The tide was in, and though she couldn't see the ocean, she heard it, a roar in her ears.

The stiffness had gone out of the corpse and it felt strangely light, as if no longer weighted down by soul and emotion and heart and will. There was a sweet odor about it, which caused the woman's eyes to water, whether from the smell of it or with tears, she couldn't tell. Perhaps both. She cradled the body like you would a child and carried it slowly up the path.

At the place between the trees, she stood for several moments and looked into the hole, considering. She laid the blanket-wrapped body on the ground and climbed into the grave, then she awkwardly pulled the body in after her. She laid it out at the bottom, straightened the limbs and folded the hands across the chest and covered the face with the blanket. Her movements were instinctive, her thoughts elsewhere. She was eight years old and she and her father were burying a dead bird that had flown into the picture window. She had cried then, and her father put his hand on her head and said it was okay. All things in God's timing. But she remembered the blue of the feathers, the way the wings folded forward and around the bird. Like a sparrow falling. A woman dead.

She climbed out, and began pushing shovelfuls of dirt onto the body, slowly at first, but then more quickly. By the time the gray light of morning was breaking over the sea, it was done.

She knelt for a long time and smoothed the grave over with her hands, smoothing, smoothing her garden. She spread leaves and moss and scrub brush over the top of it, working, raking the clods of earth through her fingers, until only the most astute observer would notice the seam where the earth had been peeled back.

Something should be said, she thought, some memorial, some service. She was openly crying now, sobbing as the magnitude of what she had done came to her. She flung herself across the top of the grave and wept.

My God, my God, why hast Thou forsaken me?

A long while later she rose, wiped her eyes with her dirt-scorched hands, and walked down the path to her house, the sea a pool of molten lead in front of her.

In the kitchen she stripped off her filthy clothing and stood naked on the stone floor, the muddy jeans and flannel shirt in a heap at her feet. She took a rag and drenched it in the cauldron of water on the back of the woodstove. She sopped it over her shoulders, her back, her neck, her face. Her movements were careful, slow, and she wept while she did this. For a long time she wept.

She unclipped, finally, the pins that held up her hair and lined them on the edge of the sink. She ran her hair, long, thick, and mostly gray, through her fingers. Clots of dirt and bits of branches fell to the floor. With the remainder of the water, she washed her hair, getting rid of the last stink of death and dirt. When it was clean she combed it, plaited it, and it hung in one long wet braid behind her back. This one act had sealed it for her. She realized that. She would cry no longer. This would be her life now.

And from this day forward she would mark her times and seasons by the rhythms of the tide and Audrey's rising and lying down. She would spend her days repairing the foundation of her house, poking in rocks and limbs to keep it from crumbling. She would climb to the top of the lighthouse and sit and look at the sea. She and Audrey would gather mussels and dig for clams at the edge of the water when the tide was low. They would fish in the pond behind the house. She would make bread from the flour, butter, and eggs that were delivered weekly from town.

In the spring she would plant flowers on the grave, and each fall the blossoms would die away to be covered by snow. And each spring she would plant them again.

This would be her life now.

1

Yes," Teri said to Jack on Saturday morning. "Carl Houseman really wants to meet with me. With us, actually."

"*Dr.* Carl Houseman?" Jack leaned forward in his easy chair and looked over the top of his *Fiddlehead Journal.*

"Well, I don't know if he's the same esteemed man of letters that you're referring to, but yes, someone named Carl Houseman is flying up to meet me—us—today." Teri was repotting houseplants that sat on the kitchen counter like soldiers in a row. She was digging around a small furry-leafed plant with a little trowel.

"From Philadelphia?"

"Yes, from Philadelphia."

"Dr. Carl Houseman from Philadelphia?"

"Yes, Dr. Carl Houseman from Philadelphia."

Jack closed the magazine and folded his hands on top of it. "Teri, do you have any idea who Dr. Carl Houseman from Philadelphia is?"

"Yes, I do, actually. He's a minister with a television program. I was able to get a couple of his books from the church library. I also looked at his website. Yes, I've done my research. I know who he is, and I've spent the better part of the last week skimming through his books."

"Teri, Carl Houseman is currently one of the most well-known Christian apologists and speakers. His books have sold in the millions."

"I know that. Yes."

"He isn't merely, as you say, a minister with a television program. His church service is broadcast internationally. His opinions are quoted by many. He's been on *Larry King.* He's been to the White House..."

Teri sighed. "I know that. Yes."

"And he wants to hire you?"

"I don't know why you seem so surprised. I'm a highly respected private investigator." The little furry plant was out of its container and would soon happily find a home in another, bigger one. "I need more potting soil," she said. "Remind me to put it on my list for today."

"Don't change the subject. How would he even have heard of you?"

"My reputation precedes me. You want some coffee?"

"Why would he want to hire you?"

"I'm having a cup of coffee. Shall I pour you one, dear?"

"You're changing the subject. If I want coffee I can get it myself. Why would he want to hire you?" Jack was in the kitchen now pouring two cups of coffee, black for himself and a hefty dollop of real cream for Teri.

"I already know why." She said it rather smugly.

"He told you?"

"He didn't have to. I have impeccable research methods. Okay, here it is. Carl Houseman's wife died five years ago, leaving Carl and four sons. The three oldest are married with children. Carl Jr., the eldest, works in the ministry office in Philadelphia, right next to Papa. I'd say he's being primed to take over. His wife's name is Mariana and they have three children; the oldest, a boy, is Carl Houseman III. Second son, Charles, or Charlie as he's known to family and friends, is a missionary in India. He and his wife have two children. Sam, the third son, is a youth minister in a rather large church in Colorado Springs. All of them are doing rather well. Papa and Mama, were she still alive, would be proud of them. It's the fourth son, Brent, the youngest, the baby of the bunch, the prodigal—he left home a year after his mother died." She added spoonfuls of soil to the bottom of a small pot.

"And?"

"He wants me to find him. And he will be hiring the perfect PI for the job since I know all about prodigals, having been one myself for a whole lot of years. I'm perfect for the job."

"And knowing you, you've already found him."

"His name is Brent Houseman. He's twenty-three years old, lives in Orange, New Jersey. He works at Pizza Hut where his fellow employees describe him as quiet and agreeable, but not opposed to a good party. He's currently living with a twenty-two-year-old waitress named Amanda Mast. He's known to enjoy the occasional beer, but really, his favorite foods are hamburgers and french fries.

"You're amazing."

"I know. One step ahead of your clients. That's my motto. That's why famous people hire me."

She grabbed a piece of paper towel off the roll and wiped her hands. She had repotted two of the furry-leafed little ones with the tiny purple and pink flowers. She had a couple of stripy leafy ones to go, plus a huge tree-like thingy with broad leaves that she would need Jack to help her repot. She collected houseplants like some people collect stamps, but unlike stamp collectors, she knew the names of none of them, nor their particular needs. Sunlight, soil, and water—hey, she'd say, that's what all plants need, right? But, curiously, they flourished in her care. Today in Bangor after the meeting, she'd get a couple of new pots and more potting soil. She started a list.

A week ago, a man with a deep voice and that distinctive Philadelphian accent had called her office, wanting to hire her to look into an extremely confidential and personal matter. "I'll be flying into Bangor next Saturday," he told her. "I'm scheduled to speak at a conference starting Sunday but would love to meet with you and your husband about this."

"My husband?"

"Yes, is he available?"

"I work alone, Dr. Houseman."

"Oh."

"I'm sorry; is there a problem?" The nerve of some men, especially these evangelist types with their antiquated ideas about women. Her husband? Well, if he wanted a man PI, why didn't he phone a man PI in the first place? She was about to say, "I'm sorry, Dr. Houseman; I don't think I'm the person you want for the job," when he said,

"I realize that came out wrong, but I have a lot of enemies out there. If someone saw me meeting alone with a private investigator, well, I don't even want to think what they would put together and come up with. Do you understand? If I'm meeting with a couple for dinner, no one would put two and two together and get five."

Oh. "We'd love to meet with you."

Dr. Carl Houseman was also, as Jack pointed out to her the afternoon after the phone call, one of the "good guys." His name had never been linked to any kind of scandal, his reputation never sullied. He had written more than a dozen books which had been described by reviewers as "thoughtful and insightful," and "honest and revealing." As well, he and his late wife had coauthored a couple of bestselling books on marriage and the family. Jack pointed out that his commentary on Jeremiah was one of the standard textbooks in seminaries now. In the past three days Teri had skimmed it. Bible commentaries weren't her regular reading material, but she found this one fascinating, which surprised her.

"Maybe I should go to seminary," she told Jack one evening. "I could be a minister. Would that surprise you?"

"Teri, if there's one thing I've learned in eight months of married bliss with you, it's that there's nothing you could do in this entire world that would surprise me."

In the afternoon they headed into Bangor, a shopping list of plant paraphernalia in Teri's shoulder bag.

Carl Houseman's plane was on time, and Teri immediately recognized him from the picture on his book jacket.

"Dr. Houseman," said Jack, extending his hand, surprised, hesitant. "I'm James Addison. It's a pleasure to meet you."

"And it's a pleasure to meet the two of you." He shook their hands in turn, and Teri thought he had what people in politics pay image consultants good money to get—presence, charisma. They were walking through the airport terminal and talking about flights and time schedules and airline food and how one gets tired of such things after a while.

"I know," Teri said. "I do a fair amount of flying with my work. It's nice to get those airline points, though."

When Dr. Houseman took a side trip into the men's room, Teri grabbed Jack's jacket. "See, it's him. The *real* Dr. Carl Houseman. I told you."

"You're right. I am truly humbled," Jack said. "The famous Christian evangelist and writer wants to hire us."

"Me, Jack. Me."

When Carl returned and his bag was collected, the three of them walked out into the sunshine of a crisp winter day.

"You can sit in the front, Dr. Houseman," Teri said at the car. "Jack'll drive and I'll sit in the back. I don't mind."

"No reason for that. I'll sit in the back. I insist on it. And please call me Carl."

He smiled and she melted. She knew he was more than ten years older than Jack and more than twenty years older than she was. But at fifty-nine, he was fit, handsome, and charming. No wonder he was so successful.

When they were finally in the car, Jack driving and Carl in the back, Jack said, "Do you have a place to stay tonight? Are we taking you anywhere after we eat?"

"I don't have anything booked. No one knows I'm here, actually. The conference doesn't start until tomorrow night. I was hoping you could direct me to a friendly hotel for the night."

"We can do better than that. Would you like to stay with us? We have a huge old house with plenty of rooms. That is, if you don't mind sharing your living space with a couple of old, friendly cats, a dog and a living room full of houseplants."

Teri sat back in her seat and visualized the place—newspapers all over the floor, dishes in the sink, litter boxes unattended to, bits of dog food all over the linoleum, flowerpots on the kitchen counter, potting soil scattered everywhere…

"If it's no imposition, I'd love that."

...guest room bed needing the sheets changed, carpets needing vacuuming, nothing in the fridge to eat...

"It's no imposition at all. We insist."

"Yes, we insist," Teri added.

When the three of them were seated at a back booth in a downtown restaurant, Carl Houseman told them he wanted to hire Teri concerning a very important person in his life.

Teri folded her arms across her chest and smiled.

"A person who used to be very important to me."

Teri smiled, turned to Jack, smiled some more.

"A member of my family."

Teri continued to smile.

"My wife."

Teri's smile faded. "Your wife?"

Jack saved her when he said, "You want Teri to find her? But the official reports at the time were pretty conclusive. There's no way she could've survived that storm."

What storm? Teri forced herself to look as if she knew exactly what Jack was talking about.

"You want me to find your wife?" she echoed.

"No. No, not find her. That's not it, exactly. I know all about the reports. It's something else." Carl pulled a thick manila folder from his briefcase and laid it on the table. "I've saved everything. It's all here—news reports, magazine articles, police and Coast Guard reports, photographs. The file is yours. If you decide to take the case, the file is yours."

Teri moved her fish and chips out of the way and opened the folder. At the top was a newspaper clipping, "Evangelist's wife dies in boating accident." She skimmed through the article. There had been an accident off the coast of Maine. High winds were to blame. A storm. Three women sailing. Two bodies found. Carl's wife not one of them. She looked up at him. "What exactly is it that you'd like me to do?"

From the bottom of the pile, Carl pulled out a card and handed it to her. It was an embossed ivory card with a full-color picture of a large old home. *The Fundy Tide Guest Home and Cottages, St. Andrews, New Brunswick* was scripted along the bottom.

"Open it," he said. "Read it. It's why I'm here. It's what I'd like you to do."

She opened up the card.

Dear Dr. Houseman,

I know it has been five years, and perhaps you don't need reminding, and you remain in our prayers always. We always enjoyed our yearly visits with Ellen. She was almost like a daughter to us. The reason for this card is that we have begun some renovations to the old cook shed (Ellen always said we should fix that part up!) and in the process we found one of her scrapbooks. (You know how she loved to keep scrapbooks!) Would you like us to send this one on to you now? We never miss your television program.

Alma and Ted

When Teri finished reading it, she looked up at Carl and saw a kind of pain behind his eyes. He was shaking his head. "I have no idea," he said, "who Alma and Ted are. No idea in the world. And scrapbooks? I don't know anything about any scrapbooks." His voice seemed to fade off. Finally, "I don't know what to make of this. I've never been to this place..."

"Did you call these people about it?" Jack asked.

"No, I didn't. Sometimes I feel I have to be careful. Maybe this is a joke. A prank..." He paused. "What I did do was go through all the sympathy cards. I read through each one again." He blinked several times and reached into his pocket. "I found this." He handed Teri another card. It was your standard-fare flower-embossed sympathy card and on the inside, *We are so deeply grieved. Ellen was one of our favorite people. Ted and Alma Ferguson and family.*

"This card didn't stand out in any particular way at the time. I got so many cards from people I didn't know. When you go through something like this… From time to time I'd go through all the sympathy cards. I never noticed this one before."

Teri looked at Jack. His gaze was steady.

"I looked up this guest house on the web. I wrote the address down." Carl handed them a three-by-five card. He wasn't wearing a wedding ring, Teri noticed. "And the place looks nice enough. It's even listed in the New Brunswick Bed-and-Breakfast Guide. The way I see it is this, either this is some sort of mistake or joke, or that my wife had…friends."

Teri turned the sympathy card over. A dollar store card. Ninety-nine cents. "What is it you want me to do?"

"I'd like you to go up there and get this scrapbook for me. And…"

Teri waited. In her line of work she had trained herself to wait without comment.

"…find out who these people are."

"Dr. Houseman, could these people be friends from before you knew her? Maybe the yearly visits were from when she was younger? The explanation is probably very simple."

He was shaking his head. "I don't think so." He picked up his coffee and stared into it and said again, more quietly this time, "I don't think so."

While the waitress cleared their plates, plunked down dessert menus and poured fresh coffees, Teri and Jack skimmed through the folder. News articles, police reports, Coast Guard reports. At the very bottom was a five-by-seven color photo of Ellen Houseman. Blond hair coifed and gently curling toward her cheeks, gold earrings, expensive pastel blue suit, and a brightly colored scarf. She looked like an ad for Mary Kay cosmetics.

"She was a very beautiful woman," Teri said.

"Yes, she was. Beautiful, quiet, mysterious, forthright, a true helpmeet."

Teri held up a news clipping from the Bangor paper which described her as a sailor and lover of the sea.

Ellen had raced sailing dinghies since she was a child, Carl told them. They learned that Ellen was a certified scuba instructor and had her boat captain's license.

"And I can't stand boating," he said. "I get seasick at the slightest provocation. I have to take medication every time I even board an airplane."

Ellen had owned a sailboat, he told them, and once a year she would head up to Maine by herself and sail for a few weeks. "It was expected of Ellen to go home to Maine once a year. I never begrudged her that time."

"So, what you want is for me to retrieve this scrapbook and find out who Alma and Ted are?"

He nodded.

"But you gave me all this other information."

"I know. I'm hoping it'll help you to understand what kind of a person she was."

Later, when they were in the car heading home, Teri said, "I'm just curious—how did you hear about me?"

"Your website. There were a number of things on yours that I liked. For one, you're a woman. I thought maybe you might have an understanding from the woman's point of view. Plus, you're located near where the accident occurred. Your website also says that you're a Christian, you specialize in finding people, and you promise absolutely confidential service. All of those things impressed me. Plus your smile. In your picture you looked kind."

2

Carl Houseman didn't seem to mind the two hungry cats who purred and meowed around their ankles and a big springer spaniel who regarded him from the corner. "Wait a minute, guys," Jack said. "Let us at least get inside. Give me a minute to get the can opener." The cats, Tiger and Gilligan, were Jack's and had come with the house when Teri moved in. Kelly, the dog, was Teri's and had come, not altogether enthusiastically, into the relationship. We're a regular Brady Bunch, Teri was fond of telling people.

In the living room she hastily gathered armloads of newspapers from the floor and kicked a true-crime paperback she was reading under the couch, wishing they had more Christian books lying around.

"You have to excuse the mess," Teri said. "Have a seat. That seat over there. Just throw that magazine on the coffee table. Saturday's our day for cleaning. Sorry we're not organized." A couple of Jack's grad students had been over the previous evening, and the kitchen garbage was stuffed with pizza boxes.

She took an armload of papers to the garage to take to her office. She subscribed to four of them, so there were always newspapers all over the living room floor, in various stages of being read, cut up for filing, or torn apart by animals.

Prior to going into business for herself, Teri had worked both as a cop and a researcher. Her police work was with the Maine State Police where after nine years she quit after a particularly grueling case left her rattled. Her next job was as a part-time researcher on an Internet missing persons registry, which she thoroughly enjoyed. When that dot-com site was bought by shareholders and expanded, Teri didn't want to work as a full-time employee, so she quit. She worked for a short time as a research assistant at the university, which was where she met Jack. When that project was finished she put an ad in the paper—*Looking for someone? I can help*—an ad that still ran weekly in five major newspapers. The work was interesting and fun, and usually she juggled two or three cases at the same time. She loved surfing the Internet, searching through dusty microfilms of newspapers down at the library, traveling (her suitcase was always ready to go and her passport current), and talking to people. Especially talking to people.

When she came back to the living room, Carl was sitting in an armchair by the unlit fireplace, reading a *New Yorker*, a cat on his lap.

"Just throw him off," Teri said.

"I don't mind cats," he said.

"Gilligan can get to be a nuisance."

"If he bothers me I'll shoo him away. You have a lovely house here, Teri."

She looked around absently. "Oh, thanks. It's big, that's for sure. Too big. We're moving soon."

"Oh? Where?"

"Same town, just something smaller." Something ours, she wanted to add.

In the kitchen, Jack poured three ice waters, and Teri began unloading the dishes from the dishwasher, placing the glasses and coffee mugs face up in the cupboard, the way she had all her life. Jack always placed the cups and mugs in the cupboard bottoms up. Teri said that way, germs on the shelves embedded themselves in the lip where you drank from. Leave the cups open side up and you're just inviting airborne germs to land inside, is what he always said.

Teri still kept her apartment in downtown Bangor and used it as an office, even though Jack was encouraging her to give it up. "This house has plenty of rooms. We could set one up as a home office. It would save on the expense."

"I like it there," she always said. "I'm used to it and I pay my own way." What she never told him was that this house—this old house where the cups were lined up in the cupboard the wrong way and all the rooms were filled with floral drapes, floral couches, floral rugs, floral wallpaper, floral everything—just had, well, too many ghosts. She would be glad when they were in their own place.

"This place is such a mess," Teri whispered as they loaded last night's pizza dishes into the dishwasher. "I can't believe we have this famous person in our living room and our kitchen looks like this."

Jack whispered back, "It's not that bad. He seems like a down-to-earth sort, anyway."

"You finish here. I'll go change the sheets in the guest room," she said.

Later that afternoon, Teri and Jack gave Carl a guided tour of their little part of Maine. They insisted he sit in the front this time while they drove through the university grounds and along the river. Then Carl asked that if it wasn't too much trouble, and if it wasn't too far, would they mind driving down to the coast. He really wanted to see the coast, he said.

"It's a nice day for a drive," Jack said.

"At least there's no snow," Teri added.

They followed the winding road next to the Penobscot River down toward the water. It was a glorious day, windy and full of sun. In the front seat Carl followed their progress on a map.

"Ellen used to come here," he said. "I haven't been back here since the accident. I came up then, of course, but I've not been back since. She kept her boat at a place called Belfast. I regret now that I didn't come with her more. That I didn't make the effort. Didn't even try to make the effort. Are we very close to Belfast? Ellen grew up near there."

"Not far," Jack said. "We can go there if you'd like."

Teri leaned forward in her seat. "What kind of a boat did she have?"

"An Alberg 29, a good, sturdy boat. Or so I'm told. I was only on it a handful of times. Sometimes Ellen would drag me up here, and I'd get on the boat, sit in the corner, life jacket tightly fastened, and be throwing up over the side practically before we were out of the harbor. It was not a pretty sight." He laughed, but there was sadness there. Teri looked at the back of his head, the way he bent forward to look at a place on his hands.

Eventually they reached Belfast, and Jack drove down toward the waterfront.

"That's the place," Carl said. "That's where she kept her boat." He rolled down the window and looked toward the wharf. "I remember this."

Jack pulled into the parking area, and the three made their way down toward the wharf. Jack took Teri's hand as Carl tried to remember the last time he was here. Carl regretted that he'd not paid closer attention. There was so much he wished he'd paid closer attention to. Such memories it was bringing back, he was saying. All of this. The docks. The way it smelled out here. The freshness of the air.

It was January. Christmas had been two weeks ago and there were only a few boats in the water. Most were on land, supported by boat stands and shrink-wrapped in white or blue.

At the end of the wharf the three of them looked out into the cold harbor, and Jack asked Carl where he and Ellen met. Jack's arm was around Teri now, and she leaned into him, breathed the familiar smell of him while a cold wind whipped at them. It was still amazing to her that at age thirty-six she had found love for the first time in her life. She who had thought she would never get married, had, in fact, given it little thought, was now the wife of a lettered professor of English literature.

"We were both so young," Carl said. "I was only twenty when we met, and she was seventeen. It was between my second and third years of Bible college, and I was working at a summer camp in New York. Ellen was there. She was the lifeguard, and also taught swimming and sailing. We met the first day of camp…or, no, I shouldn't say we met. I should say that I noticed her the first day. Long blond hair, tan. Always a smile on her face. Strong, athletic. And I'd sit on the beach and watch her during my hours off. She was so good with the kids. When she offered to take me sailing, I jumped at the chance. Now, I had never, I don't think, ever even been in a boat in all of my short life, but being a twenty-year-old guy, there was no way I was going to admit that I was scared to death." He chuckled.

"So we sailed, and by the end of the summer I had convinced myself that I almost liked it, but I didn't need to convince myself that I was in love. We married three summers later, and Carl junior was born a year after that. So long ago. A life time ago."

"You miss her," Jack said tightening his arm around Teri.

"There's not a day goes by," he said.

They were heading back to the car now, their feet clacking on the boards.

"Hey!" A stubby man in paint-covered overalls was ambling toward them. "Hey."

The three stopped and looked at him, but he was peering at Carl. "Don't I know you?" And it got Teri wondering just how often this sort of thing happened to him. Carl took of his sunglasses and the man said, "Yes! I thought I knew you. You're him. I recognize you from your picture. You're him."

Carl smiled.

"Ellen's husband! You're Ellen's husband, aren't you?"

Carl chuckled. "Yes, I guess I am."

The man put out a paint-flecked hand and said, "It's a pleasure to meet you. Hey, Janey," he called to a woman on the shore. "Come 'ere. This here's Ellen's husband." Then back to Carl. "I'm Fred, by the way, Fred Goodkins. I used to take care of her boat. Sailed it, too. She never minded, especially when she only used it a couple weeks out of the year."

The woman, also wearing loose paint-covered pants, wiped her hands on a rag and walked toward them.

"Jane Jarvis," she said. "But I won't shake your hand. We've been painting the inside of the shack."

Teri made a mental note of the names. Fred Goodkins. Jane Jarvis.

"We felt some terrible when Ellen…when we heard about that accident," Fred added. "It was just such a freak thing. She was too fine a sailor for that. She knew these waters like the back of her hand. Still can't understand it." He was shaking his head.

"I have to tell you that practically every week someone around here says, 'Wasn't that a shame about Ellen and Moira and Cheryl.'" Jane said.

"She was a fine woman," Carl said.

Later, when they were seated in a café in Belfast eating lobster chowder, Teri asked, "Why did she keep her boat in Maine when you lived in Philadelphia? Weren't there closer places she could've kept it?"

"She grew up here. She always said that the best sailing in the world was along the coast of Maine." Carl looked away from them.

"I hope this isn't too painful for you," Jack said. "Opening all this up again."

"I'm prepared for it," he said, turning back to them. "It's something I need to do. I have to make peace with the past before I can move on." He looked down at his chowder without saying anything. Then, finally, "I'm getting married again."

"Congratulations," Jack said. But Teri only stared at him. At both of them.

3

The woman adjusted her reading glasses, wrote one word on the top of the first page of the empty notebook, and stared down at it. The wind blew a sudden gust against the small window in the lighthouse where she sat, and she wondered if it would shatter. And if it did, was there a board that size that she could nail up here? She put her pen down. Audrey was sitting cross-legged on the floor lining up pieces of firewood of different sizes into perfect order, her hair clean and glinting yellow in the candlelight.

Later the woman would warm them some milk, and they would sit in the kitchen by the woodstove and drink it together from chipped white mugs. Much later she would put Audrey to bed, and then settle herself beside the woodstove and lose herself in a book.

The two of them had spent the day chopping and stacking wood—she chopping, Audrey stacking, carrying one piece at a time to the woodshed, waving it in the air on her way and singing to herself. The woman had patiently showed her how to carry more than one, a whole stack if you held your arms out together, palms up. But Audrey needed to carry the long, fat ones first. They had to go on the bottom, followed by the medium-sized ones. The smallest ones lay on the top. Theirs was the most orderly wood pile on the whole of the island.

"Mam-mam-mam," Audrey was vocalizing, lining up the wood.

"Hey Audrey."

"Mam-mam-mam."

The top floor of the tiny lighthouse, where they now sat, was accessible by a set of steep wooden steps which led from the front room of the house. A tiny triangular window offered a view of the real lighthouse, Southwest Head. Her lighthouse was not a real one. All it was was a glorified summer home built in the nineteenth century with a turret designed to look like a lighthouse. Will had told her the whole story. Fitting, she thought, that she should live out her days in a phony lighthouse.

The candle on the table flickered again. When she was a little girl, her friend's mother used to say that a flickering candle meant a ghost was nearby. But in all the years she had lived here she had seen no ghosts, heard no ghosts. Still, the townspeople said there were ghosts all over the island, but especially here, especially in the old stone house. Will said that someone was murdered in here, a woman, and whenever the wind came from the northeast, she wandered through the rooms.

The woman looked out of the tiny smudgy pane and thought about the grave on the hillside. If there was a ghost, she would know about it. She would be the one who would know about it.

Earlier that day the boy from the Save Easy had driven in with a load of groceries. She had stayed near the woodpile, while Audrey helped him carry them in. She didn't acknowledge him, didn't even say hello. Just the crazy old lady, he would tell his friends later, the crazy old witch-lady and her retard of a daughter. They would have a good laugh about it. He might even embellish the tale, have her, witch that she was known to be, chase him off her land with a shotgun, her broomstick, or an evil eye. Oh, she was well-known on the island. Everyone knew her. She was famous.

After the wood was stacked, she had washed Audrey's hair, a twice-weekly ritual that the girl hated. The woman would undo her hair from the two ponytails, brush it out, then leaning over the sink she'd pour pitchers full of warm water on it, then suds it up with cheap shampoo. Audrey would shriek and shake, her thin body shuddering. Her hair was long and thick and such an extraordinary deep mustard gold that it looked as if it could not possibly be natural. When she brushed it she thought of the dolls in her childhood, a Betsy Wetsy with real hair that you could comb. Hair golden, like Audrey's.

The candle flickered again, and the woman moved it away from the window. She had come up here intending to begin the true account of what had brought her here, the reason she was compelled to stay. The reason she had no choice. She chewed thoughtfully on the end of her pen and stared down at the word centered across the top of the page: *Betrayal.*

4

With the advance money from Carl Houseman, Teri went shopping. She bought a ream of printer paper, three different colored highlighter pens and tape flags, plus a package of 0.5 mm lead for her favorite mechanical pencils. She never used pens. Ink had the bad habit of freezing in the winter, and since a lot of her writing was done sitting inside cold cars or standing outside wearing her hooded parka and finger-flap mittens, she used pencils. At a military surplus store, she bought a new pocket notebook. She kept a separate notebook for each client, and she liked the hard-backed field notebooks favored by the military.

As she drove down I-95 toward her Bangor office, she thought that this new job had come at just the right time. One week ago she had reunited a twenty-seven-year-old yuppie lawyer with his forty-five-year-old birth mother, a never-married commercial artist living in Chicago. Along with his final check, the young lawyer had written a glowing letter of thanks. He and his mother were getting along famously and were even planning a cruise together to Bermuda in the new year. "Hope you're still speaking to each other after your cruise," Teri muttered, depositing his final check into her account. She'd been in this business long enough to know that reunion fantasies seldom lived up to reality.

There was a hint of snow in the air when she parked her Honda Civic in its usual place behind the bagel shop, a parking space she didn't give up when she moved in with Jack. She hefted her leather shoulder bag and locked the car behind her.

"Hey, Teri," a familiar voice called as she stepped inside.

"Cold out," she said.

"Snow," he said. "They're predicting it for all up and down the coast."

"'Bout time I guess."

"Yeah, we didn't have a white Christmas, guess we were in for some sooner or later. It's this whole global warming thing."

"Thought that was supposed to make things warmer, not colder." She blew on her fingers. "Give me a large coffee—"

"Double cream."

"You know me too well, Lou."

"So, how's married life treating you these days?"

"Just fine."

"I can't entice you to divorce him and marry me?"

"Not today, Lou."

"Rats."

She also ordered a toasted blueberry bagel with cherry cream cheese. She carried them plus her computer in her satchel up the back stairs to her office, and once inside she turned up the thermostat. Then she dumped the contents of her bag onto the table in the kitchenette and drank the coffee.

She had made two photocopies of everything that Carl had given her. The spare photocopy was kept at home, and this one, her working file, would be the one she would read, study, highlight, and make notes all over. The originals went into the fireproof safe in her office.

Her computer up and running, she opened her database and munched on her bagel while she created a new file. She leaned back in her chair and considered what to call it. Even though her iBook was password protected (not that that would ever keep out serious hackers), as an added means of protection, she gave her working files circuitous names only she would recognize. It was a sailing accident. A shipwreck. High waves. Wavy hair. Hair cut. Cut throat. She leaned forward and typed *Cut Throat* as her file name. Now, forever afterward, Carl's case would be called Cut Throat.

She always put her case notes in a database so she could easily rearrange things and call up items she wanted to bring to the top. She brushed a few bagel crumbs off her keyboard and remembered those rules when she was back in high school—no drinks and no eating in the computer labs. She knew that if you took the keyboard out of her iBook it would be embarrassingly full of bagel crumbs. Once she had even spilled half her coffee onto the keyboard. She dried it off and took it in to the computer guy, who said they got a lot of those. He spent fifteen minutes cleaning it, handed it back to her, and it had run fine ever since.

She put the photocopied reports and articles in a kind of chronological order. By the end of the day they would be highlighted and tape-flagged, and Cut Throat would be an empty file no longer. Items highlighted and tape-flagged in pink were possible points of interest, blue was for names, and yellow meant vitally important. A yellow highlighted passage along with a yellow tape flag meant to drop everything else and get to this pronto.

She highlighted Ted and Alma's name in blue on the photocopy she had made of their card and typed their names and address into her database. She called the number of their bed-and-breakfast, but the phone rang and rang. She hung up and dialed again. Again, no answer. *How can people not have voice mail? Especially people who run businesses?*

Her reports in chronological order, she read through them. Ellen Houseman was fifty-one when she and two other women, Moira Neddick and Moira's niece Cheryl Ryder, left the Belfast Marina, August 8, 1998, on her twenty-nine foot Alberg sailboat, *Beloved.* The *Bangor Daily News* described Ellen as an experienced sailor who sailed every summer, often single-handed, and had raced small boats in her youth. Teri tapped her pencil on the article.

It had been a clear day when the three left Maine. They were on a course toward Nova Scotia, arriving in Yarmouth on August 14. Moira's husband, Frank, had flown up from Boston to join them for four days. He later described the women as happy and content. They had experienced clear weather, and Cheryl, an amateur photographer, had been taking many photos along the coast. After five days the women sailed down the coast of Nova Scotia and headed over to Grand Manan Island on the final leg of their trip. On August 20, they "limped into Grand Harbour" (according to the article) with engine trouble. They stayed on Grand Manan tied up to a fishing boat for three days, making repairs to the engine and reprovisioning the boat. Ellen and a fisherman named Earl Wood looked at the diesel engine, and the two of them replaced a faulty impeller and cleaned and bled the injectors.

The night before they left, the trio ate supper at a café called the Coffee Perk with two other sailors, a couple named John and Pat Gibson, who had sailed their 42-foot steel sailboat over from England. The Gibsons were planning on staying on Grand Manan an extra day, and the group made plans to meet again at Rocque Island, Maine. They described Ellen as anxious that she had stayed away from her work too long, and needing to get back to her family. The repairs had taken longer than anticipated.

The following morning, the three women headed south in twenty-knot winds, which were gusting to thirty. An uncomfortable sail, but nothing that the boat and experienced crew couldn't handle.

Four days later, fishermen aboard the *Debby Jane* spotted a life-jacketed body floating off Southwest Head, Grand Manan. The body they fished out of the water had been dead for at least two days and was identified as Moira Neddick. The United States and Canadian Coast Guards and the Royal Canadian Mounted Police were immediately dispatched. The following day another life-jacketed body, that of Cheryl Ryder, was discovered floating up the west coast of Grand Manan. Both women had died from hypothermia. A third life jacket, belonging to Ellen Houseman, was picked up near where the bodies were found. Despite a massive search, Ellen's body was never recovered.

The accident was reported in the Bangor newspapers and a number of other papers in New England, plus it received national coverage in *USA Today* and *People.* The Sunday following her death, Carl's weekly television program was dedicated to the memory of his wife, with clips of their early life together. Teri highlighted this in pink. It might prove useful at some point to watch this video.

She called Alma and Ted's guest home again, but there was still no answer. As soon as she hung up, the phone rang.

It was Jack.

The first thing she said was, "Do you believe there are people who don't have answering machines? Who doesn't have an answering machine in today's world? Tell me that."

"Well, hello to you, too!"

"I'm sorry, my frustration is showing. I've been trying all morning to get a hold of these Ted and Alma people and their phone just rings and rings."

"Maybe they're not home."

"Oh, duh. Ya think?"

"We could always just go there."

"You and me together?"

"I was thinking how about next weekend? It might be nice to get away. We can leave Friday afternoon and get back Sunday afternoon. I can get Stephan or Peter or one of my other students to look after the animals."

"If I ever get a hold of these people I'll see if I can make reservations."

"We could always take our chances. I'm sure there's some motel that's open. We could drive up and take it as it comes."

"Whoa, that's rather daring for a staid academic person such as the man I married."

"I'm not all that staid, darlin'."

"And don't I know it."

"You want to take a break?"

"I just got started."

"I was thinking about lunch. Can you be persuaded?"

"I can be persuaded. You coming into Bangor for some reason?"

"No, they're having Chinese buffet at the Faculty Club. I've got a class this afternoon anyway."

"You want me to drive all the way back? I just got here."

"It was a thought."

Teri sighed. "I'd love to see you, but I can't drop everything. I wanted to get a good start on this today."

"You see, Teri, love, if you'd take my advice and move your office to one of our empty bedrooms, you'd be that much closer, plus not to mention the money we'd save."

"I like my office."

"I know. I'm sorry. It was just a thought."

"I'll see you at supper."

After the phone call, Teri felt mildly disconcerted, restless. She went downstairs and bought herself another coffee, took it upstairs and paced around her office drinking it down. Through the thin walls, she could hear the neighbors arguing, a sound she often went to sleep to back in the days when she lived here by herself, a sound that made Kelly whimper and nose at the floorboards. She tried Ted and Alma a few more times. Still no answer.

At noon she went downstairs and got herself a bean sprout sandwich on a pita and ate it grumpily by herself at a table beside the window. If she wasn't so stubborn she'd be eating Chinese food at the faculty club with her husband now. Back upstairs she put Bonnie Raitt in her CD player and started what she called her Extreme Search. After a thorough web search she'd drive to the library and go through old microfilms of newspapers. Sometimes her Extreme Search involved traveling to other cities and digging through more records. It wasn't until after her Extreme Search was finished that she would begin the talking to people part. If they were going up on the weekend to see Ted and Alma, she'd better get started now.

At the end of the afternoon she had read everything Carl had given her, plus every available reference to the accident on every available search engine on the Internet. She even hacked her way into the police site using her old password. And after all of it, certain facts remained a mystery, and the inquest shed no light on them:

1. Why was there no Mayday call? The last radio contact the trio had was the day they left the harbor. Moira had talked to a Grand Manan fisherman, Bud Williams, who asked how their engine was working, and Moira said that everything seemed to be working perfectly. And since the wind was surprisingly in their favor, they didn't think they'd have to use the engine much. They

said they were making good time, six knots on a straight steady course. The youngest member of the crew was suffering with a bout of seasickness, but that was the extent of their problems. He told them to dig out the ginger pills, and they both laughed.

2. Why was Ellen Houseman not wearing her life jacket? Ellen was known for her safety consciousness, and according to those who had sailed with her, in any kind of a blow she wore her life jacket and tethered herself to the boat and demanded that all crew on deck do likewise.
3. Why did they not deploy their life raft or EPIRB? The boat was fully equipped for offshore cruising with a life raft and EPIRB (emergency position-indicating radio beacon), which when deployed would emit a signal to satellites which would relay the signal to land-based stations which would notify the Coast Guard. Neither the life raft nor the EPIRB were ever found.
4. And finally, where was the boat? Only a few cushions had washed ashore, but nothing of its structure, its mast and sails and provisions. Not even a cooler was found floating.

Theories abounded—everything from a lightning strike (lightning was reported in the area) to a rogue wave at the mouth of the Grand Manan Channel to a "Bermuda Triangle" off the coast of Grand Manan. It was this last theory that generated the liveliest debate as sailors recounted past stories of lost ships and wrecks and ghosts off the island.

Just before it was time to leave for the day, she called Ted and Alma again. After five rings it was answered. Teri explained who she was and made reservations for two for the weekend.

5

You're awfully quiet," Teri said to Jack on Friday as they drove northward along the coast to St. Andrews and the Fundy Tide Guest Home and Cottages.

"Thinking," he said.

"About what?"

He was quiet for a while and then he said, "Wreaths."

"Wreaths?"

"Every single house we've driven past has a wreath on the front door. Have you noticed that? Every single house."

"Jack, it's Christmas. People put wreaths on their doors at Christmas."

"Christmas is over. But it's not just Christmas, not around here. You drive through here in the summer and it's the same. Wreaths. On every door. In the spring you have your pastel-colored wreaths decorated with spring flowers. In the summer those same wreaths are twined with summer blossoms, and then in the fall it's autumn colors, pumpkins and such."

"Twined. What kind of a word is twined?"

"Entwined. Like rope. Twine."

"Boy, am I glad I married an English professor. I get to use words like twined in normal conversation."

He reached over and took her hand and placed it on his knee, held it there for a while. "I'm glad I married you," he said. "I wasn't really thinking about wreaths."

"I didn't think so."

"I overheard what Verna Plant said to you on Sunday." He was playing with her fingers.

"I try not to let those kinds of things bother me."

"It bothers me, though." He held her hand tightly. She wouldn't have been able to pull it away even if she had wanted to. Which she didn't. "You don't have to be on that committee."

Teri said, "Why do I feel this coldness every time I'm around some of them? Like I'm at the bottom of the food chain or something. I just don't get it."

Jack looked at the road thoughtfully for a couple of minutes, then, "I know this isn't something you and I talk about a lot. But I think it's partly to do with the fact that Jenny and Verna had this special—I don't know—bond." He turned to her. "You knew that Verna's daughter and Jenny had the same kind of cancer?"

Teri nodded.

"And that they were about the same age when they died?"

Teri nodded again.

"It's nice that they do this every year in her memory. Maybe it helps someone else out, but I'm not involved anymore; did you notice that? And you don't need to be either."

"Thank you."

They were quiet after that. Jack went back to concentrating on the road, and Teri went back to the thick Ellen Houseman file on her lap. But she was thinking about Jenny. Jenny, Jack's first wife, died of cancer four years ago, and there were people in their church who had the odd and completely irrational belief that Jack shouldn't have married again, that four years was way too soon. And not to someone like Teri. Especially not to someone like Teri. Jenny was a kindergarten teacher wonderfully beloved by all children and parents. Jenny also volunteered at the seniors' home and taught them how to paint. Jenny crocheted lap throws for them and wrote poetry that the church secretary still printed sometimes on the back of church bulletins. And when Jenny got sick everyone prayed that she would get better. Everyone was so sure that there was going to be this great and grand miracle, because there was no one more deserving of a miracle than perfect, sainted Jenny. When that didn't happen and she died, a university scholarship was set up in her name for young women in their church who were going into home economics or early childhood education. Jack had always been the major contributor to the scholarship—and Teri had no problem with that—but funds were also raised by the Ladies' Missionary Society of which Verna Plant was the president, and this group had asked Teri to serve on the fund-raising committee. When Teri had said no, she didn't think so, Verna had said something like—Teri couldn't recall her exact words; it wasn't a conversation she particularly cared to remember—everyone still missed Jenny so much (did that include Jack?), and what an example she was to the young women (meaning Teri wasn't), and how tirelessly she volunteered in the church (meaning Teri didn't), and how much we all (meaning Teri) could learn from Jenny's life.

Teri looked out the window. Sometimes it amused her to think that when Jenny was teaching seniors how to paint ceramic leprechauns down at the nursing home, Teri was dressed up as a prostitute working undercover on mean streets.

After a little while she looked over at her husband. "Jack?"

"Yes?"

"Were you really ready to get married after four years?"

"Oh yeah."

"Are you glad you married me?"

"Oh yeah." She liked the way his eyes crinkled up at the sides when he grinned.

"Even though I make fun of your classical music?"

"Even though."

"Even though I read true crime?"

"Even though."

"And even though the only Jane Austen I ever read was Cliffs Notes in high school?"

"Now you're pushing it." Then he said, "And how about you, Teri? Are you coping being married to an old man like me?"

"Oh yeah."

They stopped for lunch in a roadside fish and chips place, and when they were back in the car, Teri again began going through the thick

Cut Throat file on her lap. It was now four days since Teri had begun her Extreme Search. This was work she loved: this snooping around in other people's business, rooting through strangers' closets, smelling their dirty laundry, fingering through the garbage of their lives. Not everyone would like it. Being by nature a nosy person, she loved it.

She was looking at the pictures of Ellen now. There was Ellen on the cover of *Today's Christian Woman*; another of Carl and Ellen on the front of *Christian Century;* publicity shots of Ellen at various ages and stages of her life; with her husband, the two of them receiving the Evangelical Christian Publishers Association Gold Medallion Book Award for their book on creating a couple's devotional life; an obviously staged shot of the Houseman family at the Grand Canyon. There was a young Ellen in her midthirties, fair hair sweeping her shoulders, face freckled and tanned. Smiling. Then there was the Christmas card portrait of Carl and Ellen and four boys ranging in age from what looked like five or six to late teens, the slouch-shouldered oldest son towering over his mother. There were various other poses of Ellen—Ellen and Carl; Ellen and groups of women at retreats, wearing matching T-shirts, their arms around each other; Ellen and Carl on the back of their book jackets. Teri pulled out the most recent five-by-seven publicity shot. Something about the woman's face caught Teri in a way she couldn't explain. There was something about the eyes that made her almost gasp. She looked again at the family shots. The youngest son, Brent, had those eyes, down-turned at the sides, thick with lashes, contemplative looking. Sad eyes. Sleepy eyes. Some would call them bedroom eyes.

"She looks so sad," Teri said.

Jack glanced over. "That one? You think she looks sad?"

"Her eyes. I don't know. Don't you see it?"

"To me that one looks like a staged publicity shot. Complete with the airbrushing. She's not smiling, but so what?"

Teri continued rifling through the pictures. A few minutes later she said, "Why do people quit smiling?"

"Quit smiling?"

"Yeah. Why do people who once smiled all the time suddenly stop?"

"Sadness or pain. Sadness, I think," Jack said, his eyes on the road.

"Somewhere along the way, Ellen Houseman quit smiling. She smiles in these early pictures. But her later ones, she doesn't smile in any of them."

"You think it's significant?"

"When I'm working on a case, everything's significant."

"And you have no indication why?"

"I've read every article written about this woman, and she has a totally unblemished past. No one has a totally unblemished past. But here she is, a perfect, supportive, loving, super mom, minister's wife, coauthor of award-winning books on how to have a wonderful marriage, yet in her pictures she doesn't smile. And there's another thing. There's nothing—not one word in any of these articles, in any of her books, in her husband's books—about sailing. Not one word. Why didn't she ever tell her interviewers about sailing? Why didn't she bring it up even once in her books? Sailing is this great metaphor for life. She could have milked it for all it's worth."

"Metaphor for life?"

"Yeah, there's the storms of life and the quiet harbors and the anchors holding and the billows rolling and the lower lights burning. I could go on."

"Please don't."

Not long after lunch, they easily found the Fundy Tide Guest Home and Cottages following the directions Alma had given over the phone. You take the second exit, turn right and keep going and going past the Irvings on the left and the Tim Hortons on the right. After the pedestrian crosswalk, it's the third driveway to the right going down to the water. Their tires crunched on the gravel driveway that wound downhill through denuded winter trees whose branches offered glimpses of cottages. Eventually, the winding drive opened up to a large paved lot. Theirs was the only car. Shrubbery and ivy, leafless and brown, clung to the large white house like fingers scrabbling for climbing holds. They parked close to the house, and as soon as they got out of the car, a cold gust seemed to come at them from all directions at once. Teri pulled the hood of her jacket up over her head and struggled against the wind. Jack bowed his shoulders against the wind, his balding head snowplowing into the wind.

A woman on the porch said, "We had a lovely morning. Now this wind."

She wore wide jeans and a man's well-worn red and white checked wool jacket with several buttons missing. Her short, steel gray hair was tucked behind her ears. "I'm Alma," she said. "You're Teri and Jack, I presume?"

They said they were.

"Come in, then, get out of this cold. I was working out in the yard all morning, clearing brush, but now it's gotten so cold. I was just about to put on a pot of coffee. Ted should be in any minute. He's out hauling wood up from the old cook shed that we want to redo. Not often we get guests this time of year."

"I hope we're not an imposition."

"Not at all. It'll be nice having the company."

In the kitchen a glass-fronted woodstove spread warmth into the room. An oil painting of a lighthouse was on one wall, and on a wooden mantle sat a little sailboat inside a dusty glass bottle. Alma unlaced her dirt-crusted leather boots at the front door and placed them on a rubber mat and hung the jacket on a wooden coat tree.

"Let me get the coffee on. Then I'll show you around the place. I'll let you have the pick of the place." She scooped coffee grounds into an old-fashioned metal percolator, set it on the stove, and then they followed her up a wide carpeted staircase. At the landing, Alma said, "Oh, can you feel that wind? Can you just feel it? I've got to get the heat on or you folks'll freeze to death up here." They followed her down a hallway wider than most people's living rooms with numbered closed doors on either side. At the end of the hall, she opened a door on the right. "This room is the nicest. It's my personal favorite because it overlooks the water. But I'll let you decide. They all have private flushes. Even though this one has the nicest view, some people don't like it because it's smaller than some of the others and more exposed to the wind, being in the front. Then there's this one..." They followed her across the hall. "Bigger, with sitting chairs, even, but the view's not as nice. All my rooms have views of the sea, but some views are nicer than others. All the rooms are clean. I cleaned them all. So you choose. Once you get settled in, come on downstairs for some chocolate cake and coffee. We'll have ourselves a good talk about Ellen then."

Teri and Jack walked from room to room, finally settling on the first one they had seen, Alma's favorite. "I couldn't stand to be in that one across the hall," said Teri. "Did you see that wallpaper?"

"I thought it was charming."

"All those flowers! You'd wake up thinking you were being strangled by green things. The revenge of the killer aloe vera plants."

"You love flowers, Teri. We have so many houseplants there's no room for anything else."

"Real flowers, Jack. Real flowers. Not artificial ones and that includes wallpaper," Teri said, hanging her jacket on a hook on the back of the door.

They unpacked quickly, and in a matter of minutes the four of them were sitting in the front room on overstuffed chairs, with cups of coffee and huge helpings of chocolate cake dripping with chocolate frosting. Ted sat in the corner, a vacant expression on his face, a bib tied around his neck. On Alma's lap lay the famous scrapbook.

"I have a letter from Carl authorizing me to pick up the scrapbook," Teri said.

Alma waved her hand. "Oh, pooh, I don't need no letter. I'm sure you're legitimate. I wrote to Carl and said I'd mail it. No need for him to send an emissary. But, you know Carl."

"Did you know Carl very well?" Teri watched her face.

"He was always on the road. Always busy, that one. Ellen always arrived by herself and then would tell us that Carl had wanted to come, had meant to come, but at the last minute something had come up, some emergency with the ministry. Always something, you know. He always sent his regards though."

Teri took a forkful of cake and looked at Jack.

"He's on television," Ted said.

"Yes, Ted," Alma said in a voice you would use to address a child, "he's on television. Yes, he is."

They could hear the wind outside and no one said anything for a while.

Teri finally asked, "How well did you know Ellen?"

Alma smiled widely. "She practically grew up here. Ellen's mother and I were best of friends. We were old school chums."

"Does Ellen's mother live around here?" Teri asked.

Alma shook her head. "June and Arthur passed away some time ago. Arthur has been gone, let me see, coming on thirty years now, and June close to twenty. But before they died, they came all the time. All the time."

"He's on television."

"Ted, dear, we're talking about Arthur and June now, not Ellen's husband." Then she looked back at Teri and Jack. "Before she died, June came every summer. Would help me out here. I have girls come now. Two nieces come every summer to help me out. Otherwise I couldn't keep this place up. Not all alone. But let me backtrack. June, Ellen's mother, was Canadian. We both grew up here. Right in St. Andrews. Arthur was American, so when they got married they moved to Maine, but she came back here every summer and brought the girls with them, Ellen and her two sisters. It was here that Ellen learned to sail. Right down there." Alma pointed through the window.

Ted looked at Teri and Jack. "Do you want to sail? Ellen's dinghy's in the shed." He rose. "I'll get it for you."

"Sit down, Ted. The dinghy's long gone by now. Long gone. And our guests don't want to sail. It's the middle of January, Ted. No one wants to sail in the dead of winter. Finish your cake, Ted." Then to Teri and Jack she said. "Ted has his good days and his bad days."

"And after Ellen and Carl were married, Ellen came back on a regular basis?" Teri asked.

Alma shook her head. "Oh no, oh no. Ellen didn't come for

many years. Not until June died. She and her mother had a falling-out, I'm afraid. But at June's funeral I took her aside and invited her back. I said, 'Ellen, why don't you come back. My house is your house.' That's when she started coming back."

"What was the falling-out about?" Teri asked.

"That I don't know. I never did get it out of June, and I'm afraid the both of them took it to their graves. Hopefully, now that they're together in heaven they've sorted things out." A faint smile played across her mouth.

"So she never told you?"

"The only thing June said was that Ellen was going through some problems and she would be the one who had to sort them out. But after her mother died, Ellen's mood picked up. She enjoyed it here, I believe. It was kind of a retreat for her. Sometimes she brought friends of hers, that Moira who died with her. They'd often sail up here. We have a mooring out there that she'd tie her boat to."

"Did their sons ever come here?"

Alma shook her head. "Ellen only started coming back here after her mother passed away. The boys were grown by then."

Ted mumbled. "The boy came, Alma. You remember the little tyke, don't you Alma?"

"Ted, Brent came only once." She turned to Teri and Jack. "Brent was the youngest. I guess he was the only Houseman boy to make it here. But just the once."

"Ellen's two older sisters, are they still around?"

"Isabelle and Elizabeth are both out west somewhere. I've lost touch with them, too. They didn't like this place nearly as much as Ellen."

"They had a nice wedding," Ted said.

"Who dear? Who had a nice wedding?"

"Carl and Ellen. It was nice."

"Yes, it was, Ted. Very nice. Now eat your cake. Look at us, we're all finished and you're barely started."

Ted looked at Teri and said, "Are you like the other detective?"

"Ted, what are you talking about?" Alma couldn't hide the exasperation in her voice. "These people just want to take the scrapbook home to Carl and spend a lovely two days here."

"What other detective?" Teri asked.

"This is like the other time, isn't it Alma? When the detective came the other time?"

"Ted, no detective, no police ever came up here and asked about the accident. No one did." And to Jack, "He watches a lot of television."

"No, Alma, you were shopping. I told him about Ellen. All about her."

"Ted sometimes gets confused," Alma said, looking at Jack. "As far as I remember, no one came to ask questions about the accident. I really apologize that we're wasting your time. You probably want the scrapbook and then spend a lovely couple of days in St. Andrews."

Later in their room, Teri and Jack went through the scrapbook page by page. Across the first page was the date: August 7–14, 1995. And inside were pictures, drawings, taped-in photos and scrawled notes. Along on this particular sailing expedition with Ellen was another woman, identified as Jane (Jane Jarvis? Teri studied the photo for a resemblance to the Jane Jarvis they had met at the wharf in Belfast. Yes, it could have been her.) and a fifteen-year-old Brent. Some of the anecdotes took up half a page, like the story of the whales coming right up to the boat, or getting the dinghy snared in a lobster trap—not the sailboat but the dinghy—and Ellen diving underneath to free it.

"She sure smiles a lot in these pictures," Jack noted.

"They all smile a lot, including Brent. But I have to say, he's a strange teenage boy who likes going sailing with his mother and his mother's friend."

Jack said, "Do you want to hear my theory?"

"Okay."

"I don't think there's any so-called 'secret life.' I think she just needed a place to get away from the demands of her life. I mean, think about it. She was living in a fishbowl. Every action would be analyzed and reanalyzed. I think she just needed a place to kick back. Be herself."

"But she didn't even tell Carl."

"Maybe she needed a place to call her own. All her own. Carl was busy. That's my opinion. I don't think there's any great mystery or secret life."

"What about the estrangement between mother and daughter?"

"That may not have anything to do with anything."

Teri was looking at the last page of the scrapbook, a full-color photo of the three of them sitting in the back of the boat, their arms around each other, a sunset in the background. "Fond Farewell" was calligraphied across the top.

"Fond farewell," Teri said, "to Ellen. And even to Brent." She closed the book.

He held out his arms and she came to him. "I say we take this back to Carl after we've enjoyed the rest of the weekend."

For the next two days they hiked along the water at low tide, scoured the gift shops and bought a watercolor painting of a lighthouse, made love in the room high above the water with the wind threatening at the windows, ate more chocolate cake with Ted and Alma, shared more Ellen memories. On their last morning there, they lay in each other's arms and through the wide window that faced the sea they watched the sun rise. It took exactly four minutes.

6

The woman's back was to him, but she knew he was there, big and bulky in the doorway, bringing the cold in with him and the smell of the sea. She was peeling apples into a cast-iron pot in the sink for applesauce. Audrey liked applesauce. The peels were falling into a plastic bucket with little thuds. Later she would take them up the hill and spread them out on the compost.

The woman planted a garden in that sheltered spot under the trees, and each year the harvest grew. The root crops were the best: potatoes, carrots, parsnips and onions. But next to the lean-to she had built to keep the wind off, she had even grown tomatoes. Not enough to can, of course, but certainly enough to enjoy fresh.

At the end of the table, Audrey hummed softly and rolled pats of colored modeling clay into shapes and said over and over, "No Ma, no Ma, no Ma."

He made a sound like a sigh, but she didn't stop the peeling, didn't turn. She knew what he would look like: large and square-bodied in his mustard yellow canvas coat. She hadn't heard his four-wheel drive. Audrey's hummings were louder now and her clay rolling more frantic.

"Will," she said finally, still facing away from him.

"Hello, Garda." He set down four plastic Save Easy bags on the table, took off his coat and hung it on a hook. "Is there coffee?"

"There's always coffee."

He clumped his way to the counter and took a mug down from the shelf, then over to the woodstove where he poured himself a cup.

The woman kept at her work. She remembered the first time he had come after the funeral almost four years ago now. (She had begun calling it "the funeral" and she had also begun measuring time by it.) She and Audrey had been outside weeding a little flower patch that grew by the steps. She hadn't seen him come, hadn't interpreted the flinchings of Audrey as anything but her normal fidgeting. It had been such a long time, after all, him working over at the sardine plant in Black's Harbour the way he did, for all those months.

When she felt a tug on her braid, she had spun around with a gasp. It was him, and he was laughing. Laughing!

"Garda, is it now? Garda?"

"Hello, Will," she had said evenly.

"Brought some stuff, Garda," he said today. "Food. Cans. Some soup. Plus a couple papers, one from Maine. Books for you, too. I know how you like books." He lay a bunch of tattered, coverless paperbacks on the table and ran his hand through Audrey's shiny hair. She squealed, not in delight but in a kind of pain.

"She doesn't like to be touched," Garda said. "You know that."

He emptied the grocery bags and began putting the cans on the shelves.

"We don't need all this food," Garda said. "I had some sent over yesterday." She stared down at her chapped hands which held the paring knife, roughened and veined, her knuckles scabbed over in places. The hands of a very old woman. "I need some hand cream," she said.

"I'll bring some next time." He sat in the chair next to the woodstove with his coffee and began reading the newspaper he had brought with him, a *Telegraph Journal*, from New Brunswick. Audrey was hitting her back against the back of the chair like a metronome, and strings of modeling clay lay like little colorful worms all over the table.

"She needs to be in a school."

Will grunted. "She's too old for school."

"She needs more than what I can give her. I try, but there's only so much I can do."

"And who will take her in? Who will drive her in every day? You, I suppose?"

She shrugged. She hadn't thought of that.

He finished the paper in silence. He was in no hurry to leave. He never was. She continued her peeling and her stirring, her hands working the knife methodically while Audrey hummed tunelessly and Will made snide comments about the government, the Americans, the banks, the world in general.

When he finished with the paper, he folded it and lay it atop the wood basket. On his way out he said, "You want me to take the compost up to the garden?"

Garda nodded.

He took the bucket from her. "Never can tell what may grow in that famous garden of yours, Garda. Never know what may spring up there." He winked at her and walked out the door.

When he left, Garda stirred the applesauce around and around, while Audrey's adult hands made their child shapes with clay.

7

Back in her office on a gloomy day at the end of January, Paul Simon's *Graceland* in her CD player, Teri wrote up her final report to Carl. She included everything she had found about Ellen. She wrote down as much as she could remember from the conversations with Alma and Ted. She concluded her report with her opinion that the only kind of "secret life" Ellen had was the need for a quiet place of her own:

> There are only two minor points of note. The first is that Ellen does not smile in any of her recent pictures. The only other curiosity is that in all of my research and in all the articles written about her in various magazines, nothing is mentioned about her sailing. It seemed to come as a surprise to the public that she even owned a boat. I have no idea why she would fail to mention this to her interviewers.
>
> The only answer I have is that being in the public eye the way she was, she perhaps wanted some solitude, some place of her own that no one, not even close family members, knew anything about. Under separate cover, I'm FedExing your folder, plus the scrapbook, plus a hard copy of this report.

With a click of her mouse, she e-mailed the final report to Carl Houseman. Then, humming along to "Under African Skies," she closed down all active Cut Throat files, saved them onto a Zip disk labeled "Best Solitaire Games for the Mac" (another one of her attempts at subterfuge), then locked the disk and her photocopies in her safe. The second photocopy she put through her paper shredder. Then she organized all of Carl's originals into a huge FedEx envelope, which she put into her leather bag.

She went downstairs and bought herself a large coffee, double cream, and a bagel and lox and found herself a booth by the window where she ate, read the newspaper, and watched the traffic in the street. She made plans for the money Carl would send her. A new pair of jeans. Maybe some boots. She needed a good pair of winter boots. Maybe a new classical CD for Jack. She'd have to figure out which one he wanted. Maybe someone he worked with would know.

If she left now, she'd have time at home to make a nice supper for the two of them, show Jack that she did so know how to cook. She'd choose a recipe from one of their wedding gift cookbooks. Then she'd go to the little local market near the university and buy what they needed. Try something fancy. If she left now, she'd even have enough time to take Kelly for a jog along the river.

She'd call Jack. Surprise him. She knew this was the day he only had morning classes. She was about to punch his number into her cell phone when she noticed her message reminder flashing. She punched in the message and listened.

"Teri, this is Carl Houseman. I want to talk to you about your report. I just got your e-mail. Can you call me at your earliest convenience. Today? As soon as you get this? And please, not at my office phone. Please call me on my cell." He gave the number and she punched it in.

"Teri, I'm glad you called. There are some things…" A long pause. Teri waited. "Would you be willing to stay on the case?"

She wanted to say, "There is no case." Instead she said, "And what would you like me to do?"

"I'd like you to see what else you can find out."

"Dr. Houseman…"

"I know what you're going to say. I read your report. I've read all the reports. They were my nightly reading for months. I know she needed time away. That makes sense; she was a very private person. But there was more to it than that. There was more to her than that. You mentioned about the not smiling. That really hit home. I knew there was something wrong at the time, but I didn't know what."

A man at the table next to her removed the pickles from his pastrami sandwich, one at a time, then licked his fingers. Carl was still talking. "I want to get married again. I don't want to make the same mistake again. There were so many things we didn't talk about..."

She shifted in her chair and looked out the window. It was drizzling. "What exactly do you want me to do?"

"I need to know about her. I need to know what was troubling her."

"Dr. Houseman, I have a question of my own. Why didn't Ellen ever mention her sailing to anyone?"

"I...I don't know. I really don't. I guess I just never figured it was all that important to her. The ministry, God's work always came first with her. When she would get home from one of her summer trips, she never even talked about what she did. Usually her trips coincided with one of mine and we ended up arriving back at the office on the same day. When she was back here in the office, it was all business."

"She never told you about her trips?"

"No."

"And you never asked her?"

"No. There's something else, too." Another pause. "I've never been fully satisfied with the theory that she died at sea. There was no body, for one."

"The evidence on that is irrefutable," Teri said. "She was immediately presumed dead. There wasn't even the prescribed waiting period in this case. All of the reports are clear on that one."

"There were all kinds of theories at the time," he said. "They hit a rock, or something on the boat malfunctioned. There was some trouble with the engine, you know. Another theory was that they were boarded by pirates, that was one theory. They never found the boat either. Did you know that?"

"Parts of it washed ashore."

"Just cushions. Just a few things. Bits and pieces. They never found the boat itself. That's always been a question for me."

"They found her life jacket, Dr. Houseman."

"That could've been a ruse to put everyone on the wrong track.

Maybe they, whoever they were, needed the boat plus an experienced sailor to smuggle whatever it was they were smuggling. They never found the boat. They never found her body. I know it's probably stupid and presumptuous, but all I'm asking is this, that you have one more look at the case. I'll be satisfied with one more look."

"One more look."

"That's right. One more look."

"Dr. Houseman, I'm not going to say yes right away. I personally think you're wasting your money. I want you to think about this and pray about it. And I'll pray about it too. Give it a week, Dr. Houseman, and if at the end of the week you still want me to look into the case, I will."

Later that evening over curry shrimp that she did make herself, she told Jack that Carl wanted her to stay on the case.

"One more look, he calls it. Get this," she said pointing with her fork, "he thinks pirates boarded the boat and took her hostage, plus took the boat and killed the other two."

"You're kidding of course."

"I'm serious." She took a forkful of curry. It was good, if she did say so herself.

"He doesn't seriously think..." And then Jack started laughing.

"It's not funny, Jack."

"I know and I shouldn't laugh, but I'm getting this image of swashbucklers and old sailing ships and eye patches and peg legs, and people walking planks. And all this in Canadian waters."

"You know your trouble, Jack? You read too much fiction."

"Teri, he seriously thinks that? You're not just putting me on? That there are pirates in Canadian waters? Doing what? Running rum?"

"Not rum, Jack, drugs. And I hate to say it but it's not so farfetched. That's the way a lot of drugs get into Canada, you know, on recreational boats coming into quiet ports along the picturesque coast of Nova Scotia. Did you know that?"

"You know your trouble, Teri? You read too much true crime."

8

Eight days later Teri received an overnight courier letter from Carl Houseman with a check for two thousand dollars "for expenses incurred to date and to get you started on the next phase of the investigation," plus a notarized letter "authorizing Teri Blake-Addison to have the full use of any documents she deems needful in pursuing the investigation into the death of Ellen Houseman." Then, in a short note to her with the Carl Houseman Ministries logo across the top, he had written:

> *Teri, I have prayed about this. Something was bothering Ellen during those last months. I'd like you to find out what that was. Plus, I'd like you to have one more look at the accident, one more look and we can put it to rest. I think you're the person for the job.*

And then across the bottom, *Carl,* in huge scrawl. And underneath it, *I don't need to tell you and your husband that this is to be kept confidential.*

On the coffee table was a stack of all the books Carl Houseman had ever written, thirteen in all. Eleven written alone and two with his wife. A few were from the church library, and the rest Jack had purchased here and there in the last couple of weeks. And on the top was the uncashed check. Teri kept looking at it. She really did need new boots.

Jack was sitting in an easy chair critiquing student poetry. He looked at her over the top of his reading glasses. "Do you want to know what I think?" He put down the papers and picked up the top book on the stack of Houseman books. "I've done a little bit of research on my own, Teri, into him."

"You have?"

"I've skimmed through his books, skimmed them thoroughly enough to get a pretty good picture of the man."

"Really?"

He was sorting through the pile. "He wrote a lot of heavy theological stuff. The only relationship-type books were coauthored with his wife. You have—" and he picked up a paperback with a cover featuring a lot of blue—"the award-winning *Couples Devotional Guide* and," he put that one down and picked up another, "*Prepared Paths*. These are the only two books where he gets personal at all about his life. And, I should add, they never talk about sailing. They write about family camping trips, family adventures, suggestions for setting up a family devotional time. Never sailing. Never Maine. Never St. Andrews, New Brunswick. Never the metaphor for life that you talked about. The rest of this stack are Bible commentaries or books on topical things. His favorites seem to be the prophets. And here's the one that got him so much recognition, *Jeremiah: Path to the Possible*. He was most well-known for his looks into the prophets, both minor and major. Here's *Path to the Godhead*."

"He liked paths," Teri said.

"It would seem."

"So what's your theory?"

"I'm coming to that." He picked up a slim hardcover in forest green titled simply *Mercy*. "This one is significant." He tapped it with his finger. "This little book is his only published work since his wife's death. And this book isn't original material at all, but simply a compilation of other works—some of his columns for his newsletter, some sermons. And incidentally, all were written before his wife's death."

"And your theory?" Teri asked.

He took his glasses off. "Before his wife died, you had a man rising to the pinnacle in Christian power. He had it all. Perfect family that camped together and stuck together through it all, as evidenced in *Prepared Paths*. Beautiful wife, all four sons in the ministry with him."

Teri shook her head.

"I'm right, Teri. The youngest, Brent, was working at the church there in Philadelphia. He was a high school senior and on weekends worked in the sound room at the church. After his mother's death and after he graduated, that's when he left."

"And moved to New Jersey where he works at Pizza Hut and lives with someone without the benefit and blessing of the clergy," Teri said.

"Exactly. Before Ellen's death, Carl was a busy man, so busy that he never even knew where his wife went during her summer vacation. *Her* summer vacation, Teri. What's wrong with this picture? She could've been having an affair with the prince of Iran and he never would've had a clue. He was so busy saving souls that he barely made it to his own mother-in-law's funeral. Here's a man who was writing a thick book like this—" he picked up *Unforgiven*—"every year or so, and they always made huge splashes in the media. And now in five years all there is is this little book titled *Mercy*. Which isn't a new book at all."

"So maybe he's still grieving."

Jack nodded. "He may be grieving, but one thing he's not doing is writing. When he stayed with us and you were out jogging with Kelly, Carl and I had quite a talk about writing. He asked me about my own, and of course, I showed him my masterful books of poetry."

"Of course."

"Then I asked about his. He kind of shrugged and told me that the demands of ministry were so great now that all he had time for were a few articles here and there and his newsletter. No books. But I don't think it's that. One would think he would have more time now in which to write, with his wife gone, his children grown. I think his wife's death was a wake-up call. That it was possible for even a godly man of such renown to lose something that meant the world to him and to know that it will never be returned. He lost both his wife and his son that day."

"But he's going to get married again. He told us that. What's that all about?"

Jack looked thoughtful. "He told me about his fiancée. He seems truly in love with her, and she with him. He said he didn't want to make the same mistake."

"Which is?"

"The overwork, the impossible schedule."

"If that's all it is, why not just get good counseling and get on with life? He must know hundreds of Christian counselors. Why hire me, a private investigator he doesn't even know?"

"Maybe he's been through the counseling route. Maybe what he needs is closure on the actual event. And maybe he wanted—needed—an objective look. Someone he didn't know but felt he could trust. Plus, maybe there *was* something overlooked. Have you ever thought of that? And I think he really wants to find out about his wife's last days on this earth. I believe that letter from Ted and Alma opened up the wound again, that there was so much about his wife that he didn't know, that he didn't even *care* about. Plus her body was never found."

"Hundreds of people—no, thousands—die in accidents on the water and their bodies are never found. The ocean's deep. It's the rare occasion when they are found."

The following morning, Teri decided to call Carl to tell him she'd do it, she'd continue working on this case. It was a rare warm morning in January, and Teri had flung open the door to the tiny balcony off their bedroom and was wrapped up in a fleece housecoat and sitting cross-legged on the cold wood deck. Below her Gilligan and Tiger were chasing each other through the brown garden, and Kelly, ears back, was sitting under a tree watching them.

A woman answered Carl's private line when she dialed.

"Oh, I'm sorry. I must have the wrong number," Teri said.

"Who are you wishing to speak to?"

"I'll try back later."

"Are you wanting Carl?"

Confidentiality. That's what Carl wanted. That's what all her clients wanted. She never took chances. "Sorry. Wrong number."

"Don't hang up. Is this Teri Addison? The detective?"

Teri was quiet for a moment.

There was a soft laugh. "Yes, this is Carl's private line, but I know all about you and his hiring of you. And I understand your reticence. My name's Peg Pellerman; I'm Carl's private secretary. My husband, Paul, and I work with Carl. He's told us all about you."

"Okay."

"We're his closest friends. His and, of course, Ellen's when she was alive. We've been through all of this with him. Many, many times."

"Okay then. Could I speak with Dr. Houseman?"

"He's in a meeting right now. And I'm glad you called, actually, because it really might be easier for me to handle your reports and expenses. You can send them on to me. And it might be a good idea for you to check in with me periodically. Carl's away so much, and he's getting ready now for a Far East tour."

"I should get Dr. Houseman's okay on that."

"Well, just a minute. Hey, you're in luck; the meeting must've finished early. Here's Carl now." A pause.

"Teri?" It was Carl. "I should've told you about Paul and Peg. They know about you. And so does Daisy, of course."

"Daisy?"

"My fiancée."

"Oh." Down below her Gilligan was circling Kelly, who was still wanting to play, still wagging her tail.

"Peg and Ellen were particularly close friends."

"Okay."

"I decided that my closest confidants should know that I've hired, or wish to hire you. Have you made a decision in that regard?"

"I'll stay. I'll do it."

"Thank you. You don't know how much this means to me."

"There are just a couple of things..."

"Name them."

"I may need to talk with your family, so I'll need their names and phone numbers."

"Done. I've spoken about this with my eldest son, Carl Jr. He's agreed to cooperate with you fully. I've also sent e-mails to my other sons. Charlie's in India and Sam's in Colorado. Both e-mailed me saying that you can e-mail them or call at any time with questions. I haven't heard from my youngest yet, but I expect to shortly. Have you got a pencil? I'll give you their e-mails and numbers."

"I do, yes." She wrote as he dictated. Then she said, "I want to talk to you about confidentiality, too, Dr. Houseman. You have my contract so you know that I will keep the investigation as confidential as I can. Also, you have my word that I will not use the information I receive for any kind of personal gain."

"In other words, you won't write a book about all this later. I appreciate that."

Gilligan was tormenting Kelly, grabbing at her tail, and Kelly was barking. Teri went inside and closed the French doors. It was too cold outside anyway. Poor Kelly would have to learn to fight her own battles.

"I'll be very discreet with my questioning," Teri said, "but I can't promise that someone won't pick up on this. And your secretary..."

"Peg? Like I said, Peg's a saint. Peg can be trusted. I don't know what I would've done without Paul and Peg."

"Do I send my reports to you or to her?"

"Hmm." He paused. "Try me, but if I'm not available try Peg or Paul. He's my right-hand man, my business manager."

"Okay. And just to get things straight, you want three things. One, the location of Ellen's body; two, what was bothering Ellen in the months before the accident; and three, you want the whole accident reviewed one more time."

"Right."

Because it was as good a place to start as any, she sent e-mails to the sons after the phone call with Carl. She also called the Royal Canadian Mounted Police on Grand Manan and both the American and Canadian Coast Guards. The Coast Guard had nothing to add, they told her, but she was welcome to come and look at their reports, which were probably the same as the reports she had. The

RCMP on Grand Manan invited her to come and see them if she ever made it to the island, but they doubted they had anything new. The case was closed as far as they were concerned.

9

The following morning, after an evening of reactivating Cut Throat, Teri drove over to Belfast. It was a wet snow she drove through, but by the time she got there, the snow had turned to a slushy rain, and she was glad for the new snow tires she'd purchased with money from her last case. Her windshield wipers barely kept up with the windswept rain. Maybe new winter windshield wipers would be next on her list. Boots, though, she definitely needed boots.

The little supply shack, the one Jane and Fred had been painting, was locked up tight. Still tacked up on the bulletin board outside were faded notices of sailing races long past, boats for sale, bean suppers and corn boils, their tattered edges wet and dripping. She flattened them out with her hand and read each one. She tried the door, locked. She peered in the smudged windows but saw nothing of interest. She wandered over to a nearby café, and ordered a coffee to go. She said to the woman behind the counter underneath a sign that read, *We're famous for our pies*, "I'm looking for Fred Goodkins or Jane Jarvis."

"Fred? You just missed him. He was here just a minute ago."

"Know where he is now?"

The woman yelled over to a man by the doorway who was zipping up a yellow slicker. "George, you know where Fred went?"

"Who wants to know?"

"Me," Teri said.

He squinted at her. He looked around the same age as Fred Goodkins, but with limp gray hair that straggled down his forehead.

"Fred might be over in the shop."

"The shop?"

He indicated with his hand. "Next to the boat house."

"Thanks. I'll check there. I'm looking for Jane Jarvis, too."

"Jane's probably up home by now."

"Where's that?"

"The big white house behind the library."

"Thanks." And then something occurred to her, and she walked toward him. "Maybe you can help me. I'm investigating the death of Ellen Houseman. Did you happen to know her?"

"Yeah." He shoved his hands into his pockets. Outside, the rain intensified. "I happened to know her."

"Did you know her well?"

"Well enough. Most everyone around here knew her well enough."

"Were you here at the time of the sailing accident?"

"I was."

His expression was guarded, his hands deep in his pockets. She looked down at the Styrofoam cup in her hand. "Look, would you like a coffee? It's cold out. Let me buy you a coffee. My name is Teri and I'm talking to people who knew Ellen."

"What for? You with one of those newspapers?"

She laughed. "Not hardly. Not me. I can't write two words together and have them make sense."

"The police then?"

"Private." She began to make her way to a far booth and he followed her, like she knew he would. She sat down and smiled at him. He sat across from her and unzipped his slicker. Teri poured her coffee out of the Styrofoam cup into the thick white coffee cup on the table. The waitress, also following out of curiosity, poured coffee into his mug.

"So," she said pulling out her notebook after the waitress left, "what can you tell me about Ellen?"

"She grew up here. Everyone around here knew her. Ellen even bought her boat off me."

"Beloved?" Teri chewed thoughtfully on her pencil eraser.

"Yeah. Wasn't named that then, though. Named *Sea Witch* when I had her."

"How long did she have that boat?"

He shrugged. "Seven, eight years maybe. It was a good boat. It shouldn't have gone down. That boat didn't go down. It was a good boat. That's what I told the cops then, and that's what I'll tell you now. She was a sturdy, solid boat made for anything the ocean could throw at her."

"How do you account for what happened?"

"Terrorists."

"Terrorists?"

"That's what I said."

"What makes you say terrorists?"

He stirred three sugar packets into his coffee carefully, one at a time. Teri waited. Finally, he said, "I said terrorists because it wouldn't be the first time. I've heard of them in these waters before, drug smugglers, the like." He stirred his coffee. "They needed her. She's excellent at the helm. They needed her and they knew it. It happens. World's a crazy place now. You got these terrorists hijacking airplanes. You got those same terrorists hijacking private boats."

"How about the other two on the boat with her? They weren't needed?"

"The other two saw what was happening and grabbed their life jackets, for all the good it did them. Water's so cold out there. They'd've died within the space of half an hour."

He looked across the table at her. His eyes were incredibly blue and clear. "Ellen had her captain's license—did you know that? They needed her, needed someone who knew the boat, knew the waters. They used her, these terrorists did. Then got rid of her and the boat."

Teri had read this or variations on this theme in numerous newspapers. She tapped her pencil on the notebook. "Okay, I'm also thinking of Ellen's state of mind before the accident. How was she? Do you remember?"

"What do you mean, her state of mind?"

"Did you know if she had problems of any kind?"

"Ellen was a good sailor. She never took her problems to sea, if that's the new tack the police are taking. She was not responsible for the accident. No way."

"Did you see her before she left that time?"

"Sure I did."

"And how did she seem to you?"

"She seemed fine. She was fine."

"No problems of any kind? You didn't happen to know if anything was on her mind?"

He glared at her, then rose. "I'm sick of you people with all your questions. Trying to pick at things that aren't there and never were." He zipped up his jacket and walked away. She watched the back of him go, a hunched figure in a grimy yellow slicker. He hadn't drunk more than two sips of his very sweet coffee.

Teri plunked down three dollar bills and waved cheerfully to the waitress on her way out.

She found Fred Goodkins in the boathouse on a stepladder sanding down the hull of a lobster boat named *Valerie II* with a power sander.

"Hello," she called.

"Yeah, hey." He turned off the machine. "Hello. I remember you."

"Nice job," she said. "Big boat."

"Oh," he shrugged. "Been refitting lobster boats for as long as I remember. You develop a knack."

"You a lobsterman yourself?" she asked him.

"Me? Never had my own boat, if that's what you mean. Worked for a while as a sternman, though. That's about it." He found a dull spot on the hull and began finger wiping it with his cloth. "I like this sort of inside work. Not many people do."

Three boats, looking enormous with their whalelike hulls, rested on jack stands in the boathouse.

"I'm here about Ellen," Teri said.

"What do you want to know about her?"

"She grew up here, right?"

"Her people have all left."

"Did you know Carl at all?"

He wiped his hands on his coveralls, gave a kind of guttural snort. "No one could believe she'd gone off and married a preacher. Ellen? Her? That was the biggest surprise. But she kept ties here. Even with her people gone, she kept ties here."

"Ties here, how?"

"Oh, with Jane Jarvis. They were the best of friends. Used to sail together betimes."

"What do you think happened?"

"I've heard tell of a Bermuda Triangle down there at the bottom of Grand Manan. You got Nova Scotia, Maine, and Grand Manan Island, with them two bodies of water vying for each other. I've heard tell of boats that head down there and never come back." He was walking around the hull now, and Teri followed, stepping over boards, old anchors, thick decayed pieces of rope, odd bits of machinery whose function she could only guess at.

"The currents?"

"Not only the currents, but...all the seamen gone down before. They exert a kind of, um, pull."

"You mean like ghosts?"

"Ghosts. Whatever. It's not impossible."

The rain was intensifying, making conversation difficult. "Did you talk to Ellen before she left?"

"Yeah, o' course. She came to see me, always did."

"How did she seem to you?"

He scratched his head. "Same as always."

"Not upset about anything? Problems?"

He shook his head.

"I talked to a man at the coffee shop who was quite incensed that I even suggested that."

"That must be George. He's been half in love with Ellen his whole life. Broke his heart into ten pieces when she ran off and married the radio preacher."

Rain water splashed over her jacket and ran down her neck as she raced for her car. The rain would make her hair frizz, so she pulled her hood up. She patted her face and hair dry with a paper napkin left over from her take-out coffee after she climbed into the driver's seat.

The big white house behind the library had a name. *Ashburton House* was written on a small brass plaque next to the door, along with a date, 1785. There was a huge metal door knocker in the center of the door, which Teri clapped down a few times. She stood as close to the house as she could under the overhang. Still the water pelted her back.

Jane Jarvis answered. "Yes?" Still that attractive freckled face, that short graying hair swept back behind her ears. It was a strong face, a rugged face, the face of a woman who spends a lot of time outdoors.

"Hello, Jane. I don't know if you remember me from the other day..."

"Well, yes I do. You were with Ellen's husband on the wharf there."

"That's right. Actually, I wonder if I could ask you a few questions?"

"About what?"

"About Ellen. About the accident."

Jane raised her eyebrows.

"To be perfectly honest, I'm a private investigator, and I've been hired to give the Ellen Houseman accident one more look-through."

"May I see some sort of identification?"

"Of course." Teri pulled out her wallet and showed her. She watched Jane examine her ID. Did she really know what she was looking for?

"The reason I ask is we've had so many people come here. You've no idea. It was distressing."

"I understand."

"And why after all this time are you here again?"

"As I said, I'm looking at the accident once more before it's finally put to bed."

"And they hire private investigators to do that?"

"Sometimes. Actually, I've been hired by a private individual."

"Who would that be?"

"I'm not at liberty to say."

"Well, come in then, out of the rain."

Teri followed her through a dim wide hallway, water from her jacket dripping onto the rug. This house was not unlike the house she shared with Jack, large and lots of wood, high ceilinged and built a couple of hundred years ago. It was cool in here, dark and oppressive, but that could have been the rain. She glimpsed rooms on either side of the hallway, with stiff Victorian chairs in formal seating arrangements. All this place needed were the velvet ropes. There were a lot of clocks.

"This is quite a house," Teri said.

"A monstrosity, isn't it? It's been in my family for generations, but that's a whole nother story. I'm ready to turn it over to the historical society and move into an apartment. Ellen would stay here when she came to Maine."

"So, you knew her well?"

Jane shrugged. "You could say that."

They were in a solarium at the back of the house, obviously added much later, which gave out onto a garden. Here and there were potted cactus plants, many of them in bloom. It was a great room, and Teri told her so.

"I live in only a few rooms of this place. This is one of them. Gardening is my hobby."

"I like plants, too," Teri told her.

They were sitting in white wicker chairs opposite each other. The tops of Teri's knees were wet, and despite the cheeriness of the flowers, she felt thoroughly chilled and damp.

"So, tell me about you and Ellen," Teri said.

"We grew up together. We were classmates here, friends. Sailed some together. If anyone *could* know Ellen well, I guess that person would be me."

Teri opened her notebook to where she had written precious few words from her previous interviews with Fred and George.

"I'm especially interested in the last weeks or so leading up to the accident. There was some suggestion that Ellen may have had something on her mind, that something may have been troubling her."

Jane didn't look at Teri, but looked out onto the brown, ragged garden when she said, "You'd like to know about Ellen's state of mind then."

"I would. Here's my observation—Ellen never smiles in her recent photos. There were dozens of them taken, ministry shots, her and Carl. Lots of them. But she seldom smiles. Or if she does smile, it's a sad kind of a smile."

Jane looked at her and said softly. "There was a sadness in Ellen. It wasn't there when she was a child. She sailed. She won races. There was even talk of her getting onto the Olympic team. Then she left, married Carl, and life changed for her. I think not living here was a great sadness for her. She would come back here two or three weeks every year and that kept her sane. It was something she needed."

"She never talked about her work? The church? Her life with Carl to you?"

Jane put her hands on her knees. They were knuckled strong hands, wide and broad, gardener's hands. Somewhere a clock ticked and outside the rain continued. "The only thing she said about the church in all those years was that she hated the uniform she had to wear."

Teri looked up. "Uniform?"

"She called it the uniform. First, there was the church uniform: The pastel suits, just skimming the knees, the panty hose, the gold earrings, lipstick, eyebrows plucked to perfection. Those were her exact words. I quote her when I say that. She had such a way with words. But it was odd..."

Teri waited.

"She only mentioned this the once. I remember asking her at another time about the 'uniform,' and she looked at me as if she didn't know what I was talking about. But I remembered it so plainly, because it was the one and only time she ever talked about this other life of hers."

Teri drew curlicues on her notebook and thought of the five-by-seven she had, the pale blue suit, the scarf tied just so. "There are a couple of things that trouble me," Teri continued. "The first is that she doesn't smile. And the second thing is that she's written up in scads of magazines and in none of them does anyone mention her sailing. It's as if it never existed."

"She wanted to keep it separate," Jane said. "This place was her salvation."

Her salvation. Teri wrote that down. "So, she never talked about the ministry to the people here, and she never told the people she worked with in Philadelphia about her Maine friends. I can't help saying how very odd that seems to me. It's like she's two different people."

The lead in Teri's mechanical pencil broke, and she replaced it while she listened to Jane agree with her that it was odd. And Teri began to think it was odd for another reason. If Ellen Houseman truly believed what her husband preached, why was this place her "salvation"? Wasn't that an odd word choice? Also, if Ellen truly believed what her husband wrote about and talked about, wouldn't she take every opportunity to tell people about Jesus, even the people here? Where was her missionary zeal? Why did she need to take a week or two *off* every year? To Teri, just newly back in the fold, there was no other word for this behavior than *odd*.

"Did Ellen ever talk about Carl? About her sons?" she asked.

Jane rubbed her knees. "You mean aside from the fact that Carl never came up with her, and how that any minute now he was going to show up? You mean aside from that?"

"Tell me about that."

"Okay," Jane said. "She'd arrive. She'd unpack here. She'd go down to the wharf and begin to get her boat provisioned for whatever trip she was going to take. Sometimes she stayed on the coast of Maine; sometimes she went up to New Brunswick. Sometimes I went with her, sometimes not. But she would tell everyone, and I do mean everyone, that when Carl shows up to send him down to the wharf. Not *if* he shows up, but *when* he shows up. It got to be a joke, because we all knew he was never coming."

"How sad," Teri said.

"That's why she didn't smile. She was married to a man who didn't love her." Jane became quiet when she said, "I've thought a lot about her since she died, and I think Ellen married the wrong person. I think she would've been far happier if she had married someone from town. A fisherman. A lobsterman. She hated the limelight. I always thought she would've been happier if she had her own little lobster boat and kept a few traps. The money meant nothing to her."

"What about the other women who died, Moira Neddick and Cheryl Ryder? Did you know them?"

"Less well. Moira and Ellen were friends, but not from here. Moira sailed mostly near Boston. I don't know how they met. Cheryl was Moira's niece, and I didn't know her at all."

"Did you see the three of them before they left?"

"Everyone did. There was a big party over at the Clam Digger, and they were there. And Ellen seemed...well, she seemed her usual self. You could never tell whether she was happy, sad, whatever. That was Ellen. She and I were such good friends once."

When she didn't say anything more, Teri finally asked, "Do you think she loved Carl?"

"The problem was that she loved him too much." Jane smoothed her hair behind her ears. "I've sailed to Grand Manan where the bodies washed up. Sailed into there with Ellen. It's a beautiful place."

10

Garda dreamed. At night, her dreams were mostly of the sea, and sometimes the sea was a terrible place where the rising tide caught in her nostrils and suffocated her, her cries drowned by the scream of the wind. She fought those dreams and would wake breathless and gasping, the sheet caught around her neck like a rapist's fingers.

By day, her dreams were memories that would take hold of her and make her pause. She would be working in her garden and suddenly she would hear her sisters laughing, and she would look up and there they would be chasing each other down by the house, their dog barking, and then just as soon the vision faded and she would go back to her weeds. Sometimes she would be at the window, and the feel of the curtain would be a lover's hands on her face. And she would remember—she couldn't stop herself—being gently guided, pressed against the garage wall in the night and the deep hungering kisses that went on and on. And these memories would take hold of her with new guilt. She was not free of it, even here, even now.

Sometimes these memory-dreams would clutch at her with such force that she would stop in the middle of something—sweeping the floor, chopping apples, kneading bread—and have to suddenly sit down, overcome with weariness. Oh Audrey, she would say. Oh Audrey, oh Audrey.

On this night, three weeks after Christmas, Garda was asleep and dreaming, but it was not about the sea that she dreamed nor her lover's hands. She dreamed of Christmas. Every Christmas, all of them, she and her sisters and her parents would pull on their heavy boots and hike into woods for a Christmas tree. It was a magical time, for sometimes they would not find the tree her mother deemed 'perfect' until the sky was littered with stars, and they saw their breath against the moon.

In her dream it was Christmas morning and she was a child again and they were around the Christmas tree. Her father was reading the Christmas story from the second chapter of Luke, long, slow, ponderous, in the King James version, taking his time with it while the children waited, fingers drumming on the floor, eyes on their packages. Audrey was there in her dream, impossibly there, and a Christmas stocking lay across Garda's lap, its lumpy offering still inside. One of the sisters finally said, "You're supposed to open it. You're supposed to open it, stupid. Don't you know anything, stupid? Stupid!"

Garda reached inside the stocking. There was only one item in there, stuck way down in the toe, and she maneuvered it out with her fingers. She gasped. It was a small green book with the simple title, *Mercy*. "Let's see what Santa brought," said her mother, but Garda took the book and ran down the cliff toward the water. She waded into it and felt the cold wetness around her ankles. And in the faded distance she heard the sound of the church carillon playing "Silent Night, Holy Night," just those two lines over and over, while the tree lights blinked on and off, on and off, her ankles cold in the water, the book *Mercy* pressed against her face.

Garda woke gasping from the memory of it, tightly coiled in the sheet and covered in a sheen of sweat. The light of the lighthouse moved rhythmically through the windows of her bedroom and the Christmas carillon was the bell buoy out in the channel.

Another storm. She got up and tied the faded blue robe around her waist and went to the window. The wind had come up in the night. She watched the trees moving, and beyond them, although she couldn't see it, the Grand Manan channel, churned frothy by the wind.

Will had left the book, *Mercy,* a slim volume with the green cover, along with the stack of paperbacks and newspapers he had brought. She hadn't noticed the book until he was well gone back in his place in Grand Harbour. She could picture him, brewing himself a pot of tea. She pictured him sitting there, bobbing the tea bag up and down, smirking to himself.

It was meant as a taunt, a reminder that he knew all about the woman buried up in the garden. And that he had power over her. And he would never let go this power.

Outside the trees moved in the wind like dancers on a stage.

11

By morning Teri had received four e-mails. Carl Jr. had written her a long reply, telling as much as he could remember, he said, about the accident, which wasn't a whole lot. But it was evident to Teri that he liked being a part of things, and he thanked her many times for "taking on this undertaking." He wrote about where he was and what he was doing when the accident happened. He ended by saying that although it had been five years ago, it made him even more thankful for his wife, Mariana, and their three children, who missed their grandma. And he knew that all things work together for good. It was interesting stuff, thought Teri, but not a lot of solid stuff. Except for one interesting tidbit. His signature on his e-mail read, Dr. Carl Houseman Jr., author of *Mercy*.

Author of *Mercy*? Carl Jr.? Since when? She reached for the book and went through the opening pages. No mention of Carl Jr. Wait—here it was, small print: *Thank you to Carl Houseman Jr. of Carl Houseman Ministries for compiling these sermons and talks and writings of his father.* Odd, she thought, as if Carl Sr. was the one who had died, and not Ellen.

The e-mail from second son Charles Houseman was much shorter and matter-of-fact. It came from India and said that he'd be happy to help in any way he could, but since he had been overseas at the time of the accident and had only flown home for the memorial, he didn't know what he could add.

The third from Sam Houseman, youth pastor out in Colorado Springs, said essentially the same thing. He knew even less. He didn't even keep track of his mother's friends and had never been on her boat. He had never even seen it. That stunned her. Had never even *seen* it? Her own son?

The final e-mail was from Peg Pellerman. It was cheery and full of smiles and exclamation points, asking to be kept abreast of the investigation, and asking for an update of her work ASAP.

No word from Brent, the New Jersey Pizza Hut son. But then she wasn't expecting one from him. She'd been there; she knew how it was. She punched in the only number she had for him, and it was answered by a female. Amanda Mast if her research was correct. Teri was told that Brent was at work.

"Is this Amanda?"

"Yep. Who's this?"

"Can you get me his work number?"

"Hold on a sec."

A few minutes later Teri punched in the number for the Pizza Hut and was told that Brent was out on a delivery and would be back in maybe twenty minutes or so.

When she got off the phone she packed. It was a four-hour drive from their home in Maine down to Boston where Moira's and Cheryl's families lived. May as well start there. While she packed, Jack tried to talk her into staying overnight with some friends of his, Craig Muster and his wife Monica. Craig was an English professor colleague of Jack's who had moved to Boston. He and Jack had coauthored a number of papers, which they had presented at conferences, on the life of female poets of the seventeenth century. Craig and Monica had been longtime friends of Jack and Jenny's. *No thank you, Jack, I think I'll stay in a motel.* "I don't really know them," is what she said.

"Sure you do. They came to the wedding."

"A lot of people came to the wedding."

"No, there weren't. It was a small wedding."

"I don't think I remember them."

"Sure you do, Teri. I go back a long way with them. Jenny and I used to go camping with them. Our kids practically grew up together. You'd love them, Teri."

"I'll visit them, Jack. I promise I'll visit them, but to spend the night? When I'm on a case it's always easier when I'm by myself. You know how I get. All business. All work. It isn't like this is a social call."

Jack was leaning back on his heels against the dresser in their bedroom. He was thinking, remembering, and Teri never knew what she was supposed to do when Jack remembered. "They're great people, Teri. Good people. You'd like them. They'd like you."

She zipped up the duffel bag with a force that surprised her. "Okay, I'll call them when I get there. Give me their number and I'll call them." She slung her duffel bag over her shoulder. "Oh, and if Patsy Mellon from church calls? Tell her I'd like to see the Sunday school curriculum as soon she has it. If you can pick it up for me, I'd appreciate it. It's only like three weeks until I'm supposed to start teaching that class. I've left a couple messages on her machine, but she hasn't gotten back to me." She was aware that she was talking fast, stumbling over her words. "And I'll leave my cell phone on if you need to reach me. And I'll be sure to call the Musters when I get there..."

"Teri." He drew her to him and his kiss was long and lovely, but Teri wondered, was this kiss for her? Or was he thinking about Jenny?

When she filled up with gas at the Irving on the corner, she also filled her travel mug to the brim with coffee. Pulling onto I-95, she thought about that faraway look she sometimes saw on Jack's face. She felt the beginnings of a headache and rooted through her purse for her Advil with her right hand while she kept the other on the steering wheel. She veered once onto the shoulder, and the loud noise of the rumble strips brought her quickly back to reality. *Get a grip,* she said to herself, steering with both hands back onto the road. *Get a grip.*

It could make her crazy when she thought that finding romantic happiness for the first time in her life was dependent upon another person dying. Think about the case, she ordered herself. You've got a job to do.

On the passenger seat next to her were two maps. Frank Neddick, husband of the late Moira Neddick, and his new wife Philipa had said they were "more than happy" to help with the investigation, that Moira and Ellen had been good friends, and even

Philipa knew Ellen. Would she come for lunch? Good, it was settled then. Cheryl Ryder's parents, Archibald and Laura, were "agreeable to the prospect," but a bit less enthusiastic than the Neddicks.

Tonight from her hotel room she'd try Patsy Mellon again, too. They had been playing telephone tag for a couple of weeks now, and it was time she got this thing nailed down. She didn't know Patsy well, but she seemed nice enough. She worked as a receptionist in the hospital, was close to Teri's age, and had two dark-haired twin girls named Kristen and Karla. The last time she talked to her face-to-face was before Christmas when she learned that the teacher for the senior high girls' class, an elderly woman named Ida, was going in for surgery in March and would be retiring after that. It came to her while she was sitting in church that she could teach that class. That she *should* teach that class. She had something to offer them. Not only did she like teenagers and generally get along with them, but it was during those years, after her mother died when Teri was fourteen, that she had strayed from God and left the church. After the morning service she found Patsy.

"Oh, that's wonderful," Patsy had said touching her arm. "I think you'll be wonderful. I'll get the materials to you just as soon as I get them from Ida."

Partway to Boston, Teri stopped at a roadside turnout, bought another coffee, a bag of nacho chips, and some Gummi Bears. She also called Brent Houseman. His phone was busy.

Back on the highway she tuned in to a light rock station and spent the rest of the drive singing along. Traffic on the way into Boston was surprisingly light, which didn't hurt her feelings one bit.

The Neddicks' square, brick home was reached via a series of turns on winding back streets with signs that weren't always visible behind high shrubs and fir trees. But following the Internet map she'd printed off at home, Teri finally found the house and pulled into the driveway and parked behind a Volkswagen Jetta. The two of them, Frank and his wife, answered the door. He invited her in and introduced himself and his new wife, Philipa, who was a short, blowsy woman in a pink tracksuit and white sneakers. In the kitchen a huge crock of beans simmered deliciously on the stove.

"Sit, sit," Philipa said, pointing with a wooden spoon. "Would you like some coffee? Frank, would you make some coffee, pretty please?"

Frank grinned and got the coffee pot out.

Teri liked kitchens. She had learned that people who brought you into their kitchens were generally friendlier and more willing to share information than those who sat you down in their living rooms. And this kitchen was friendlier than most. Painted a cheery yellow, every wall and spare countertop was covered with knickknacks: matching Dutch boy salt and pepper shakers, matching oven mitts hung on tole painted hangers, a whole row of miniature lighthouses on a shelf with wooden pegs underneath on which hung little decorations that looked like they belonged on a Christmas tree. There were calico prints on the windows and framed needlepoints of Bible verses. The table was covered in a daisy-printed tablecloth with a lot of huge sunflowers, nice on a winter day. Glass milk bottles painted with winter scenes lined the window ledge. The two of them stood beside the stove, arms around each other.

"We're newlyweds," Frank said, "in case you wondered."

Philipa said, "Oh, Frank."

She served their lunch on sunflower plates, and the spoons and knives had sunflowers on their handles. There were also chunks of homemade bread and a bowl of jellied cranberry salad. After a brief grace, they dug in. The beans were every bit as good as they smelled, and Teri didn't realize until then just how hungry she really was.

"So, how long have you been married?" Teri asked.

"Three months."

"Ah. I'm a newlywed myself," Teri said. "Eight months. My husband was a widower for four years before we got married."

"Just about as long as me," Frank said.

"Seems like everyone's getting married these days," said Philipa. "Even Carl Houseman."

"Carl, yes," Teri said. "Do you know him well?"

Frank shook his head. "Not too well. Not anymore. I used to. A bit. But we've been sort of out of touch completely since Moira and Ellen passed away."

"How did Moira and Ellen meet?"

"Oh, they met in Maine. Moira was just up there by chance, taking a sailing course. Ellen needed crew and Moira went along. They became good friends after that."

"Did you see Carl before that last trip they took?"

"No. He was supposed to come to Yarmouth, but he never made it."

Teri buttered a piece of very good homemade bread. "But you went up to Halifax?"

"Of course. So did Cheryl's boyfriend."

"How did Ellen seem when Carl didn't show up?"

"Disappointed. I would say disappointed. But she didn't show it. I do remember one thing though, that we thought odd at the time. I remember the four of us were walking around Yarmouth—that would be me and Moira and Cheryl and her boyfriend—and all of a sudden we realized that Ellen wasn't with us. No one had realized she was gone. Later, we met her at the bed-and-breakfast, and she said she was going to stay on the boat. We had rooms booked and everything, but she decided to go back to the boat and sleep there."

"She was disappointed then?"

"I would say so. But she didn't say. A little while later Moira remembered that she had left her makeup case on the boat, and when we got back to the boat Ellen was down in the cabin on her cell phone and talking rather loudly to someone. She was saying, 'I can't keep doing this.' And then I heard her say, 'You won't tell him though.'"

"Do you have any idea who she was talking about?"

"None. I don't know. Is this the sort of thing you're looking for?"

"Exactly," Teri said.

"We tried to make some noise as we stepped aboard the boat so she wouldn't think we'd heard her or anything, and there she was sitting down below, the cell phone to her ear. I remember thinking, there's a woman who has it all—famous husband and money—and there she sits all by herself. When she saw us, she smiled and waved us aboard, and all of a sudden her phone conversation got very happy and she said something like, 'We'll see you soon,' and hung up and that was it. The three of us sat down in the boat and chatted like old friends."

"She didn't tell you who she was talking to?"

"No, and we didn't ask. Because suddenly she was showing us all the things she had bought and saying things like, 'Do you think Carl will like this?' and showing us stuff she had picked up for her grandchildren, saying 'Oh, they have such cute things here in Nova Scotia, don't you think?' She was chatting on like that. I remember having this funny feeling about the whole thing."

"This wasn't her usual behavior, to be chatty?"

"Not really. She was usually very serious."

"And then there was her premonition, Frank," Philipa said. "You told me about this premonition."

"Philipa, I don't think anybody cares about anybody's premonitions. It's facts they're looking for, aren't you?" He turned to Teri.

"Right now we're looking at anything that might help," Teri said. "No stone unturned, so to speak. Did Ellen have a premonition?"

"No, Moira did," Philipa said. "Frank told me that Moira definitely didn't want to go on that last trip. She was definitely afraid about that last trip. Moira was known for her premonitions."

"Oh, Philipa, it was nothing we talked about." Frank sighed. "Okay, about a week before the trip, Moira said she had a funny feeling. I said, 'What kind of a funny feeling,' and she said she couldn't put her finger on it, but that there was a part of her that didn't want to go on that trip. She almost didn't, but then didn't want to disappoint Ellen. And then, too, there was Cheryl to think about. Cheryl was really looking forward to it."

"I'm going to see Cheryl's parents after this."

Philipa snorted. "Well, good luck on that one!"

"They're very bitter," Frank said. "Very bitter still."

"About the accident?"

"Cheryl was their only child. Archie used to do some work for Carl. He doesn't anymore. They moved up here and broke all ties. And this after they used to be such grand friends of the Pellermans and Carl and Ellen."

"They blame Carl," Philipa said.

"How can they blame Carl?" Teri asked as she turned to a new page in her notebook.

"They find a way to blame everyone else for their problems," Philipa said. "They blame Carl because if he had been a better husband, Ellen wouldn't have been upset. But because she was upset and not thinking straight, they went out in poor weather and died."

"That's kind of circuitous reasoning."

"You have to know the Ryders to figure that one out."

Philipa got up and started clearing the table. "They've stopped going to church altogether, will have nothing to do with us. I don't envy you visiting them this afternoon."

Philipa put a pound cake on the table with a knife and three plates, and they spent the rest of the lunch hour eating and talking about boats and sailing. The Neddicks had a huge powerboat that they lived aboard in the summer. Philipa couldn't stand the way a sailboat heeled, Frank said, so they had sold his and Moira's Hinckley and bought a big cabin cruiser they were planning to take down through the Intracoastal Waterway to Florida. The boat had all the comforts of home, Philipa said, including a washer, dryer and dishwasher. And Teri said how nice that sounded, and spent the rest of the lunch hour noting to herself the difference between Philipa and what she was learning about Moira. *Maybe that's what widowers do, marry women who are the total opposites of what they married first time around.* She left them her card in case they thought of anything else.

Archibald and Laura Ryder lived right on the water in a sprawling home in an upscale neighborhood just outside of Boston. Teri knew that Archibald was into real estate, and by the looks of his house, she guessed that he sold the homes of the rich and famous.

She arrived around four in the afternoon and was met at the door by an elegant, dark-haired, very trim woman wearing what Jane Jarvis might call, "The uniform—casual style."

"I thought you would be here earlier," was the first thing Laura said.

"I'm sorry," Teri said. "I thought we said midafternoon."

The woman made a show of looking at her watch, a gold one on a bangle bracelet wristband, and sighed loudly before she said, "I wouldn't say four in the afternoon is midafternoon. Archie came home, waited for you, and had to leave for a meeting."

"I'm sorry. Perhaps I should've phoned."

"That would have helped, since we absolutely had no way to reach you."

She was not offered coffee or tea, but ushered into a parlor where they sat on straightbacked wooden chairs. "Cheryl was our only child," was the first thing Laura said. "Our only child."

"I'm so sorry."

"But according to all the newspapers at the time, and your investigation, you'd think it was only Ellen who died. There were two others. Everyone seems to have forgotten that. You have to remember, I lost two people in that accident. Carl lost only one. Frank Neddick lost only one. But I lost two. No one seems to remember that little fact. But you would've thought with all the press she got that Carl lost his whole family. There was nothing about that that was fair at all. My daughter, my sister."

Teri opened to a clean page on her notebook.

"And I hate to think of what Frank and Philipa said about this. Carrying on the way they do. And Moira barely gone. It's disgusting, him marrying so soon. It's like Moira never existed." She flicked a stray hair with a ringed hand. "It's awful. And then going to church like they're not doing a thing wrong. I even went to our pastor about it, but he was the one who married them, after all. Archie and I haven't been back to church at all. We're not inclined so much after the way we've been treated."

Teri longed for a glass of water. "I'm sorry for your loss," she said.

"You're not sorry. You don't even know us. We told Cheryl not to go, but she was all fired up to go with her aunt. The two of them." Laura shook her head. "How could they be safe, I ask you, out on a boat like that? We practically ordered her not to go, but you know young people. There was no arguing with her. And then when we heard about the accident, well, I for one was not the least surprised. Archie and I went right over to Carl's and demanded to know what had happened. And then all the news people, well you'd never know there were two others who died that day. It was just Ellen, Ellen, Ellen!"

"Did you know Ellen well?"

"Ellen was an extremely unfriendly person. Very hard to get to know, in my opinion, which I'm sure doesn't count for much. No, I did not know her well, but what I did know I was never very impressed with."

"Why's that?"

She waved her hand as if swatting away a fly. "No substance to her."

"I understand that your husband worked for Carl for a while?"

Laura rolled her eyes. "I'd like to know who told you that bit of fabrication."

"I also heard that you and your husband were grand friends of Carl and Ellen."

"Another lie. Another fabrication."

"So it's not true?"

Laura smoothed her skirt. "We all used to be acquaintances. Occasionally we'd be at the same function. When our daughter passed away, I told Archie that I didn't feel comfortable being associated with Carl Houseman Ministries in any way, shape, or form. We moved back to Boston then."

"Philipa said that Moira had a premonition about the trip. Do you know anything about that?"

"She shouldn't have gone. None of them should have. They

should've listened to my sister. I have absolutely no respect for the man."

"Carl?"

"No, Frank, never paying attention to Moira's suspicions."

"What about your husband? Can I call and talk to him?"

"He's an extremely busy man, and frankly I resent being harassed about this all over again. It was bad enough at the time. We're trying to get on with our lives. We're trying to put the pieces back together. We don't relish the thought of digging it all up again and again, every time someone gets a whim. All this painful nonsense..."

Teri quietly closed her notebook. And while she listened to Laura Ryder continue on about how life had treated them so unfairly, Teri began to make plans to go to Grand Manan Island. That would be next on her agenda. Go to the place where the bodies washed up. And in her mind she was already driving home.

12

My mother should've had daughters. My mother should've had a whole lot of daughters. Gentle, pretty, long-haired daughters instead of 'four strapping sons,' as my grandfather always called us. Four strapping sons to make our father proud. Four strapping sons to make our church proud. Four strapping sons to make God proud. That's what he always said.

Brent Houseman pounded pizza dough against the wooden table and thought about his mother. If he hammered at it hard enough, he could block out the restaurant sounds: the babies crying, children screaming, the clanking of dishes, people yelling orders, laughing. Sound seemed to seep out of the restaurant itself, as if the very pores of the walls were infused with sound. And then there were the sounds of his thoughts—insistent, drumming, like the sound of Amanda's machine-produced music, which she played and played until he would yell, "Turn that thing down."

"Who are you, my mother?" she would yell right back at him.

There was noise in his childhood home, three older brothers who stormed in and demanded things of his mother. *Daughters would've been quieter,* he thought. *My mother would've liked that.*

It was the e-mails. That's what had started all this. First there was the one from his father:

> Brent, I've hired a private investigator to look into your mother's accident. There are certain things that have come up after five years, and I believe the whole thing warrants one more look. I'm not going to go into these things in an e-mail, but I would be glad to share these with you in person if you would deign to call. I trust that you will give this detective your fullest cooperation. Her name is Teri Blake-Addison.

And he had signed it *Love, Carl* of all things. Not *Dad,* not *Pop,* not even *Father,* but *Carl.* And *love?* Since when?

Well okay, *Carl.* I thought you were getting married again, *Carl.*

Then not a day later he gets an e-mail from her (*Her!* What kind of a *woman* goes around being a private detective?) asking for his "impressions" of what happened back then. Was there anything that had come to mind that he may not have remembered back then? He put the e-mail in his trash, emptied his trash, and told himself to forget about it. But she had even called. Amanda had told him that.

"What did she sound like?" he asked, trying to keep his voice nonchalant while his fingernails bit into the palms of his hands.

"I don't know. Normal. Who is she? Old girlfriend?" Amanda was painting her nails at the kitchen table. She was all in black from her skinny black sweater to a pair of skinny black jeans and skinny black boots. All knobs and sharp angles, she was. Her fingernails were a kidney bean red. She would paint one nail and then lift it up and examine it. If it passed her scrutiny, she would go on to the next one. The biting, acetone smell of polish was everywhere.

"That stuff stinks."

"I like the smell."

"So, then, what'd you tell her?"

"Tell who?"

"That person that called?"

"That you were at work. She wanted to know the number, so I told her."

"You *told* her? You shouldn't have done that, Amanda."

She sat forward, placed her palms on the table and looked up at him. "Who is she?"

"Just someone I don't want to answer questions from right now."

She had cocked her head at him. "What, like the police? Are you in some kind of trouble, Brent?"

"No."

"Well, then who?"

"Just someone." He ran his hand through his stubbly hair.

Amanda blew on her nails, and then using the pads of her fingers, she screwed the cap back on the bottle and unwrapped herself from the kitchen chair and stood up. She was tall, easily as tall as Brent, and when she stood a span of white stomach showed along with the top edge of her butterfly tattoo. "Sometimes you are so weird. Do you know that? You're so weird. Everyone thinks so."

It was raining now and people were coming into the Pizza Hut with dripping umbrellas and stomping feet and talking about the downpour. A big guy with rain dripping off his nose stood at the counter and shouted out an order to him, and all Brent did was point to the guy at the counter, a smiley-face guy named Nathan. No kidding, Nathan's head looked like one of those round yellow smiley faces. Brent used to tell his boss, Molly, that he'd like to wait tables occasionally, but she never put him on a shift. It was probably because he never smiled. He should be more like Nathan. Then he'd get some tips maybe.

He had left his parental home on a day like this, a rainy day in January when the world was depressed and dark and rainy and snow-laden. He had emptied his bank account and had thrown his clothes into his backpack. Then he put all of his mother's scrapbooks plus the money he had stolen from his father into an old duffel bag he had found in the basement, probably belonging in a former life to one of his Little Leaguing brothers. Then he had taken an old car that belonged to the Pellermans and just driven away. He could imagine dour, spiritual Peg Pellerman pursing her thin lips, the crease between her eyes deepening, putting her hand on his father's arm and saying something like, "We'll pray for the boy, Carl."

He had no direction in mind. Just away. He needed to be on his own. It was just the two of them, Carl and himself, now in that big house that easily fit six family members plus guests. There was something too familiar about seeing his father, whiskery and tousle-haired, heading for the bathroom in the morning wrapped up in his satiny red bathrobe.

He had thought of going north, maybe Maine where his mother grew up. He had been there a few times. And unlike the rest of his family, he liked it there. He'd even been out on his mother's boat. He decided against it, though. People knew him there. Too much would be expected of him. Too many questions would have to be answered.

So he had driven across the river into New Jersey. The first place he applied was Pizza Hut where Molly Cedars, the manager, had taken him into her office, talked with him a few minutes, and hired him on the spot. He stayed in a cardboard-walled motel room you could rent out by the hour. Amanda was working at the Pizza Hut then, and six months later he moved in with her. She had since left Pizza Hut and was working at a bar a few blocks from their apartment where the tips were better.

As he spread sauce on a large Meat Lover's, it was suddenly fifteen years ago and he was walking home from school. At the back door he called for his mother, and when there was no answer, he headed down the hall to his room. But the door to the bathroom was open and there was his mother, rubber gloved, towel secured around her neck, combing hair dye through her hair. He had stood there for several seconds, watching her, the smell of the stuff causing his nostrils to clench. He had coughed. "Whew, Mom, what's that?"

"Brent, oh!" She turned to him, startled. He caught the embarrassed flutter of her fingers, the way she jumped back. "I didn't see you. I didn't know you were there. Goodness, what time is it?"

When he told her she said, "I had planned to be finished with all this mess before you got home." And then she had turned and looked in the mirror at herself and frowned. "You know what I should do?" and there was a tremor in her voice, hardly discernible. "You know what I should really do? I should just not do this. Make my hair this blond color. I should let it go gray. See what your father says about that." Then she giggled nervously.

Brent shrugged and walked away. But something about the event pasted itself onto his mind, his mother doing that phony thing. Like the fictions she had created about them all in her scrapbooks.

Because his father was away so much. When Brent was little, he unconsciously tried to make up for that lack. He would bring her stickers from school, special drawings he'd done up in art class, poems he wrote, and valentines. She always praised him. And on the rare occasions when Carl did come home, she would point to the fridge where she had magnetted his offerings. "Look, Carl, look at what Brent did. Isn't this nice?" And he would say "Nice work, Brent," and smile down at Brent, as if that made up for his many absences.

And now Carl had hired a detective to do what? Make him give over the scrapbooks? Make him give back the money he took? Find out about him? No thanks.

He hadn't been to Maine in a whole lot of years. But maybe it was time to do a little detective work of his own. Maybe he owed it to himself to find out if what he had suspected all along was true.

During his break, he found Molly in the back, on the phone. He waited. Finally, "Yes, Brent?"

"Molly, I have a family emergency. I need to leave for a couple of days. Maybe longer."

She raised her eyebrows. "I'm sorry to hear that. Is there anything I can do?"

He shook his head. "I don't know how long I'll be. I have to clear up some stuff."

"Do you have any idea when you might be back?"

He shook his head again. It was unfair of him to do this to her. Faithful, kind Molly who had given him a job without even checking his references, Molly who had given him a break when no one else in his entire life had.

He went to the bar where Amanda worked. "Hey Brent, what're you doing here?" Two strings of black hair hung down on either side of her face. She flicked them back with a spiked nail.

"I just came to say good-bye."

Her smile faded. "What do you mean?"

"I have a family thing I have to take care of."

"Family?" He had never, ever mentioned family to her. Whereas he knew all about hers. He knew about her divorced parents and her loser brothers and little sister living up in Queens, and her down here because she couldn't take her mother's rules any longer.

He nodded. "It just came up. Something I have to take care of."

"Is this about that phone call?"

"Sort of."

She moved closer to him, and in a voice uncharacteristically gentle said, "Well, you could've told me, Brent. We're supposed to be friends. I know you're a little weird, but you're nice, too. You want me to come?"

"No. I have to do this by myself."

He gave her a quick kiss, then walked out.

At the apartment, he packed his backpack, grabbed all of his mother's scrapbooks, the duffel bag from his closet, all the loose money he could find, and loaded up his gray van. (He had long since sold Pellerman's car.) He headed out of Orange and up to the interstate to New England and Maine.

13

Teri sat cross-legged on the bed of her motel room compiling the day's interviews into her computer while she watched a very old episode of *Columbo* on the television. Her evening with the Musters had gone fine, better than expected. She had expected them to regale her with tales and photos from "the good old days of Jack and Jenny and Craig and Monica," but they didn't. Instead, they talked about crime and handguns, and Monica surprised Teri with her knowledge of criminals and punishment. She showed Teri her new Glock 17 with a ten-round magazine. She and Craig were members of a gun club and were taking shooting lessons at the range. Teri looked at them in surprise, these university people. Jack barely knew the difference between a handgun and a sword, while there they sat in the Muster's recreation room looking at handguns and discussing with great animation the new crime bill currently being debated in congress. Teri sort of regretted her decision not to stay there, but by nine-thirty she was in her motel and working on her notes.

She decided to make a few calls before it got too late. She dialed Patsy Mellon's number, and lo and behold, the woman herself actually answered. It was a breathless hello, answered after three rings.

"Patsy! Hello! This is Teri. I finally reached you! I've been trying for days. I hope this isn't too late. I was just wondering about the Sunday school materials."

A pause. "Oh, Teri, yes. Where are you calling from?"

"Where am I calling from?"

"Your number didn't come up on our caller ID."

"I'm on my cell. I'm in Boston. I'll be home tomorrow. I was wondering if maybe, could we meet tomorrow night? I could get the curriculum from you then. I'd really like it if we could fit this in because in another day or two I'll be away again for a while, and if I could have the stuff with me on my trip I could spend some time in the evenings working on it. I have to tell you I'm really looking forward to the girls. I had a pretty rough childhood, myself. I feel I have lots to offer them; I'm really—"

"Teri, it's wonderful that you volunteered for this position, but the Sunday school board is still in prayer about the matter, and then there's Ida. I still don't have the lesson books from her. I'm sorry that the board is moving so slow on this, but you'll have to bear with them a little while longer. With all of us." And then she laughed, a kind of tinny high laugh that made Teri feel slightly uncomfortable and she didn't know why.

Next she called Jack. She got the answering machine. She called Jack's cell, but it rang and rang. *Figures,* she thought, *he never uses the thing.* The cell phone was this year's Christmas gift from Teri, but he always forgot it. Or if he did remember it, he didn't turn it on. She called the house and left a message this time, that the Musters were great, but she ended up not knowing a great deal more about the accident than when she arrived. She'd be home tomorrow around lunch, but then she was going to be heading, probably the next day, up to Grand Manan.

Next she phoned Brent again, and Amanda told her that Brent was gone.

"You mean at work?"

"I mean gone. As in gone."

"Gone, where?"

"Gone, like I don't know where gone. It was some sort of family emergency. That's all he told me. Are you the same lady who phoned a few days ago?"

"Probably. He leave a number?"

"I didn't even know he had a family, much less one with an emergency." She seemed pleased with her turn of phrase and giggled.

"If he calls, can you get him to call me?" Then Teri recited her cell phone number.

By the time she got back to her computer notes, Columbo was

solving the case, some high-society female who'd killed her husband's secretary.

Family emergency? Teri picked up the Houseman family photos and leafed through them. She liked looking at people's faces. A raised eyebrow, a half-scowl, a crooked smile, a somber expression. They all said so much. She looked down at a Christmas picture of three young Houseman boys and Brent, a babe in Carl's arms. But something seemed wrong with it. She turned the photo this way and that, but couldn't figure it out. There was Carl, full of confidence, holding his baby son, and the boys—Carl Jr. (thirteen at the time), Charles, and Sam. No, that part looked okay. What was wrong with it had to do with Ellen, as if her picture had been pasted in later. Teri ran her fingers over the photo just to be sure. No, that wasn't it. Maybe it was the way she stood there, slightly apart from the rest of them, mere inches, but apart nonetheless.

She set the pictures aside and lay back on the motel pillows.

She was standing at the window, and outside someone was walking toward her, calling for her and frantically waving her arms. It was her mother. She was wearing the clothes she wore that day she went grocery shopping and never came back: green corduroy jeans and a faded, striped sweater with loose threads at the shoulder.

"Mom, you should get rid of that sweater. It's falling apart," Teri had said.

"I like it. It's the most comfortable thing I own, Teresa." Her mother and father were the only people who called her Teresa.

And now Teri strained to open the window, to find a way to get to her mother, but the window wouldn't open. She pushed, she shoved, but the window held fast. It was painted shut, she could see. She retrieved her nail file from her makeup case and began scraping away at the paint. The file broke. Then she took her shoe and hit the window hard, but her shoe bounced back and went skittering across the floor. There was her mother just outside of her Boston hotel room, and she couldn't get to her, couldn't rescue her. And overhead a bird shrieked at her, mocking her. Screeching. Screeching.

Her eyes jerked open. She glanced over at the window, draped solidly closed with motel-issue heavy navy. Her cell phone was ringing and she grabbed for it. She knocked her satchel onto the floor and looked at the red glinting numbers on the bedside clock. 10:56.

"Hello!" she screamed into the phone.

"Teri? This is Peg Pellerman. Did I wake you? I'm sorry."

"Oh, hello." Teri tried to make her voice sound normal. She was angry with Peg suddenly, Peg who had broken the dream spell. She wouldn't see her mother anymore tonight, and her mother-dreams were becoming scarcer. Peg was asking for an update.

"An update?" Teri rubbed her eyes.

"Yes, I expected one before now. I e-mailed you a while ago."

Teri leaned up on one arm. "I promised Carl weekly reports. So far I have done just that."

"Is it too much to ask, really, Teri, that you send me one as well? Just duplicate it and e-mail it to both me and Carl."

"Carl hasn't told me I should do that."

"Carl's so busy with the running of things it's a wonder he gets his shoes tied most days." She chuckled, but to Teri it was a mirthless sound.

"I'll talk to Dr. Houseman when I get home tomorrow."

"When you get home? Where are you now if not home?"

"I'm in Boston," was out before Teri had a chance to think about it.

"Boston! Whatever for?"

"Doing my job. And after this I'm heading up to Grand Manan Island." *Go for it,* she thought.

"Is that really necessary?"

"I think it is." Teri stifled a yawn.

"What Carl wanted was for you to look through the police reports again, not all this traipsing around."

"I'm doing the job Carl hired me to do."

"Which was to find out about that card. That started this whole thing. It's just so upsetting to all of us. We wish he would've left well enough alone. The ministry is even suffering because of it, and poor Daisy is beside herself."

Too bad for poor Daisy, thought Teri.

"She was the one who actually found your website, who actually told Carl to hire you."

"Daisy did?"

"Well, the three of us, but mostly it was Daisy. You know who Daisy Best is, I'm sure?"

"His fiancée."

"My goodness, Teri, she's more than that. She's one of the most popular writers of Christian romance that there is today."

"Oh."

"She was impressed with your qualifications. So, you see, it's not just Carl who's hired you, it's all of us." She sighed audibly. "Ellen is long dead and it's time Carl got on with his life. We all feel that way. Everyone feels that way."

"I guess Carl Houseman is the only one who can make that decision."

"I shouldn't be telling tales out of school, but all of us on the ministry team have noticed that Carl's gone a bit downhill since Ellen died. All of us here are worried about him. Well, let's just put it this way, some of his choices lately aren't as rational as they could be."

"Can I ask you a question, Mrs. Pellerman?"

"Fire away." Cheerful voice.

"How well do you know the Ryders and the Neddicks?"

There was a silence. "The relatives of the other accident victims? Not well at all."

"Didn't Archibald Ryder work for Dr. Houseman for a while?"

"There are so many people involved with the ministry, it gets to be impossible to keep track of all of them."

"I thought you were all grand friends."

"Grand friends? What an odd way to put it. Through the course of my work with Ellen, we became close, and I expect I'll become close to the next Mrs. Dr. Houseman. We're already becoming good friends. But really, the Ryders? No. They were merely acquaintances."

"What is it exactly that you do there?"

"Administrative assistant is my official title, but Paul and I do a variety of things. I worked with Ellen a lot coordinating her schedule. She was often called upon to speak at women's retreats, conferences, that sort of thing."

"And she did that? Ellen did a lot of speaking?"

"She never felt totally comfortable with it, but I coached her. She was always a little reluctant, but together we were a team."

"So, she's like a regular first lady then?"

"Well, I guess." Peg Pellerman laughed again. "What a strange analogy, but yes, in a small way, that's exactly what it was like."

When she hung up the phone, Teri picked up the Christmas photo and looked at Ellen, standing apart from the rest of them.

14

When Teri left the next morning to head home to Maine, there was another traveler on that same highway. Instead of singing along to Bonnie Raitt on his CD, he drove in silence, kept company by his thoughts alone.

He tried to remember the last time he was up this way. It must have been on a sailing trip more than a dozen years ago now, with his mother and his mother's friend Jane. Even as a teenager he never minded the way Jane would touch his hair. To him, she was always Aunt Jane. That seemed to please her. Another woman who insisted on being called "Aunt" was Peg Pellerman. But he hated it when Peg touched him.

"Why does she always touch my hair?" he would ask his mother.

His mother's eyes would crinkle up into a grin and she would say, "It's because you have a headful of cowlicks, Brent. Your hair goes every which where all over your head, and mother types can't help but want to straighten it around."

He had been around ten at the time and had scowled. "But why do I have to call her Aunt Peg? She's not my aunt."

"Well, you call Aunt Jane *Aunt.* What's the difference?"

"Aunt Jane is nicer."

She had leaned toward him, and he could smell her perfume, a sweetness like cinnamon. "You just like the sailing. That's all you like. That's why you think Aunt Jane is nicer." She had roughed his hair then, and he had shrugged away from her.

People were always touching his hair. Even his father, before church, would wet his hands under the tap in the kitchen and attempt to calm bits of his hair that sprang up all over. His hair was thick and dark, unlike his brothers whose hair was the color of bones.

Women still commented on his hair. He had dyed it yellow with the help of Amanda, and when it started growing in, he looked like a skunk. So one morning Amanda said, "You should shave your head," and he did. It was just beginning to grow back, and when he ran his hand over his head he could feel the soft prickles of it, like a brush.

By evening, Brent had arrived in the town his mother had grown up in. He found a little café, bought a basket of fish and chips, and sat listening to the conversation around him. Lobstermen in yellow overalls and baseball caps, families with food-spattered little kids in high chairs, and right next to him, a chubby woman trying to manage five little kids, which included one set of twins and a cranky baby. He turned away from them and read the place mat, which advertised a lot of local businesses.

After this, he'd go and visit Jane. He hoped he remembered where she lived.

15

When Teri arrived home, only Kelly greeted her with any kind of enthusiasm. "I know. I know," she said bending down to scruff her under the ears. "It's hard being here with two cats. I know all about it. Poor you."

She threw her duffel bag on the back stairs and opened the fridge. That brought Tiger and Gilligan running. They purred and meowed around her ankles while she grabbed orange juice, mustard, some wrapped sandwich meat, and a hunk of cheese. She balanced all of this precariously while she kicked the fridge door closed with her foot. Both cats were still insistent. "You hypocrites," she told them. "You only like me when I can get you food. Well, you'll just have to wait."

In the end, however, she relented, realizing there would be no peace while she ate unless she did the deed. She put down her sandwich fixings and got out the Puss 'N Boots from the fridge and put scoops of the pâté into two bowls.

She made herself a sandwich and thought momentarily about heading into her Bangor office, but decided that what she really needed was to take a run beside the river with Kelly and then unpack, do a load of laundry, and pack again for tomorrow. She got out the coffee fixings and saw a poppy seed coffee cake in a box from the market. She opened it and looked longingly at the white drippy icing. I better not, she decided. Jack had obviously bought it for tonight's poetry group.

Early in their marriage, when she was still trying to impress Jack, she had accepted an invitation from one of Jack's students, whom she fondly referred to as Stephan the Underwater Poet, to sit in on their group. Big mistake. It was two hours of listening to young earnest poets reading their poetry in quiet, serious monotones. After about half an hour, she was trying to figure out a way to gracefully leave. In the end, she stuck it out, but vowed to herself that ever after she would be "busy" on those nights.

Stephan wrote all of his poetry underwater. He was a scuba diver who found the underwater environment "more conducive to creative thought and reflection on the deeper meaning of life." His words.

Then there was Peter, who always brought a small set of congas and drummed on them with the heels of his hands while he recited his memorized verse. And there was Alyson, who wrote about the worldwide oppression of women and recited her poetry quite tearfully, and Olivia, who took the part of historical figures and wrote poems and essays from their viewpoints. There were others, too, and it usually ended up being a group of around a dozen.

After that one time, Teri said to Jack, "Are these kids for real?" To which Jack replied, "They're all good kids who are searching, and if I can be an influence for God in their lives, an influence for good, I'll take that as my mission."

Her coffee ready, she poured herself a cup with her usual quarter-cup dollop of cream. Then while her iBook booted up, she sat down at the kitchen table and spread out her maps. Tomorrow morning first thing, she'd head east on Route 9 to Calais and then up to New Brunswick and her eventual destination, Grand Manan Island.

She plugged her modem into the wall, dialed up, and after a few false starts found a listing for bed-and-breakfasts on Grand Manan Island. She called the first one on the list, Marnie's Bed-and-Breakfast, and a female voice told her that she was normally closed this time of year.

"Do you know where there might be a place to stay, then? I need to come in tomorrow and stay one, maybe two nights. I really prefer a bed-and-breakfast, but is there a hotel?"

"There's a couple of motels up Grand Harbour way, but I don't even know if they're open. We don't get many visitors this time of year."

"No bed-and-breakfasts? I always like to stay in bed-and-breakfasts when I travel." When she wanted to find local information she stayed in bed-and-breakfasts. When she wanted to rest and sleep, it was motels. Proprietors of bed-and-breakfasts were often fountains of local information.

"Oh dear, well let me think about this. Is it just you?"

"Just me."

"And are you a bird-watcher by any chance?"

"Bird-watcher? No."

"Well, I was going to tell you that there's no bird-watching on the island this time of year. All the birds have gone south. In case that's what you were coming for."

"Smart birds."

"You'd be surprised at the number of people who don't know that."

"I'm not coming to look at birds."

"Okay then, well, normally I don't take people this time of year, but it might be nice to have some company. That might be nice. Sure, you come. As soon as we hang up here I'm going upstairs and get a room ready for you. I usually turn the heat off in that part of the house, and it's off now. But I'll go get that ready. That'll give me something to do. This will be nice. You'll have to tell me what you like to eat, too, and I'll go out to the Save Easy. I'll probably give you the front room. You can see the water from there. From the back all you can see is the woods. The front is better. I'll make the bed up there."

After Teri got directions, she told Marnie that anything foodwise was okay. She hung up and said, "Bingo!" Not only did she have a place to stay, but she had a talker as well.

Before heading upstairs, she threw her dirty clothes down the laundry chute. She'd get to them later. Then she headed upstairs to pack. Grand Manan Island in January. Warm things, she was thinking. Layers. Fleece jackets. Jeans. Rain gear, possibly. Hiking boots, of course.

When her bag was packed, Jack phoned to tell her that he

missed her and was glad she was home, and that he'd be home with a bunch of pizzas for his students and that he'd kick them out as early as he could.

"Hey, the Musters were great. They know more about guns than I do. I had a great time with them."

"I told you you would! Craig and Monica used to lose me when they would go on and on about caliber this and caliber that. I knew you guys would have a lot in common."

"I'm leaving for Grand Manan tomorrow."

"You have to go?"

"Work beckons."

"Then I really will kick the kids out early."

Next Teri called Carl Houseman to brief him on what she was doing.

"It sounds like you have a lot of good information already," he said.

"Dr. Houseman—"

"Carl. Please."

"Okay. Carl. I wonder if you could send me a copy of the video of Ellen's memorial service, the one that you broadcast on your show."

"Fine. No problem. Anything else?"

"Yes, one thing. Peg Pellerman has asked that I submit weekly updates of my investigation to her. Is this something you'd like me to do?"

He chuckled, a deep baritone sound over the phone lines. "As I've told you, I have very few secrets from Peg and Paul. If you can't get a hold of me, then by all means talk to Peg. She usually knows where I am."

"But weekly reports? Do you want weekly written reports?"

"Is that what Peg asked for?" He laughed again. "I'll have a talk with her. Weekly written reports is an awful burden. I do expect a phone call weekly, however."

"You have that. I'll call at least weekly, most likely more."

After that Teri put a load of whites in the washing machine, and while it was agitating, she took Kelly for a jog by the river. She spent the rest of the afternoon sitting on the chair beside the fireplace, wrapped in an afghan and reading *Prepared Paths* while she finished up the remainder of the pot of coffee.

Jack arrived home around five with Stephan and Peter and four large pizza boxes. Actually, it was Peter and Jack who carried in the boxes. Stephan was carrying a little bundle of books: his latest chapbook of poetry, he told Teri proudly. He flipped her a copy and she caught it in her left hand. It was titled, simply, *submerged.*

"Hey, great," Teri said.

"You can have that copy. That one's yours. I signed it for you."

"Hey, great," Teri said.

"You going to join us?" Peter asked.

"Can't. Work. Tons of it."

Soon the others arrived: Alyson in black, the color worn to show solidarity with all her oppressed sisters, then Olivia and Cassandra and the others.

Teri grabbed two pieces of pizza and settled herself at the kitchen table with her iBook. Behind the closed door she could hear the low murmur of conversation while she transcribed her Boston interviews into Cut Throat. Then she would hear Jack's voice, more solid, more sure. She listened for his voice. It always impressed Teri how Jack could steer even the most mundane conversation back to God. And the students loved him.

In the end, Jack wasn't able to keep his promise to "kick them all out early." And it was after eleven when he came into the kitchen and put his arms around her and told her how happy he was that he had married her instead of a poet.

"But you love poetry! You read poetry all the time."

"I need some sanity in my life, and you provide that, my love."

16

For the child's sake, Garda had hung a Christmas stocking. She had shown Will the stocking during the first week of December. She took him into the front room of the cottage, the one with the window facing the sea, and showed him Audrey's sock that she had hammered to the wooden mantel of the stone fireplace, a thing they never used.

"Can you find it within yourself to bring something for her? Candy maybe? Something? For Audrey's sake?" She looked long into his eyes for some softening there. Just something. Please God. But she saw none.

He never brought candy, and as December moved into January, Garda closed off the front room with its southeast winds that slithered like snakes in between pane and window casing.

She did this every winter, moved them into the kitchen where she placed wool rugs on the stone floor and kept a fire going in the stove, day and night. Sometimes on very cold nights they even slept there. Garda would drag the mattresses from the bedrooms and put them on the floor next to the stove. Audrey liked that. She would clap her hands, and to her own music she would dance on the floor around the mattresses, eventually falling onto them with a thump and a gurgling laugh.

Audrey was doing that now, dancing. A slim, young woman clad only in a white cotton slip, she danced barefoot around the kitchen to "Tales from the Vienna Woods" that came from a battery-operated radio on the counter tuned in to CBC Radio Two.

Garda sat in a cane rocker next to the woodstove drinking tea while Audrey danced. She looked so normal, Audrey did, a delicate young woman, her hands flouncing the plain white shift as if it were some exquisite gown, two butter-colored ponytails lifting and falling, lifting and falling as she moved about, barefoot on the rug. Will was wrong. She needed to be in a school. Garda should just take her, she thought. Just pack her up and the two of them walk out of here. Get on the ferry and just arrive on the mainland. What a stir that would cause now, wouldn't it?

The tinny music stopped for a moment, a station break, and Audrey squealed and raised her arms. "Don't worry. It'll be back on soon," Garda said.

Garda had turned the radio back on just this morning. It was safe now to turn it on. At the first of December she put the radio in the bottom of the linen closet in the living room, the sound of Christmas carols bringing up such a sorrow in her that she couldn't bear them.

But Garda, in private moments, was teaching Audrey about God. And on Christmas morning she had sat next to Audrey on the mattress and read her the Christmas story from the old Bible she found in the sideboard. The girl's eyes brightened as if this were something she had known all along.

Garda wouldn't leave here. Even though she thought about it, she couldn't. She couldn't. Will would destroy her if she even tried. Will knew all about her. He was the one person.

Still, if she were to leave, could her punishment—public ridicule, jail time possibly—be any worse than this? It had been four years since she buried the woman in the garden, four years since she sought some kind of redemption in this lonely, phony lighthouse that was rotting out from underneath her.

The music came back on again, and Audrey resumed her dancing. And Garda watched her strange and lonely dance while her stocking hung empty in the cold living room.

17

Like the police and that private investigator, Brent had his own information about the accident. He'd kept things. A few news clippings and photos. He'd even saved some cards. Other things, too. Plus, he had those scrapbooks. Wouldn't that PI love to get her hands on those!

Right after the accident, Brent would take the newspaper from the front porch up to his room, where he cut out the articles he wanted to save. Then he stuffed the rest in the garbage can in the backyard. Nobody missed it. Nobody asked where the newspaper was. Carl Jr. and his wife and their kids came to the house every day for three weeks after the accident and never asked once to see the paper. Carl's wife brought over casseroles of burned lasagna, her specialty.

And every day more cards came. Mostly they came to his father's office, and from his perch in the sound booth, he could see the mailman walk in with stacks. But cards came to the house as well, and he would see these when he got home earlier than his father. The cards that came to the house were generally from his mother's Maine friends. All the cards from Maine and the east coast he opened without hesitation. There was a flowery one from Jane Jarvis, addressed to his father. *Dear Dr. Houseman, I am deeply grieving over the loss of Ellen, as I know you are. She was a wonderful friend and a generous human being…*

Dr. Houseman, she called her best friend's husband. Shouldn't that tell you something right there? A plant was sent by four Maine friends: *Fred, George, Bill, and Gordon, your boat buddies.* He had placed the plant in the living room with all the others and had kept the card to himself. His father never even noticed it. Nobody watered the plant and it was dead within the month.

He also kept money. A card from Maine had a five dollar bill in it. He kept it, and it gave him an idea. For the next couple of weeks, he waylaid the mailman before he got into the church building. He took the cards, opened them, and took out money. Why people would include money in a sympathy card to his father was beyond him, but they did. A five dollar bill here, a twenty dollar bill there, and Brent would take them out of the cards and put them in his pocket, and when he got home he put them in a brown envelope in the back of his closet. It was sort of funny when you thought about it. The Pellermans, who were such money hounds, didn't even notice that the sympathy cards were coming already slit open. They would assume his father opened them. His father would assume Pellermans opened them. He ended up with more than five thousand dollars in loose bills this way.

He never spent any of it. Now, he was on his way to Maine, the money in the duffel bag safely hidden under the floorboard of his van, along with the gun he had also stolen from Pellermans. What he needed to do was to find that detective.

After supper at the café, he drove to Jane Jarvis's. As soon as she saw who it was, she threw open her door and hugged him. She smelled like apples.

"Well, Brent, hello! It's been how long?"

"Hi, Jane."

She cuffed his hair. "And you're too old now for *Aunt* Jane? Is that it?"

He smiled.

"You better come in. What brings you up this way?"

She invited him for supper. He said no, he had just eaten, and she said shame on him for not calling when he arrived and for eating by himself! Fred had dropped off a box of lobsters, and she was boiling them up for the freezer. She did have pies, though. And was just this minute getting them out of the oven. Brent said thank you, apple pie sounded nice.

She talked as she led him through to the kitchen. Fred had quit lobstering and was working in the boatyard now. The house his mother had grown up in had a young family in it. He was some kind of lawyer. Also, Jane's brother had been killed in a hunting accident. Had he heard that? Had his mother told him? Did he remember Jane's brother? He shook his head, no. While they ate pie and ice cream, she asked him to stay the night; she had plenty of rooms. He knew she had plenty of rooms. He'd been here often enough when he was little. He shook his head. "I don't know."

Then she had wiped her face with her napkin and plopped it on the table. "Okay, Brent, I know you well enough; what's troubling you? You didn't come all this way to eat pie with an old lady."

He took a moment before he said, "Did a detective talk to you? Has she been by?"

"So, she's talked to you, too? I can't imagine that the police really want to open this case after all this time."

Brent blinked. So that PI hadn't told Jane that she was really hired by his father! Well, that figures. Brent made a grunt sort of noise and said, "Maybe it's some sort of law. Maybe they have to look at every case every five years or something."

"Well, I never heard of *that* law before."

"Actually, I'm trying to get a hold of her. Do you know where she went?"

Jane paused, pursed her lips. "I don't know. She was talking to a few people here, but she really didn't tell me where she was going. I have her card if you want to give her a call. Here, let me go get it."

He let her get up, fiddle around with the message pad by her telephone, write down the number and hand it to him, even though he already had her number on a piece of paper in his wallet.

"So, she didn't say where she was going or anything?"

"I don't know for sure, but I imagine she'd go on to Grand Manan. But then again, who knows?"

He shrugged.

"So, will you be going up there?"

"Maybe."

"Maybe you shouldn't follow her, Brent. Maybe there will be things you don't want to find out."

18

Marnie Doane of Marnie's Bed-and-Breakfast turned out to be a petite, heavily made-up redhead who came outside to greet Teri wearing a loose, floral-print summer pantsuit and gold mules. Her head was a mass of pink sponge curlers, which stuck out at odd angles, but it was her lips that really stood out: fire-engine red and drawn well above the natural curve of her upper lip, *I Love Lucy* style.

"You must be Teri, my houseguest," she said.

"Yes, I'm Teri, and you're Marnie?"

"Yes, come in. Come in." She waved her hand. "I have to tell you that it isn't often that I get guests in the middle of winter like this. But you should see me in summer. Up to my ears in bird-watchers. Never a moment's peace for me then. I'm baking all the time."

Marnie took out a loose curler, combed the piece of hair—which looked already curly to Teri—through her fingers and redid the curler, pulling it tight against her pink scalp.

"Oh, Teri, just to let you know, before we go inside I want you to take a look at that bird feeder over there." She pointed. "Do you see it?"

Teri looked. "You mean that green one?"

"Yep. I'll be giving you a key to the place, but if you forget it, I always keep a spare one in that bird feeder. You just got to reach your hand in at the bottom. And regards to paying me? I take anything. MasterCard, Visa, you name it. Even cash. Just whatever suits."

"Great."

"Let's go inside then. It's cold out here. I've got a nice coffee cake on. I found a new recipe on the Internet."

Teri followed her up the steps to the back door, which led into a mudroom where Teri was instructed to remove her boots and hang up her jacket. Then she followed Marnie into the kitchen, which was warmed by an electric fireplace made to look like a real one with log-shaped pieces of ceramic with flames licking around them. In the center of a table covered by a Christmas-print tablecloth was a delicious looking apple pie. On another smaller table was a bowl of fresh fruit.

Marnie led Teri through the kitchen and down a hallway and up a wide staircase lined with framed photographs. They stopped at every one while Marnie introduced nieces, nephews, cousins, and other relations whose associations to her were no longer clear.

The room Teri was finally brought to had two single beds and a small table and lamp between them.

"I figured you'd want a desk," Marnie said. "Now, I know you're not a bird-watcher because it's not the season. So, I thought, what reason could there be to come to the island by yourself in the winter? So I thought, maybe she's a writer. Sometime we get writers on the island. I once had a writer stay here. In this very room. For two whole months. Strange fellow. Never said *boo.* Kind of creepy, too. I'd wake up at all hours and hear him walking up here. Heavy footsteps. Now why would he be wearing his shoes in the middle of the night? He had these haunted eyes, like ghost eyes. My girlfriends said to me, Marnie, are you safe with him by yourself there? But he never bothered me *that* way, if you know what I mean. Do you like the view?"

"It's beautiful," Teri said. They were high on a bluff, and down across the trees and the highway was a distant view of the Bay of Fundy.

"It is, isn't it?" Marnie straightened both beds and fluffed the pillows while she talked and talked. "I've lived here all my life. I get this view all day long any time of the day I want it. You know, I haven't even been to the mainland in...well, I don't know how many years. Hate that ferry ride. How was the ferry ride over? Rough?"

"Smooth as silk."

"That's good, because it can get some miserable out there. You see any whales?"

"Whales? No. I probably should've been looking."

"You make sure you look for them on the way back. They have these whale watching boats you can get on, but I say, phooey to that, you just ride the ferry and you'll see plenty. We got all kinds of whales. Hundreds of them. Right whales and finbacks. Every summer my bird-watchers tell me about the whales they see."

"So, where do these bird-watchers come from anyway?" Teri asked, placing her duffel bag on the closest bed.

"Oh, from all over. Anywhere and everywhere." She laid towels at the foot of the bed and told Teri that she was to help herself from the linen closet in the hallway if she ran out. And that dirty towels could be placed in the hamper at the end of the hall. Marnie did laundry every day when she had guests, never missed a day, and winter would be no exception; the only thing was, she wouldn't be able to hang the towels outside. Too cold.

While Marnie talked, Teri unpacked a few things and set up her computer. She was told that the bathroom was right across the hall and that since she was the only visitor here just now, she'd have it all to herself, and wasn't that nice.

There were plants around the room, too, with fuzzy leaves and purple flowers, and a hanging plant in the corner with perfect white flowers. Teri tentatively touched the leaves. Artificial.

"You like my flowers?" Marnie said. "I find artificial plants so much easier to care for."

Teri smiled.

"So, are you a writer or what?"

"I guess I'm a *what.* I'm a researcher, of sorts."

"A researcher. Well. That's a new one." She paused, took a curler out and put it in again. "So, is that like a scientist or something?"

"Sort of, I suppose. Actually, I'm here to research that sailboat accident that happened five years ago off the island. The one that killed the three women. Were you here then?"

Marnie stopped, eyes widening, her hand to her heart, "Oh my, of course I was here then. Of course I was. Where else would I be?"

"Maybe I can sit down and talk to you about it sometime?"

"Oh, yes. By all means. I'd love to help you with your research. Oh my, I could tell you things about that! When you get unpacked why not come downstairs. I've got a nice coffee cake heating up and I'll make us some tea."

"Great. I'll unpack and be down in a minute."

After Marnie left, Teri sat down on each of the beds, testing them. There seemed to be a wind coming through the edges around the windowpanes, so she decided on the bed farthest from the window.

A waist-high bookshelf ran the entire length of the wall opposite her bed. It was crammed full of magazines and books. On closer examination Teri saw that they were all romances, every single one of them. Nothing but romances. And on the floor in front of the bookshelf stood a pile of bridal magazines, going back a dozen years. She looked past the magazines and books, and out onto the bay.

The ferry had been full on the ride over, and a fellow about her age in a plaid wool jacket asked if he and his very pregnant wife could sit across from her in the booth.

"I don't mind at all. Have a seat," Teri said.

He told her that he hoped she had a nice visit on the island.

"It shows that much? That this is my first time?"

"Saw your Maine license plate when you drove on. We were right behind you."

"Oh."

"In the truck there. Most people come to Grand Manan in the summer. Not many in the winter."

"I guess I'm odd doing my sight-seeing in the winter. Beats the crowds though. And I get my choice of places to stay."

"So, where you staying?"

"A place called Marnie's Bed-and-Breakfast. You know it?"

He grunted. "Everybody knows Marnie."

"Oh yeah? Is her place okay?"

"Good enough. She talks a lot, though."

"And if she says anything," the woman said, "don't believe her."

"She has a great imagination," the man said. "So, what're you coming to the island for?"

"Research." When they looked at her blankly, Teri said, "Well, to be absolutely truthful, I'm a PI and I'm doing some research on the accident where those three women died in a sailing accident five years ago. You remember that?"

"You the police?"

"Private."

The man wrapped his long fingers around his coffee cup and opened his eyes wide. "Really? Like you're a private detective?"

"Yep."

"Well, isn't that something, eh?"

"Yep. So, what's your take on the accident? Were you here then?"

"Yeah. There was something wrong with the engine. That's the plain and simple of it."

"Oh? I thought whatever was wrong with it was fixed."

"It wasn't. Not entirely. There was this part that the engine needed, but those women took off in the boat without getting it fixed. They wanted to get home in a quick hurry. That's what I heard."

"I hadn't heard that about the engine."

"It's common knowledge around here."

"What about the storm?"

He snorted. "What storm. Most of us have been out in worse in dories."

"Oh yeah?" Teri took a sip of her coffee. "So you don't go with the pirate theory?"

"Tell her about the witch, Mark," the pregnant woman said.

"What witch?" Teri said.

"There's a witch on the island," she said.

"Really?"

"She's not a witch," he said. "Just a crazy old lady. Don't be going around saying that, Jessica."

She stared at him, a defiant look in her pale eyes. "There are some who say it was her. You know that's true."

"It was engine failure, Jessica."

She pouted into her Coke. "I'm just saying what some people have been saying. You know I'm right. That it was a witch or ghosts. Or evil spells or something."

Teri stood on the second floor of Marnie's Bed-and-Breakfast and watched the fog roll in from the ocean. And rolling was what it was doing, great round clouds turning end over end. It sort of did look like ghosts.

"Yoo-hoo!" Marnie was at the bottom of the stairs. "Yoo-hoo! I've got coffee cake on, Teri."

Downstairs Marnie stood at the counter peeling bits of plastic off the bottom of the coffee cake. "Oh, my dear, you weren't supposed to see this. Here I go, heating it up in the oven and I leave the plastic on it. But it'll be fine. I'll just get this off. Ouch, that's hot. I could burn myself on this. I put it in the microwave, but maybe I had it in for a bit too long.

"I'm sure it'll be fine," Teri said.

"I hope so. We'll just have to sit down and try it."

"Your pie sure looks good though," Teri said.

Marnie began laughing. "You go look at that pie carefully, Teri. Touch it. Go on."

Teri walked over to it, peered down at it, touched the edge of the crust. It was ceramic. "It looks so real. You had me fooled."

"Isn't it lovely? I got that from a gift store in San Diego. That's in California."

"Were you there recently?"

"Oh no, not me. Like I said, I haven't been away from this place in years. I ordered it from their website. Couldn't resist it. I could show you the website I got it from if you're interested."

"That's okay," Teri said.

"The tea's ready. I like a nice cup of tea in the afternoon, don't you?"

Teri didn't, but she didn't say so. She drank coffee, but if the mood was right, tea was okay as long as it was strong. Very strong. When she made tea, she put two tea bags into a mug, covered them with boiling water, and kept the tea bags in there the whole time she drank it.

"So, tell me about your research." Marnie said. "What do you want to know? I was thinking about this when you were upstairs that I think I know every single person on this island. Every one."

"The reports say that the accident was caused by high winds."

"That's what the TV said, but most of the locals say the wind wasn't that bad. Now, you ask me, I say it was pretty bad. You take wind and the kind of tidal rips and currents we get around here, and a boat could be easily caught off guard. I've seen it happen."

"So, you just think it went down?"

"My theory?" She licked her fingers and adjusted a curler. "I go with pirates."

"Pirates?"

"Pirates needed that boat, so they boarded it and...well, they killed the women and just took it." She took a sip of her tea.

"So they killed the other two, but kept Ellen alive to sail the boat for them?"

"Not a chance. No, that's not what happened. If that's what happened, don't you think she'd find some way to get back here? Back to her husband? He looks so handsome in his pictures. Do you think he's handsome, Teri? I think he's handsome. I'll tell you one thing, if I had a man like that waiting for me and I was taken by pirates, I'd find some way to get back to him, believe you me."

"So, why didn't they find her body?"

"She didn't have her life jacket on. So she sunk and became lobster food. Did you know lobsters are bottomfeeders? Everything and anything that goes overboard they eat. Think of that the next time you sit down to a lobster dinner in a fancy restaurant. Bottomfeeders."

"What about ghosts? A witch?"

"So, you've heard about our witch, have you?"

"Someone on the ferry mentioned her."

Marnie looked outside. "When we finish here, why don't we go for a walk. I'd like to show you something."

Her weak tea finished, Teri went upstairs, pulled on a fleece jacket, wool hat, mittens and hiking boots. Downstairs, the only concession Marnie had made to the weather was a floral silk scarf tied around her curlers, and some fluffy white socks with Keds. She was still wearing the wide silky floral pants, and over it she had pulled on what looked like a man's gray wool sweater several sizes too large for her.

Outside, Marnie said, "It's so beautiful this time of year. This is my favorite time of the year."

Teri looked doubtfully at the gray cold skies and the leafless brown trees, felt the edge of wind, tasted the fog moving in. "You like winter?"

"I love it. This is the only season where you can see clear through the brush to the water. You can't always do that the rest of the year. It makes everything wide open. That's why winter's my favorite time." They drove in Marnie's ancient, rattling K-car down a winding foggy road to the south end of the island and parked beside a lighthouse, Southwest Head, Marnie told her. They took off from there on foot.

Marnie's walk quickly turned into a hike, as she led Teri on a path that bordered high jagged cliffs. Ten minutes later, Teri, who thought she was in shape from her years as a casual jogger, had to scramble to keep up with the woman. The only moments she got to catch her breath were when Marnie stopped to reclasp an errant pink curler or to refresh her lipstick. And Marnie talked the entire time, while Teri, not hearing most of what she said, made little noises of assent every so often.

They were now walking perilously close to a cliff. Teri hung back, but Marnie walked right along the edge. Every once in a while vistas of steep cliffs with jagged edges and trees scrabbling for rootholds would break through the fog. Two hundred feet below, flames of ocean spray licked the rocks.

Teri stopped and looked. "This is so beautiful. So rugged. So breathtaking."

"I come here every day," Marnie said.

Aren't you a little close to the edge? Teri wanted to ask, but held her tongue.

"There are paths like this all over the island," Marnie said. "People come here for two things—the birds and the paths, and I've hiked most of the paths. Then when my bird-watchers come back, I can tell them the best places to go. I don't bird-watch myself, just go out and let them know where they're likely to see birds. That way I get the same people back every summer. I don't like to rent my rooms to just anyone. I like to know who they are, after that strange writer guy." She rolled her eyes. "And you know something else. He's never written anything that I could find, and I tried on Amazon. I tried everywhere. Some writer, I say. I think that's a bit fishy, don't you, Teri? You can't be too careful nowadays. That's what I think. A lot of lovers come up here, too. It's a favorite place for that. But people die here all the time. Fall off. They're not wearing proper hiking clothes, that's the main thing." She said it so matter-of-factly. "We had a couple just this summer from Vermont, maybe you heard about them. Everyone thought they'd been kidnapped or murdered or taken away. They just disappeared. But I know what happened to them."

"You do?"

"I do. Do you know what it was?" She stopped and turned to Teri. After a few seconds Teri realized a response of some sort was required.

"No, what?" she said.

"They fell. One of them slipped and the other tried to help, and they both toppled over. And the current took them out to sea. Lobster food now, I suppose. You don't like lobster, do you?"

"Sort of. Well, I used to."

Marnie kept this up the whole time.

At a clearing up ahead Teri pulled her wool cap more firmly over her cold ears. And she marveled at Marnie still in her loose cotton pants and silk scarf, now fallen down around her shoulders.

Then Marnie pointed ahead of her down about a hundred feet to an odd looking squat lighthouse perched out on the rocks, and next to it a small cottage. "This is what I wanted to show you."

"That couldn't be a real lighthouse, could it?"

Marnie chuckled. "Nope. That little lighthouse-looking building has a story behind it. It was built by a rich duke from Scotland who decided he always wanted to be a lighthouse keeper. The problem was he was a drunk, and no one could trust him to light the lights at the right time. So he built his own, a miniature one. It has a real light in the lighthouse part, but it's never been lit. The tourist people wanted to buy it for a sort of tourist attraction. Fix it up, you know? But it's condemned. It would need to be almost completely rebuilt before it's safe. But it's inhabited. A hermit woman lives there with her retarded daughter. That's the witch you heard about."

"Really?"

"Yes, but that's not what I want to show you," Marnie said. "You look at that beach down there in front of the lighthouse. See it?"

"Yeah."

"That's where the stuff from the boat washed ashore. Right down there. When it all happened, I remember being up here watching all those police boats, up and down the water there. It was quite something to see. Being up here was better than CNN, that's for sure. Quite a show."

"I bet. Is it possible to hike along the bottom of the cliff? Maybe get a better look at the water?"

"It's getting late today. We're losing our light. We could go tomorrow."

"Great." Teri looked again at the lighthouse and cottage. "There's really a woman down there with a child? I can't imagine it."

"Well, she's not such a child anymore. Girl must be in her twenties by now. Should be off going out with boys, and here she is stuck down there with a very strange mother."

"Really?"

"She's Grand Manan's true recluse. But it's not her that's supposed to be the witch. It's the daughter."

"Really!"

"Yes, really." The woman's name was Garda, Marnie told her. She had been engaged to someone named Will, but then at the last minute, ran off and married Will's brother Jerome and moved to Saint John. It broke Will's heart into a million pieces, she said, and he's never been the same. The next thing anyone knows, Jerome's dead from a car crash, and Garda is back on Grand Manan with a new baby girl. When Garda arrived back with her baby, neither Jerome's parents nor her own parents wanted anything to do with her. When they found the baby was retarded, they said it wasn't their son's, that Garda must've had an affair. Because if she stepped out on Will, who's to say she didn't step out on Jerome?

"They took one look at the girl's eyes and said she was devil's spawn. Can you figure such a thing? That's where the whole witch thing comes from," Marnie said.

Teri looked at the tiny run-down cottage. "That's so horrible. What about her parents?"

"Wanted nothing to do with her, either. She was kind of a wild child back in those days. Everyone said the car accident was a little fishy. I thought that, too. You see, Jerome and I were an item way back when. We were going to get married, and then next thing I know, Garda's off with him."

"And his brother, Will, is he still around?"

"Yep. Lives over in Seal Cove. Well, when Garda gets back here she has nowhere else to go, and the next thing you hear, Garda's taken her baby and they're living in that old lighthouse."

"It's so hard to believe. Does she ever come into town?"

"Hardly at all. She and I were never on speaking terms in the first place. She taking Jerome right out from under my nose like that. She was a wild child back then. Well, don't get me wrong—I was a wild child, too, but we were wild in different ways. Lots of water under the bridge since then. Lots of water, Teri."

Marnie dug out her lipstick, flipped up a little mirror attached to it, refreshed her lips, and then blotted them on a handkerchief she had in her pocket.

"Well, let's go back," she said. "A nice cup of tea would go down nice right about now, wouldn't it?"

19

If Garda had to find a beginning, if she had to go back to when it started, she would tell you that it was the prescription filled by the young pharmacist with the dark hair and the kind eyes. That was the beginning of it, when their hands touched and she looked at him and felt as if he was seeing something inside of her that no one else was bothering to look for.

She'd read about these sorts of things since in magazines, in books, psychologists who studied the phenomenon of what causes two people to be attracted to each other. She never did find any answers. Not for her. There probably weren't any.

But if she were honest she would say that the chance meeting in the drugstore really wasn't it at all. Her story really began years and years before, and was born out of loneliness. Too many evenings alone while her husband spent all of his time and money on his mistress.

When the pharmacist counted out her change, placing the bills in her hand, his hand touched hers. It could have been nothing. That could have been the end of it. But she went back. The next day she went to his counter and asked about possible drug interactions. A stupid question really, since it was all spelled out on the bottle. Did he sense that? Could he see why she was really there?

She liked the white jacket he wore, the way his thick hair gently fell forward, the way he pushed it out of his eyes. He wore no wedding ring. She noticed that.

Garda audibly sighed, and Audrey looked at her. It was a mild day for January, and she and Audrey were out in the front of the cottage. No breeze blew, and down below the Grand Manan Channel looked like a sheet of solid steel. A large rock was in danger of slipping out of the foundation at the front of the cottage, and if it did it would compromise the entire structure. The winds and erosion were eating away at her place like maggots, and it wouldn't be long before the cottage fell into the sea along with the lighthouse. With her pickax, Garda attempted to place another large rock next to it. Futile work. They should leave.

While she worked, Audrey sat on a log and drew shapes in the frosty puddles with a stick. She was wearing an old jacket of Garda's, having outgrown most of her childhood clothes in the last few years. They really needed to take a shopping trip to town, even to the mainland.

After she had filled that prescription, she began making excuses to go to the drugstore. She needed shampoo in the middle of the afternoon. She needed to buy a birthday card. She would stand beside the card rack and pretend to go through them until he would come over. "Can I help you with something?" And she would say, "I'm looking for the perfect birthday card." That's what it was mostly like that first summer—just casual conversation, her leaning against his counter, him smiling down at her, talking about the weather, the price of lobsters—which affected his business as well as the lobstermen's—who's out on what boat and where they were fishing.

A few days later, or it could have been closer to a week, he had leaned over his counter and said, "Would you like to have coffee? I have a few minutes. Are you free now?"

That struck her as ludicrous. Free. She was very much *not* free. But she told him she was. The first in a string of lies that would ultimately lead to the deaths of four people and two friendships.

It's odd the way you can justify your actions, she thought as she wedged the rock into place. My husband has his own mistress, and so I rationalize. I've a right to be happy, don't I? I deserve this little island of happiness in a sea of loneliness, don't I? Don't I have that right?

There were letters that winter between the two of them, letters in which they shared their lives, their hopes, their dreams. He would write little anecdotes of his day, and she loved reading these, imagining herself there at his drugstore, watching while he swept the snow away from the front door, watching while he mopped up a water spill in the basement, laughing with him when he described the lopsided cakes brought to him by his landlady, crying with him when his old cat died.

She knew exactly what she was doing. She knew that with every letter she was crossing some bridge for which there was no going back. Ever. By the following summer they sat together openly at the café and drank coffee and ate pie. Hers was peach, and his was apple with vanilla ice cream. The place was famous for its pies. Funny the things you remember.

Four days later, on a warm summer night he kissed her. She had come to the drugstore to meet him after it closed. Sometimes she did that so she could walk him home. We're just friends, she had told herself. I'm allowed friends, aren't I? They had stood outside of the pharmacy and talked for a long time in the dark, while across the street the neon light from a pizza parlor glinted, the *a* flickering on-off, on-off. They talked. Oh, how they talked! Married couples can sit in silence through an entire meal, but lovers have so much to say to each other.

And then he had reached out his hand. She remembered it still, the way he had placed it on her cheek. It lingered there. And then he had leaned down and kissed her on the mouth. She moved to him, closer, closer, and they held each other while the *a* flickered on-off, on-off across the street.

Before this happened she used to laugh, like all busy wives and mothers, How could I possibly have an affair? Where would I find the time? But people do, you know. Moments here and moments there. Time can be found if time is truly what is wanted...

"Mama fly, Mama fly, Mama fly." Audrey, standing with arms outstretched at the cliff edge, brought her back to reality.

"Audrey!" Garda lunged, grabbed her and pulled her away from the cliff. "Audrey, oh Audrey, no." She held the girl to her, clung to her, wept and rocked the child, ran her hands through her hair.

She needed to get it right. She needed to get this one thing right. Audrey would be her redemption. Her one last chance.

They went inside then, and Garda made tea and the wind came up.

20

The following morning Marnie, her hair still in curlers, remembered to undo the plastic wrap on a couple of sweet breakfast rolls before she popped them into the microwave. She poured Teri a cup of coffee the color of weak tea, then set a container of milk in front of her. Not cream. Skim milk, even. She sat across from Teri and told her that her boyfriend called last night and was coming for a visit.

"How nice for you." Teri poured the milk into her mug, turning it a grayish color.

The microwave dinged and Marnie pulled out the sweet rolls and separated them onto a plate. "Do you have children, Teri?"

The question startled her. "No. Well, my husband has two children, but they're grown."

Marnie stared at her, eyes wide. "That's just like my boyfriend. Exactly. He has two grown children. I knew you and I had a lot in common. I said to myself when you walked up the stairs into my house, now here's a girl who's a lot like me. I don't know. I just felt it, you know, a connection. I knew we had a lot in common. You remind me of me when I was your age."

Teri drank her coffee and ate her rubbery bun. Marnie hadn't applied her makeup this morning, and without the harsh eyes and the red unnatural lips, she looked, well, pretty. It was her eyes that made her so. They positively sparkled. Maybe it was the coming visit from the boyfriend.

"My boyfriend is divorced from a real witch who took all his money and turned his children against him," she was saying. "Does your husband have a good relationship with his children?"

"Yes, an excellent one."

"And do you, Teri?"

"I guess. I hope so. I haven't spent too much time with either of them."

"Same here! I've hardly spoken at all to my boyfriend's children. Was your husband's former wife a witch?"

"No. My husband was a widower for four years before we got married."

"Widower! That's the worst kind, Teri. The worst kind. Oh, Teri, you want to watch out for widowers. I wish I'd known you before you got hooked up with him. You want to get involved with a divorced man rather than a widower. I've had boyfriends who were widowers. All they talk about are their dead wives. Those poor dead wives become saints. And nothing you do can ever match up to them. Nothing. I've seen it time and time again. I know what I'm talking about here." While she talked, she wiped out the inside of the microwave, wrung out the rag and ran it over the front of the fridge. "Give me a divorced man whose wife is a witch any day. But, I've never gotten married. Call me chicken. Call me whatever. But I never got married. Had many opportunities too, including Jerome...well, before he ran off with Garda, before Garda bewitched him." She turned to Teri. "Why did you get married?"

"It's a long story."

Marnie beamed. "We've got time, and I'd love to hear about it." Her eyes were so wide and she looked so innocent that Teri told her.

"When I was fourteen my mother disappeared. She was probably murdered, but her body was never found. When I tell that to people, the first thing they say to me is, 'Oh, what a terrible thing. That's so sad.' Well, Jack was the first person who said to me, 'And that's where your life began, isn't it?' I remember thinking, what an odd thing to say. Because this is where my life ended, not began. And I told him that and then he said, 'No, it's where it began. It's the reason you went into police work, the reason you're such a hotshot missing persons researcher. This has defined you.' I guess his reaction so surprised me that I fell in love with him on the spot."

Marnie put her hands over her heart. "That's such a nice story,

Teri. You should write that one down. That one should be in a book. And you've been happy?"

"So far, so good." Teri finished off her sweet roll, wiped her hands on her napkin and said, "Well, thank you for breakfast, but I better get on my way. Maybe you can tell me where to find that path that goes down below the cliff."

"Better than that. I'll come with you. You forget. I know these cliffs like the back of my hand."

"You don't have to. You must have things you need to get done."

"My boyfriend's not coming for a few days yet. I've got time. You wait here; I'll just go get ready. Get my makeup on. Oh my, I'm a hag without my makeup. Can't believe I even let you see me like this! You must be thinking, what an old hag woman she is. It's kind of a rough path, rougher than the other one, so wear boots." She consulted a tide chart pinned to a bulletin board by the door. "We're in luck, too. This is just the perfect time. Low tide, and we'll have it around four more hours. One thing you don't want to be doing is hiking along that lower path during high tide. Parts of it are okay, but the rocks below the cliff are some dangerous."

A quarter of an hour later they were driving in Teri's car to the Southwest Head lighthouse, where Teri parked it according to Marnie's instructions. Teri wore her lace-up hiking boots and her parka with hood. In her big pockets she carried a small camera and her notebook and pencil. Marnie wore her white Keds and a pair of wide, pink, fleece lounging pants, her hair still in curlers. She carried a small bag over her shoulder. Teri would put money on it that it contained her lipstick.

The path was narrow, rough, full of rocks and roots, but Marnie was surefooted as a deer. The path wound down, and as Marnie coasted down it, Teri found herself holding on to roots and branches to check her fall. And all of this while Marnie talked nonstop about people who had fallen to their deaths right here on this very spot, this very path. She also talked about Jerome and all the boyfriends she had had through the years. Teri learned where Marnie went to school (on the north end of the island, a little one-room schoolhouse that had since burned down), and when Teri asked her how it was to live on such an isolated island, Marnie said, "Isolated? What's isolated about this?" She told her that she had everything she wanted right here. Things she couldn't buy on the island she bought from the Internet.

Then Marnie stopped and turned to Teri. "Do you like romance?"

"You mean as a concept, or what?"

"No, I mean romance books. I love reading romance. I read them by the dozens. Hundreds. Well, I'm always after the drugstore to get more in, but they never get enough." She was back to walking. "Only five or six new ones a month. That's not enough. Not for me, anyway. I found a place I can get them on the Internet. I also read a continuing love story on the Internet. Every day a new chapter. I wouldn't miss it. Plus, this lipstick?" She stopped suddenly, and Teri held on to a scrub weed for balance. Marnie pulled out her lipstick with the little mirror that flipped up for use, and then flipped down and became part of the case. "I got this off the Internet, too. I showed them this down at the drugstore. I said, 'You should get stuff like this,' but they said it wouldn't sell here. I said, 'Sure it would. We ladies on Grand Manan like to look like ladies, don't we?'"

"What'd you do before the Internet?" Teri was huffing and puffing while Marnie scurried on down, not the least bit breathless.

"I had catalogs. Me and my catalogs. I was known for my catalogs. All over the island, anytime anyone needed anything, they knew where to come. I still get catalogs, but now you can get everything on the Internet. It's so much easier."

They were walking along the water's edge now, making their way over gray rocks, brown vegetation, and pools of murky water.

"Watch your step now," Marnie said. "Tide's out, so this is real slippery. We'll just have to remember to get back in a few hours. Don't want to be caught out here."

To their left was the water, oily and violent, and to their right cliffs loomed high above them.

"Isn't this beautiful?" Marnie said.

"Yes, it is."

"Now, you tell me, how could I feel isolated with all of this nature?"

A little while later they reached a place where the beach widened. No longer were they scrabbling over huge rocks, but there were patches of sand and clumps of seaweed. They walked over tiny pebbles and stepped over tufts of grass. To their right a narrow path zigzagged up the side of the hill.

Marnie pointed. "That's the way up to where Garda lives with her girl. And here's where some of the cushions from the boat came ashore. Right on this beach. Right here. And out there? That's where the bodies were, floating in their orange life jackets. You could see them from here. Looked like little bobbing pumpkins."

"You saw them?"

"I think I saw them first. Didn't know what they were. Then I heard about the accident."

"Did you see anything else? Any parts of the boat?"

"Nope. Not me. Garda maybe, but not me."

Marnie was leaning against a slatted wooden dory so embedded in the weeds and rocks that it looked like it had never been anywhere else. Teri looked up the path then back at Marnie. "Do you think she'd talk to me?"

"Who? Garda?" Marnie put her hand to her chest. "Well, you won't catch me going up there, that's for sure, Teri. I've no desire to tangle with her. Not after what she did to Jerome and me. No sirree."

Teri shivered. Her hands were cold and she stuffed them in her pockets.

"Those boys down at the Save Easy who deliver her groceries? They say she's even gotten crazier, that she chases people away with a shotgun. And that the daughter puts hexes on people just by looking at them."

They were walking again. Teri had picked up a stick and was poking it into the ground as they made their way across the beach.

"Thing is," Marnie was saying. "Jerome and I would've married. That was a plain fact, as plain as the rock standing there in front of us." She paused. "You know, if you want to know more about the accident I could maybe fix you up with Flynn."

"Flynn?"

"Flynn Green. Flynn's one of my oldest friends. He and I were an item once, too. Now we're just friends. He knows everyone on the island too, like me. He even knew that minister's wife who died. Worked on her boat. Plus, I think he could arrange it so you could talk to Garda. If that's what you want to do. But don't ask me to go talk with that woman."

Later, when they were back at the house, Marnie called Flynn, who said he'd meet Teri for lunch at the Coffee Perk. The Coffee Perk Restaurant was little more than a roomful of chairs and tables of varying sizes and shapes covered with dissimilar tablecloths. It looked as if the entire furnishings had been picked up at garage sales. The effect was charming, however, and Teri got there fifteen minutes ahead of the meeting and ordered herself a coffee. The coffee was marvelous, and she needed it. The hike down the cliff and back up again had chilled some deep part of her. She was on her second cup when Flynn arrived.

"You Teri?"

"Yes, and you're Flynn."

"Had enough of that weak stuff that Marnie passes off as coffee, I see."

Teri smiled.

"She's okay, our Marnie is," he said. "A character. That's what you gotta say about her. She's a character." He pulled out a chair and sat down across from her. Flynn Green was a tiny-faced man in a pea-colored jacket that hung on his narrow shoulders. His hair was pure white and combed evenly across his small, red head.

"So Marnie tells me you want to know about that accident. You the cops?"

"Private."

"Private," he echoed. He put his forearms on the table and leaned across the table and looked at her. "So, what do you want from me?"

"Marnie said you know everyone on the island. I'd like to talk to a few people who may have had contact with Ellen when she was here. There's a fisherman, Bud Williams, who's named in the reports as the last person to talk to the women on the VHF radio. I'd like to maybe talk to him. Plus, I'd like to get your thoughts on the accident."

"I know Bud. Had himself one of those heart bypass operations. He's in the hospital over in Saint John."

"That's too bad."

"It happens."

"So, what do you think happened with Ellen's boat?"

"Me, I've a different theory altogether than anyone. I don't think the accident happened anywhere near here. I think it was closer to Maine. I think the police and everyone was searching in the wrong place. That's my opinion, and I told the Coast Guard that when they were here, but they still concentrated their search just at the south of here. But I know myself, those currents can take you places you never expected to go. Now, I fixed that engine. It was running fine when she left."

"I thought it was missing some crucial part."

He snorted. "We made do. We cut and welded a bit of metal I had lying around. It would've worked forever."

"Did you know Ellen and the other women well?"

"Ellen had been here a few times if memory serves, only staying a couple days each time. I could give you the names of some other fishermen who knew her."

"That would be great. Thanks."

He wrote down two names and handed them to her. "You can most likely find them down at the wharf in Grand Harbour. Well, speak of the devil."

Teri turned. A large man in a mustard-colored jacked was making his way toward their table.

"Well, Flynn, you didn't tell me you had a new lady friend."

"I don't tell you everything, you old buzzard."

He sat down and looked at Teri. "I'm Will," he said. "I heard you wanted to talk to my sister-in-law."

Teri put out her hand. "Teri Blake-Addison. Yes, I'd very much like to talk with Garda. But how did you know?"

"A little birdie told me. There are no secrets on this island. None."

He was staring at Teri, and there was something about his gaze that was uncomfortable. If she met him in a dark alley, she would turn and walk the other way. Fast.

"I heard that some of the debris floated onto her headland," Teri said.

Will grinned and rubbed his nose. "Well, yes, I would say that some of the *debris* did float onto her beach, and I'd be delighted to introduce you to my sister-in-law. Yes, Garda would be most pleased to meet you. Would you like to see her right now? Well, finish your lunch first. Go ahead, do that. I'll join you." He yelled, "Can I have a large fish and chips over here?" Then back to Teri, "You be sure to ask her all about the *debris.*"

Throughout lunch Teri was quiet. She took notes, but mostly she just listened to Flynn and Will talk about accidents, shipwrecks, and Grand Manan ghosts. And she watched Will and tried to figure out what it was about him that made her feel cold.

21

For the second time that day Teri drove down toward Southwest Head. She was following Will's pickup truck after having declined an invitation to ride with him. She found it hard to believe that this hard man could have had his heart broken into a million pieces, as Marnie put it. As she drove down the winding two-lane highway, she thought about what Marnie had said, that after Jerome died, Will had taken it upon himself to take care of his brother's wife and her baby. Even when she wanted nothing to do with him?

Twenty minutes later they were parking beside the lighthouse, the same place she had come to earlier that day. It was afternoon now, and a wind had come up. Teri pulled her wool hat down over her ears, glad for her thick gloves with the multiple layers of Thinsulate. If she strained her ears she could hear the bell buoy out in the water.

Will said, "Follow me."

She put her notebook and pencil in her jacket pocket and locked her car, even though Will said there was no crime on the island. It was misty and the icy wind cut into her face as she followed Will down a tire-rutted path toward the little lighthouse. Will didn't say much as they walked, despite her asking several questions. Did he know Ellen? What was his theory about the accident? Did he know the other women? Had he seen anything out on the water?

"I never saw anything. Neither did Garda."

"Marnie said she saw the bodies floating out there."

"Oh, that Marnie. You can't believe half of what she says."

"Marnie said that Garda retrieved a few boat cushions and some other things."

"Oh, that. I gave those to the police. That was all."

"Did they talk to your sister-in-law?"

"I wouldn't let them."

"Why not?"

He grabbed a branch from a tree and tore it off. Finally he said, "She doesn't see anyone."

"She's seeing me."

He didn't say anything to that.

The path narrowed and he walked ahead of her. She could hear her own breathing as branches clawed at her face. They trekked through puddles, and she could smell the vegetation, the tang of it, the moistness of the earth, the dampness on her face. In her line of work she sometimes entered fearful situations, and as she walked behind this man, she wondered at her sanity.

When they reached the part of the path that ran next to the cliff, she stayed as far from the edge as she could and was glad when it wound inland again. From the cliffs, the path wound down steeply until it opened onto a clearing. The little lighthouse and cottage were ahead of them. Up close it looked like a caricature of a lighthouse, a cartoon of one. It was as if the builders, weary after constructing only one story, added the light. The tiny windowed cottage was made of flat gray stones and looked like the cottages in all the fairy tales she had ever read. Even the smoke blowing sideways from the chimney looked like the stuff of mythology.

"I can't believe anyone lives here," she said.

Will was chuckling as they neared it. Actually laughing out loud.

The clearing at the front of the cottage sloped gently down for about ten yards to the edge of a cliff, and the front of the cottage seemed to lean slightly forward as if it were grass blown by the wind.

"It's close to the edge," Teri said.

"The whole works will go tumbling into the sea one of these days."

"Why doesn't the town or someone try to get her out?"

"You can't move Garda." And he laughed again.

Teri reached for her disposable camera and took a couple of

shots. Although there was a door at the front of it, it looked to be boarded up and dark. She followed Will around to the rear, and he opened, without knocking, a thick wooden dungeon door that led into the kitchen.

The warmth of the place was the first thing Teri noticed; the next thing she noticed was the enticing aroma of some kind of meat stew. The kitchen was rectangular and ran the entire back of the cottage. Against the north-facing wall was a woodstove and next to it a small white ceramic sink. On the wall beside the door was a row of thick nails for coats. Teri looked around for proofs of electricity, and saw a single lightbulb on the ceiling and a small, old-fashioned refrigerator.

"So there's electricity," Teri found herself saying.

"When it works. When it's not cut off. Mostly it's cut off."

To her left two mattresses were lined up against the wall with neatly folded blankets at the foot of each.

"Audrey and Garda sleep there in the winter," Will said. "The front bedrooms get too cold. The wind, you know."

Teri nodded. In the center of the room was a large, ornately carved, heavy-legged wooden table. Several chairs in the same pattern and a sideboard topped with books and dishes leaned against the opposite wall. But it was the pottery that drew her attention. Every spare inch of space was taken up by crude pottery bowls. Some were misshapen, while others were exquisite. It was all hand-formed, she could see, not thrown on a wheel.

"She makes pottery?" Teri asked.

"The girl makes those."

"Some of these are very good."

"Don't be flattering. She's very retarded."

Teri stared at him, mouth open. "Where are they?" she finally asked.

"Outhouse? Garden? Who knows?" He went to the door. "Ah, here they are just coming down from the garden. Must have taken some compost up there." His eyes twinkled when he said, "She's well known for her garden. Don't forget to ask her about her garden."

The woman who entered the kitchen wore a pair of loose jeans, a heavy denim overcoat, and rubber boots.

"Hello, Garda," Will said.

Garda formed the word *Will* and then stopped when she saw Teri. Even worn by time and the sun, she was an attractive woman. Her white-gray hair was long, and she wore it in a single braid down her back.

But it was the girl that caught Teri's gaze. She looked to be maybe fifteen, tall, as straight as a tree. Yellow-blond hair shrouded her head like mist. She looked waif-like and beautiful. She stood behind her mother, and when she saw Will she began to rock back and forth. At first Teri thought the girl was blind; she never looked at anyone directly. But then she walked, unaided, over to the mattress and turned on a little radio.

When Will did not introduce them, Teri approached Garda. "My name is Teri Blake-Addison. Your brother-in-law said I might be able to talk to you."

"About what?" There was uncertainty in her eyes. And something else, too. Fear?

"I'm reviewing the accident that occurred here five years ago. The one where the three women died in the sailboat accident. I was told that debris washed up on your beach. I was just wondering if you'd seen anything."

She stood perfectly still and shook her head slightly.

"You never saw anything?"

"No." The word came out raspy and uncertain.

"Did you talk to the police at that time?"

"No." Garda backed away from her.

"Teri would like a cup of coffee, Garda," Will said. "And we all should sit down, really. It's quite a hike in, you know."

"I'm fine, really," Teri said. "I don't need coffee."

"Nonsense; Garda will get us coffee. Garda makes good coffee."

Garda walked to the stove and poured coffee into two mugs. She handed one to Will and placed one on the table closest to where Teri was standing. There was a trembling in Garda's fingers, Teri noticed.

"Have a seat." Will indicated a place at the table.

Audrey rocked on the mattress, saying quietly over and over, "No Mom, no Mom, no Mom." She grabbed a piece of modeling clay and rolled it along the floor, leaning into it rhythmically as she did so.

"What do you take in your coffee, Teri? Cream? Sugar?" Will asked.

"Just a bit of cream."

"Garda, would you get your guest a spot of cream?"

Garda opened the refrigerator and placed a small hand-built clay pitcher on the table. Will picked it up. "Ah, this is one of Audrey's, I take it. You can see how crooked and jagged it is."

"I think it's nice," Teri said.

Will said, "Teri is a private investigator. She's been hired to find out what happened to Ellen Houseman. You remember Ellen Houseman? She was one of the women in that sailboat accident."

Garda clasped her arms around her chest and looked down, her shoulders gently heaving. Was she crying? Will was grinning. There was something going on in this room that Teri couldn't fathom.

"Ellen's the focus of this investigation," Will continued. "Isn't she, Teri? It's all about Ellen."

"I don't know anything about that," Garda said without looking up.

Audrey had turned the radio up. It was a classical music station. Neither Garda nor Will made any attempt to lower the volume.

"I was just wondering," Teri said, opening her notebook, "whether you saw anything, anything at all."

"Nothing. No," Garda said.

"She's here about the debris," Will said. "You know, all that stuff that washed up on your shore?"

Garda shook her head. She said something that Teri couldn't make out over the music. Teri said, "Pardon?"

"I said I can't help you." Garda turned her back to them and began stirring the stew with a wooden spoon.

For a few minutes no one said anything, then Will said, "I was telling Teri all about your garden. I was thinking you should take Teri up there."

Garda said nothing.

"That's okay," Teri said. "I don't need to see it. I'm sorry to have bothered you." She pushed back her chair and in her haste, Teri bumped into the sideboard and a shower of books clattered onto the stone floor.

"So sorry." Teri bent to retrieve them. "Let me get these." Most were well-used paperback novels popular a decade ago. "So sorry." On the bottom of the upended pile was the little green book *Mercy*. Teri stared at it. When she picked it up, a folded news clipping, yellowed and creased, fell out. "Evangelist's Wife Dead," she read. She looked up at Garda. A strangled sound escaped Garda's throat.

Teri said, "Do you know this book?"

"Will brings me old books. I like to read. He brings over books from the used bookstore."

"But this book isn't old. It just came out," Teri said.

"I don't know. Will brought it. I don't know. That paper. That paper must've been inside it." She was wiping her eye with the sleeve of her sweatshirt. And then she gasped and left. She walked past Will and opened the door to the front of the house, the cold part of the house, and closed it behind her.

Then Will grinned and said, "You have to forgive her." He pointed to his head. "She's not quite right, if you know what I mean. The two of them," he indicated Audrey with a flick of his wrist, "are two peas in a pod." Then he made a circular motion beside his head with his finger.

The mist had turned to outright rain by the time Teri drove back to Marnie's. What she needed was to go back and talk with the woman. She was convinced of that. She needed to go back when Will wasn't around and find out what that strange, silent woman was hiding.

22

Garda had meant to write it down. That had been her plan when she came here, to get it all down on paper and explain everything, all about what had brought her here and all about the body buried on the hillside and why she kept the folded news clipping. After all this time. But time had a way of moving ahead, day after day. It had been four years since she had buried her friend. Now with so many gardens planted atop it, it was too late.

Initially, she had been surprised that no one came. No police came with their sniffing dogs. No one. At the beginning she was almost waiting for them. They would come. The dogs would race up to her garden, sniffing, sniffing. They would dig. They would find her. But no one came. Not at the beginning, and not now. Gradually she had grown to forget the woman buried on the hillside, and had come to believe that this was the only life she had ever known. Here with Audrey. There had never been an adultery. There had never been a murder. There had never been a betrayal. There had never been a God.

And then the woman with the curly brown hair and her notebook had come to remind her of everything she lost when she made that one mistake twenty-six years ago. Why hadn't she hidden that book, *Mercy*? Why hadn't she at least put the news clipping in the drawer? She picked up the clipping now and flattened it on the table. "Evangelist's Wife Dead."

"Yes," she said out loud. "Yes, it is true. She's dead. She caused the deaths of others and now she herself is dead, and deservedly so."

She folded the clipping along its crease lines and placed it in a drawer in the sideboard. Then she opened the green book, *Mercy*. Green, the color of grass, the color of spring. Green is God's favorite color, her mother used to say. At the thought of her mother, she closed her eyes. Another life lost, another betrayal.

Centered in the middle of the first page, she read: *To my wife, Ellen, 1947–1998.* She stopped and read that page over and over. To my wife, Ellen. A beginning, 1947, and an ending, 1998. A definite end of days.

"Tea Mom. Tea Mom. Tea Mom." Audrey was standing next to her, so Garda got up and fixed her a cup of tea with two spoons of honey. Then she turned the radio volume down. It was getting dark. She pulled the cord that hung from the overhead bulb, but the power was out again, so she lit the oil lamps. Then she poured a cup of tea for herself and sat down in the wooden rocker with *Mercy.*

After a while she said, "There is nothing new here, Audrey. None of this is new." She didn't know what she was expecting, but not this. Old sermons she had read before, parts of other books, quotes from magazines. The only cohesiveness was the general theme, mercy.

She closed the book, put it underneath the stack, and then got out the blank notebook from the bottom drawer in the sideboard. She opened to the first page and saw where she had written the one word, *Betrayal.* She would write it all down now. All of it. Her affair. The sailboat accident. The death of the woman. The burial. And the betrayal that had caused it all in the first place.

23

Brent couldn't believe his luck. Here he was, a hamburger combo in front of him, and the PI, *that* PI, sitting just two tables away. She was talking on a cell phone while she ate from a plate of fish and chips. At first he didn't clue in that she was the one. He'd come in here to grab something to eat and to make his own plans, and then he heard the words *investigation* and *Houseman,* and that made him look over for sure. That person with the short, curly brown hair and little round metal glasses with dark frames had to be the PI. She was kind of chubby too, he noted, and Brent wondered why his father had hired this person when he had a whole fleet of lawyers and police he could have called on. She was talking rapidly on her cell phone and punctuating her remarks with hand gestures.

He got up and went outside, and sure enough, there was a crummy little Honda Civic with a Maine license plate. He went back inside and grabbed a newspaper from a pile beside the door. He pretended he was interested in the useless *Grand Manan Record,* when what he was really trying to do was listen to her. His waitress came over to ask how everything was, and he said, fine, fine.

"Would you like another Coke?"

He looked up at her. She wasn't the fat old lady that had brought him his hamburger, but she was about his age with brownish-blond hair tucked behind her ears and little heart earrings in each ear. It was the earrings that got to him. So sweet. Her name tag read *Tracie.*

"Where'd the other waitress go?"

"I just came on shift. Another girl was sick."

"Hope it wasn't the food. Hey, maybe some more water, Tracie," he said.

"Sure."

His attention was momentarily diverted from the PI to Tracie's retreating figure. She was short, not as thin as Amanda, but then there weren't many girls as thin as Amanda. Sometimes hugging her was like holding on to an armload of coat hangers.

Tracie came back and poured him water sideways from a clear jug. He looked up and said conspiratorially, "Don't you just hate those cell phones? People who talk on cell phones in restaurants." He indicated the PI with a roll of his eyes.

"Is it bothering you, sir? I could maybe talk to her."

He waved a hand. "It's not bothering me. It's just the nerve of some people. Well, she's not from around here. You can tell that much."

Tracie's eyes widened. "You can say that again! She's with the police or something. I heard some people talking. She's working on that boat accident."

"Really? What boat accident?"

Her eyes were even wider. Brent found it hard not to look at her cute ears while she talked to him about the three women, and how only two bodies were found, the third one and the boat magically disappearing.

"So, you were here then?" he asked.

"No, we moved here after it. But everyone told us. Would you like some dessert?"

"Sure," Brent said, even though he was full, even though he had to watch his stash of money. "What's good?"

"Pies. We have all kinds of pies. Our pies are famous. We might have some chocolate cake left, too. We had some earlier. I could check. Plus, we have all kinds of ice cream."

"You got apple pie?"

"We always have apple pie."

"Okay, an apple pie. And a coffee."

He watched her shove her hair behind her ears every so often. Maybe it would be a good thing to develop a friendship with someone on the island. It might come in handy. He looked at those earrings again. She looked awkwardly at him and smiled. "I'll get that for you right away, sir."

"You have any vanilla ice cream?"

"Yep."

"Can I have a scoop on my pie?"

"Sure."

He asked her how long she'd been working here.

"Since summer."

"You like it?"

"It's okay. I'm leaving in the spring."

"Oh yeah? Where you going?"

"Work. Then school."

"School, huh?'

"I've got a job in Fredericton. In the Pizza Delight. Then in the fall I'm going to UNB. I want to be a nurse. It's all I've ever wanted to be."

"A nurse, huh?"

"I've never lived in a city. It sorta scares me. I'll be staying with my aunt there."

"Well, have fun."

"Where are you from? That your car out there? We couldn't figure out your license plate."

"Who's 'we'?"

"Me and the guys in the kitchen. We don't get many strangers this time of year. Now we got two."

It was almost on the tip of his tongue to tell her "New Jersey," and then he stopped himself. New Jersey. And then in approximately one hour everyone on the island would know that there was someone here from New Jersey. He needed to throw them off the track a bit.

"Toronto," he said. "Here for a visit. Looking for work."

Her eyes were wide. "You're from Toronto and you're looking for work on Grand Manan?"

"It's a long story."

"Must be." Then she laughed. She balanced her plates and started to walk away when the PI put her balled up napkin on her plate, closed her notebook, and reached for her jacket.

"Hey, Tracie," he yelled. "I remembered I gotta get going. Got an appointment. Can you just bring me the bill?"

"For a job, you mean?"

"What?"

"An appointment for a job?"

"Yeah."

"The pie's good. You'll be sorry."

"I'll grab some next time, I promise."

He paid his bill and left Tracie a generous tip from his sympathy card money and was outside just as little miss detective lady drove away. He memorized her car, noted the direction she was headed, then drove his van to a back road and parked. He got the screwdriver out of his glove compartment and unscrewed his license plate and placed it under the front seat. If stopped, he'd sheepishly produce the plate and say he didn't know what happened, but it fell off. The screws had rusted through, and he was waiting to get to a place where he could replace them.

Then he drove slowly in the direction the PI went. And just outside of Seal Cove he saw her car parked in front of a big white house with a faded sign that read, *Marnie's B&B.* This was easier than he thought.

24

After a day of hiking, Teri went to the Coffee Perk for supper. She ate fish and chips while she made a list of things she needed to do tomorrow: talk to those fishermen Flynn had told her about, talk to someone in the RCMP detachment, maybe even go to the library. Possibly visit Garda again. She toyed with that idea as she ate her fish and chips.

She went back to Marnie's, said no thanks she had work to do to Marnie's offer of hot coffee cake, and then sat cross-legged on her bed and entered the interviews, as much as she could remember of them, word for word into her iBook.

In the morning Marnie stood at her kitchen counter surrounded by a flour canister, butter, a carton of eggs, and mixing bowls. She was whipping very quickly by hand something in a bowl. She still wore her pink curlers, but her head was wrapped up tightly in a scarf.

"Today's my day for baking, Teri," she said. "My boyfriend likes these cookies. He's not supposed to be here for a couple days yet, so that gives me some time. And good thing, too. I got so much to do to get ready. I can never make enough cookies for him. Help yourself to coffee. There's the mugs right there. I got them out. I never use an electric mixer. I think they're best whipped up by hand. Do you bake cookies, Teri?"

"Not if I can help it," Teri said, grabbing a mug. "The precept I live by is that if God had intended for us to bake, He wouldn't have invented bakeries."

"Oh, Teri, you should learn to bake. At least cookies. At least cookies, Teri. Men like cookies. If you want to keep your man, that's what I've found."

"Trouble is," said Teri, laughing as she poured herself a cup of the impossibly weak brew, "neither Jack nor I especially need to eat a whole lot of cookies."

"Jack. Is that his name?"

"His real name is James. Jack's a nickname."

"Oh, how nice. He sounds handsome. Oh Teri, I made some soft-boiled eggs. In those eggcups over there. And some toast."

Teri took a piece of cold toast and a lukewarm egg to the table. She held her knife to the egg and wondered what she would find inside.

"Teri, do you need me today for anything?"

"I'm fine on my own, thanks. You've been such a big help. I don't know what I would've done without you."

The egg, thankfully, was hard-boiled cold. Not her favorite, but it beat raw-and-runny cold, hands down.

"Well, that's good. Today I've got to get these cookies baked. Was Flynn a help?"

Teri looked up. "Actually, yes. He gave me some names that I'm going to check out today. And while we were talking, Will came in and took me to see her."

"You saw Garda? Oh my. Oh my, Teri. What was she like?"

"Sad," Teri said thoughtfully. "Sad and scared."

"Sad. Oh my. That doesn't sound like her. She didn't threaten you with a shotgun?"

Teri shook her head. The idea of that strange, frightened woman chasing anyone away with a shotgun seemed absurd. Perhaps life had taken its toll, and Garda had changed.

"She didn't seem that way to me," Teri said. "She was nervous. Her hands kept shaking."

"Let me tell you something, Teri. Will's heart was broken into a thousand pieces by that woman. And mine, too, since Jerome and I would've married. Are you leaving tomorrow, Teri?"

"I'm thinking about it, yes. I'm going down to make reservations for that first ferry. Then I'll be out of your hair."

Marnie opened her eyes wide. "Oh, I didn't mean it like that.

Don't think I meant it like that. I was hoping you weren't leaving today, that's what I was thinking when I asked you. I was thinking that maybe tonight, your last night here, we could have a real girls' night at home and watch videos. Like a good old-fashioned slumber party. My boyfriend isn't coming for two days so we can have popcorn and chat. Oh, please don't tell me you're busy tonight."

Teri couldn't help but grin. "I would be delighted to watch a video tonight. I'll make sure I'm back in time."

"Good. I'll even make supper for us. Do you like split pea soup with a real ham bone?"

"Don't go all out, Marnie. I could stop by and get something. Is there a pizza place anywhere? I could bring a pizza back for us."

Marnie put up her hand. "No way. I've had this ham bone in the freezer for a long time. I need to use it up before it gets freezer burned. You be back here at six. Is six okay, Teri?"

"Six is fine."

The first place Teri went was to the town wharf at Grand Harbour. It was chilly down on the docks, and snow was gently falling. The dock smelled of fish and seaweed. Teri pulled her fleece hat down around her ears and buttoned her jacket to her neck. The only people down on the docks were a few men in oily coveralls. She approached the first one, a man hosing down the back of his boat.

"I'm looking for Jasper Chase or Phil Mathewson."

The man turned off the hose and looked up at her. "You must be the one about the sailboat accident?"

"Word really gets around."

"Jasper's down the end of the dock. That's his boat, the blue one. The *Melinda*. He should be on it."

"Thanks."

When she got to the *Melinda*, a man in a tattered and grimy green ski jacket was sitting in the large back area of his boat, engine parts around him. He was fiddling at something with a wrench.

"Hello!" she called.

"Hello yourself."

"Are you Jasper?"

The man stood and wiped his hands on his grimy jeans. "I am. Last time I checked. And you're here about the accident."

She stepped closer to the boat. "I understand you worked on Ellen Houseman's engine along with Flynn."

"I did."

"Did you think the boat was seaworthy? There was some speculation that she should've stayed and waited for some part for it or something."

"That was one of the theories. But that wasn't true. That boat would have no problem making it anywhere. Yes, the alternator bracket would need replacing at some point, but she was fit to go. She could've run the engine all the way down to the Bahamas and back before it ran into problems."

"Did you know Ellen?"

He shook his head. "She seemed a competent enough sailor, but one never knows. She could get out in a blow and panic. That happens to women sometimes. She might have been unaware of the tide rips. They might've tripped her up. That's what I think happened. Them three ladies got out in a bit of a blow and panicked."

"But you didn't know her personally. You wouldn't have known if there was anything on her mind before she set out."

"Can't help you there." He sat back down and reached for his wrench.

"Thanks. Do you know where I can find Phil Matthewson?"

Jasper chuckled, revealing a missing front tooth. "You won't see him for a while. He's out on the mainland."

"And Bud Williams?"

"On the mainland too. Hospital in Saint John."

"That's what I heard."

Teri went next to the RCMP detachment office, where they were waiting for her, it seemed. The receptionist, a woman with a blond ponytail, smiled at her and introduced her to a young, very tall constable named Tom Freeley. Tom invited her into their lunchroom, where there was a little microwave and a coffee machine with what looked like real, dark coffee.

"You want a coffee?" he asked.

"Sure."

"I wasn't on the island when the accident occurred, you know."

"So you've heard about me, too? Are there no secrets on this island?"

He set the coffee down in front of her and grinned. "None."

"That must make your job a heck of a lot easier."

"One would think."

"I've also been told there's no crime on the island."

He snorted. "Someone told you that?"

"A lot of domestics, I bet."

He agreed. "When everyone is related to everyone, that makes all crime domestic." He looked at her for several seconds, then said, "And you're a private investigator."

"Yep."

"You used to be a cop, right?"

"With the Maine State Police. Seven years."

"A statie. And you quit to go private."

"I did. I quit first, did a few other little jobs before I went private."

"You like it?"

"I get to set my own hours. And I get to take only cases I want. It has its advantages. Is there anyone in here that was around during the time of the accident?"

"I think Sergeant Bauer was. But here, I got you these." He rose and brought her a sheaf of papers from the top of a metal file cabinet. "I didn't have a lot to do yesterday, so I copied all these for you. You can have these. The accident reports at the time."

"Is Sergeant Bauer here? Can I speak with him?"

"He's on the mainland today. He'll be back tomorrow if you want to wait until then."

"Thank you," she said. "I was thinking of leaving on the first ferry tomorrow."

As she looked through the photocopies, she tried not to show her disappointment. She had all of this and more. There was nothing new here. Maybe there was nothing new to be had anywhere.

She looked at him. "What do you know about Garda Stanton?"

He leaned back, intertwined his fingers behind his head. "Not a lot. We know her story—the death of the husband. The daughter. The only problem is the integrity of the place she lives in. We'd like to move her away from there. Find some suitable housing for her. That's going to be a battle. Every so often one of us goes out there, just to make sure the place is still standing. She's not going to want to move."

"And you can't get social services involved with the daughter?"

"The daughter's twenty-four. There was a time when someone could've done something, but no one did. Now, she's a grown woman."

"Twenty-four! She doesn't look much more than fifteen."

"You met her?"

"Went out to see Garda."

"Really?"

"I understand that some of the debris from the accident washed up on her headland. I wanted to talk with her about that."

"It did. That's in the report." He leaned forward. "How do you choose which cases you want?"

"Excuse me?"

"Can you actually make a decent living going private?"

"Well, there can be lean times. Did anyone talk to Garda at the time?"

"I guess you'd have to get established, get your name out there, wouldn't you?"

She blinked at him. "Yeah, I guess you would."

He grew up reading PI novels, he told her, and this was something he'd always been interested in. You might say he had become a police officer just to train for his career of choice, being a PI. Eventually, she found a crack in the conversation, and sought her way through it to the door.

"Thanks," she said. "Thanks again."

"Anytime," he said.

As she drove to the public library, she realized that the only thing she had in all of this was a nervous woman who may or may not have seen something. She parked at the community school to which the public library was attached. Librarians were fountains of information, she had learned. There were only a few other patrons in the library: an elderly man seated on a couch reading a magazine, and a few people fingering through the fiction shelves. She walked around, touched books and book displays, and waited by the desk until a woman with fluffy gray hair and Birkenstocks smiled. "Hey," she said. "Can I help you?"

"Do you have newspapers on microfiche?"

"Some. Not all. We've got a few from New Brunswick plus the *Bangor Daily News*."

"What about a local paper? That newsletter-type paper that I see around, the *Grand Manan Record*?"

She laughed. "No, I don't have that on microfiche, but what I do have is a couple of binders of them. I could let you look at those as long as you stay in the library."

"That would be great, thanks."

"You're that investigator, aren't you?"

"I was just telling the constable that there are no secrets on this island, are there?"

Her face clouded. "There are secrets. There are plenty of secrets. That's the problem with a place like this. There are too many secrets."

Teri thought about that while the librarian went into an inner office. She came back with three thick binders. "Here you go. I'm Liz Caruthers, by the way."

"Nice to meet you, but you probably already know my name." They both laughed. "Do you have a theory about the accident?" Teri asked. "Faulty engine, high winds, panicked skipper, ghosts, witches, Bermuda Triangle, terrorists, ill winds, evil curses?"

"You've been talking to the locals, I see. I wasn't here at the time.

My husband and I moved here three years ago. He's one of the local ministers in town."

"Really? That's great. I wasn't planning to be here on a Sunday, but if I was, I'd stop in."

"We'd love to have you. Where are you staying, by the way?"

"I'm at Marnie's Bed-and-Breakfast."

"Oh, Marnie, bless her heart. Is she talking your ear off?"

"Almost."

"From what people tell us, she used to be very involved in church. Something happened to turn her off."

"That happens," Teri said.

"All too often, I'm afraid," Liz said.

"She and I are going to watch videos tonight, and she's baking cookies today. I guess her boyfriend is coming from the mainland tomorrow."

"The phantom boyfriend."

"Phantom boyfriend?"

"For all her talk, no one's ever met this boyfriend."

"Oh dear."

"I feel sorry for her. There are a lot of people that just laugh at her."

Liz was about to leave Teri with the binders when Teri said, "Can I ask you something? What can you tell me about Garda, the woman who lives by herself in the little lighthouse?"

"Grand Manan's true recluse. To hear people talk, she was the Wicked Witch of the East."

"I visited her yesterday."

"Really?" She stopped, surprised, and looked at Teri. "I thought that brother-in-law of hers kept a pretty tight lid on visitors."

"He seemed almost anxious for me to come."

"That genuinely surprises me. My husband and I have tried to visit her a few times, but have been thwarted by the brother-in-law. He seems to have a sixth sense when it comes to Garda."

"It's sad." Teri toyed with the idea of telling Liz about seeing *Mercy* there, then thought better of it.

"Well, you get to those papers, and call me if you need me."

Teri sat at a wooden table and opened the first binder. It went back to 1964, apparently when the *Grand Manan Record* began. It was a weekly eight-page newsletter, stapled in the middle, and given out free. She flipped back five years ago to the time of the accident.

Island residents were horrified that three women apparently died at the hands of one of Grand Manan's famous tide rips when *Beloved*, an Alberg 29 sailing vessel, went down off Southwest Head. Teri scanned the article. It really didn't give any new information, just a different slant, a more newsy rendition, including how many CNN vans had been spotted and where, and how the Coffee Perk had to hire more staff and add items to their menu. There was even a little article about how some of the CNN news people had tried Grand Manan's seaweed confection, dulse, and what they thought of it. Teri reflected that the accident was probably good for business.

She jotted down the names of people and some of the quotes and closed the binder. For curiosity's sake she went back to the early 1980s and found what she was looking for in a small box on the second to the last page.

> Islanders were saddened to learn of the sudden death of Jerome Stanton, 21, in Saint John. His young wife, the former Garda Green (of Green's Hardware) has returned to the island with her baby daughter, Audrey.

That was all.

She packed up the binders, laid them on the counter, called out "thanks," and left.

It was after one and she was hungry. She headed over to the Coffee Perk, which actually did seem to be the only restaurant open this time of year. She ordered a tuna fish sandwich and a salad, deciding that she really needed to eat something a little different than fried fish and chips. She grabbed a new copy of the *Grand Manan Record* and read while she ate. She half expected to see something like: *Private Investigator Teri Blake-Addison is on the island investigating the accident that occurred here five years ago.* Thankfully, there was nothing.

After a quick lunch she drove down to the Southwest Head. She still had not altogether given up the idea of visiting Garda. She parked and called Jack on her cell.

He missed her, he told her.

"I miss you, too," she said.

"How's it going?"

"It's beautiful here, Jack. You and I should come here for a vacation. There are cliffs that are absolutely magnificent, and trails all over the place. We could hike for a week."

"But what about the investigation?"

"I was afraid you were going to ask me that. It's not going all that well. Nothing new. Some say Ellen was reckless and went off in a storm without getting her engine properly fixed. Some people think she panicked, and it was no big storm anyway. Everyone has an opinion, but no one has any new facts. I even talked to the RCMP constable. He was more interested in my job as a PI than anything. There is an interesting story here, but it doesn't have anything to do with my investigation. There's this reclusive old woman that everyone thinks is some sort of witch. I went to see her, and the only inkling of anything strange is that she was very, very nervous and had a copy of *Mercy* on her counter. In the middle of the book was a yellowed news clipping from the time of the accident."

"There could be a lot of explanations for that."

"I know. Like the accident was the biggest news item ever here on the island, and so of course people would keep clippings of it. Make whole scrapbooks of it. I'm thinking of going to see her again."

"When will you be home?"

"First ferry tomorrow. Maybe by late afternoon."

"Oh, I almost forgot. You got a phone message from Daisy Best."

"Carl's fiancée? What did she want?"

"All the message said is that she wanted to talk to you."

"Did she leave a number? You know, I may have to head down to Philadelphia next."

"I really will miss you."

"Maybe you could come?"

"Can't. I'm in the middle of term here."

"I understand."

25

After she talked with her husband, Teri spent several minutes gazing out at the ocean before she called Daisy. She and Jack had to come back here. Maybe they'd even stay with Marnie. While she sat there, her car engine and heater on, a gray van pulled in and parked on the other side of the lighthouse. A young man with dark hair and a leather jacket got out and made his way to the front of the lighthouse. He glanced in her direction several times. Probably wondering what crazy person was parked out here, she thought. She strained to see his license plate, but couldn't.

When she finally punched in Daisy Best's number, it was answered in a sweet southern accent. "Teri, I'm so glad you called me. Carl's told me so much about you I was hoping we'd get a chance to meet sometime."

"I'm out of the country now for a few days," Teri said.

Daisy was quiet, and Teri said, "You wanted to talk to me about something?"

"I really don't know how to say this… Oh, I probably shouldn't have called you at all."

"What is it?"

"It's about the investigation." Her voice broke. She cleared her throat, and it seemed to Teri that she fought to regain control.

"Yes?" Teri tried to imagine Daisy Best, sitting, perhaps, on a floral love seat, one jeweled, manicured finger tapping gently on the top of her oak writing desk. Despite her mental picture, Teri found herself warming to this southern woman, this second wife. Teri had done a little of her own research into the woman. A writer of more than thirty romance novels, she had married young and was widowed after only two years. She had no children and had never remarried. Until now.

"What is it, Ms. Best?"

"Do call me Daisy." She paused. "What I would like...is to have you stop this investigation."

"Stop it?"

"Carl hasn't been himself lately. It has me worried. A bit. He's become obsessed with this. Going over all the articles again and again. All of this is hurting him so. I just wish it was all over with."

"I understand."

"Is there any way you can...uh, stop the investigation? I would pay you. For the remainder of your work, I mean. The equivalent of what Carl would be paying you, of course. You could tell him that you looked and looked and didn't find anything."

"Carl hired me to do a job for him."

"We were supposed to be married in December, this time. A Christmas wedding. But Carl canceled. He's canceled twice before."

"I'm sorry." Teri looked at the lighthouse. The young man was walking back to his van. Maybe it was her overactive imagination, but he seemed to be looking too much in her direction.

"If it's any consolation," Teri said, "I'm not finding anything new."

Daisy's breath was audible. "Well, that's good news. Maybe I can even begin planning a spring wedding. A spring wedding would be nice. Oh, I'm sorry. I shouldn't have called you with this. This isn't fair."

"It's okay," Teri said. "But I've been hired to do a job, and I'd like to complete it."

A cold wind was whipping off the channel as Teri walked down the rutted path. The ruts were frozen, and Teri broke off chunks of dirt with her boots.

When the path wound inland, she no longer felt the wind. It even felt warmer, so she pulled off her hat and stuffed it into her pocket. In front of her, roots wriggled out of the ground like elbows and knees, a gnarled tree-man crawling across the ground. Several times on the path she thought she heard footfalls behind her, but when she turned she was alone. Of course she was alone. It was just the woods. This is just a path. I've been on this path twice. I know my way by now. There is no one else here. She forced herself to think about the case, about Garda, about why she was going, but instead she caught herself thinking about woods.

She grew up near woods, but she was forbidden to go there as a young child. She was never told the reason. But when she was fourteen she found out why. Every inch of those forbidden woods were combed by police and searchers when her mother went missing and her life became defined by fears and terrors. It was because of fear that she had developed a tough guy attitude. Because of fear she had gotten into trouble in high school. Because of fear she had straightened out enough to get into police work, where she cultivated a whole network of buddies but no friends. Because of fear she never stuck at one job for very long. Too many attachments, too many things to lose.

And then she met Jack. It wasn't exactly as she told Marnie. It had taken a long time, almost a year, before she consented to go out with him.

But Jack saw the frightened, lost girl behind the good buddy facade, and when they talked, he had an uncanny way of getting behind the multitude of masks she wore. Through Jack's help her barriers were broken down, and she started on the long, slow journey back to trust.

But every once in a while she thought about the woods.

Ahead of her the path opened to the clearing and the cartoon lighthouse and tumbledown cottage. She approached from behind, cautiously, looking around. Was it an animal behind her? Maybe just an animal. She wished she at least had Kelly with her.

It was then that she heard the scream, high pitched, piercing. An animal caught in a trap? What? The screaming continued. Every instinct in her wanted to run back the way she had come. She forced herself to stand still. Ahead of her the girl, Audrey, was standing tall behind the cottage and pointing into the trees and screaming. Not at her, thankfully not in her direction. What was she seeing?

Teri ventured forward. Audrey's face was red, her mouth an O.

"Hello, Audrey," she said quietly.

The sound had brought Garda outside, where she stood beside Audrey and looked at Teri. She wore jeans, black rubber boots, and a tattered V-necked sweater.

"I'm sorry to bother you, Garda," Teri said, "but I wanted to ask you a few more questions."

"I don't know anything about that accident. You better go." She looked around her, eyes darting from tree to tree.

"I'm sorry if I seem pushy, but you have to trust me. I'm not the police. I was hired by the woman's husband to give the accident one more look, that's all."

"The woman's husband." She mouthed the words.

Audrey was winding down, her screams not as piercing. She moved toward her mother, and Garda reached out and touched her hair, lightly, just her hair, moving her bangs away from her forehead. The girl flinched and walked past her and into the house.

"I'd like to talk to you since the accident happened near here." While she talked, Teri moved inch by inch toward her, backing her into the cottage. It was a skill Teri had learned as a police officer, and had perfected as a private investigator.

By the time they were inside the kitchen, Audrey was sitting quietly at the table, rocking back and forth and molding clay with her fingers.

Teri said, "I came because I wanted to talk to you when Will isn't around."

"Why?" She was standing, her hands behind her back, wringing them, no doubt.

"Garda, what did you see? What is it? What did you see that has made you so afraid that you haven't even been to town since it happened?"

Garda's hand trembled as she pushed away a few strands of hair from her face. She swallowed and looked away from Teri.

"Some of the stuff washed ashore," Teri said. "Ellen Houseman's life jacket and a few other things. But I think you saw something else. I'm not the police, Garda. You can tell me."

"I don't remember it."

"I think you do."

She shook her head.

"Why did you keep that old news clipping?" Teri asked. "Why do you have Carl Houseman's book?"

"Will brought it."

"Why?"

Garda shook her head. Audrey continued rocking, and Garda went to the door to the front part of the house and opened it and walked through. Teri followed. It was cold in there and dark. The room was sparsely furnished—a couch and a few chairs, that was all. One empty sock hung limply from the fireplace.

Garda walked to the window, and Teri came and stood beside her. The window offered a clear, uninterrupted view of the Grand Manan Channel.

"You can see everything from here," Teri said. "You saw something from here, didn't you?"

Garda was silent for a while. Then she said, "Do you know Christ's greatest miracle?"

The question startled Teri.

Garda continued, "Christ's greatest miracle was not the feeding of the five thousand. It was not giving sight to the blind; it was not turning the water into wine or healing the lame and the sick." She paused. "His greatest miracle was calming the seas, stilling the wind. His most powerful words in all of creation were, 'Peace, be still.' These three words embody all of grace, all of mercy. Peace. Be still."

26

In the back of his van Brent assembled a tuna fish sandwich. A can of tuna mixed with a bit of mayo and slathered on slabs of plain white bread. He'd dipped into the sympathy card money and bought himself a few things at the Save Easy: a loaf of bread, a bag of Oreos, a case of Coke in cans, some cheese, a little jar of mayo, and a can of tuna. When he was little his mother used to make him tuna sandwiches on white bread. He loved them then. He hadn't had a tuna fish sandwich on white bread in a long time. Amanda was mostly into dark brown breads with lots of seeds. She was also a vegetarian—a vegan, is what she called herself—which was partly why she quit Pizza Hut. Their bar-sized fridge was filled with jars of beans and rice from Sweet Life Health Foods. She would roll her eyes at his Wonder Bread and Oreos.

He and his mother used to eat tuna sandwiches on white bread on Friday nights when his father was away and his brothers were at youth group. On those nights he and his mother would play Sorry!, his mother's laugh high and false.

He shivered in the back of the van at the memory. He should start up the engine, get some heat in here. But he didn't want to waste gas, and he worried a little about the noise the engine would make.

When that crazy girl had screamed at him, he had hightailed it out of the woods as fast as he could and back to his van. Then he drove back up the island and followed the signs to the airport, which turned out to be a little strip, not like any airports he had ever seen. Next to the airport he pulled down a dirt road, then another and another. Then he eased his van in amongst some brown brush. No one would ever know he was here. Maybe he'd be safe here.

He had followed the detective, staying a bit behind her. She, for all her detective ways, hadn't even noticed him hanging back in the woods, scrambling from tree to tree. But when he reached that funny looking little house, with the silo thing beside it, he stepped out from behind the tree and stared at it. And then the girl saw him and began screaming and pointing at him. He had no choice but to turn and run. The only glimpse he had of the old lady was the back view of a long gray braid and a baggy sweater.

Into his second sandwich, he thought about that. What did that detective want with a forest fairy and her mountain woman mother? He knew his mother's boat had gone down somewhere off the bottom of the island. Maybe the detective thought these two knew something about it.

He put the lid on the jar of mayo and stuck it at the back of his van with the Cokes, then pulled out the duffel bag to put the change into the zipper compartment. At the bottom of the duffel were his mother's scrapbooks. It had been years, literally years since he had gone through those.

There were seven of them in total, all of them family vacations they had taken. His mother would paste in photos, postcards, city maps, tourist flyers, and even menus from restaurants they ate in. Underneath the family photos she wrote things like, *Here we are, all safe and sound!* and *What a great day we had exploring the caves!*

Sometimes when he was little, he would come upon her in the middle of the day at the kitchen table surrounded by papers, glue, scissors, photos, posters, and cards. And he would climb up on her lap and smell her perfume and the glue.

"Wasn't this fun, Brent?" she would say. "The clowns we saw? You remember the clowns?"

But it seemed to him that even then something was wrong, that his mother was smiling too widely, exclaiming too loudly, eyes too bright. And he would climb down and run to his room. Born almost a decade after Carl Jr., Brent wasn't stupid. He knew he was "the accident," the child that wasn't supposed to be born.

The scrapbook he held now bore the simple title, *Family Trip to the Grand Canyon.* He was seven at the time. Carl Jr. was nineteen and already a clone of his father. The three of them, Carl Jr., Charlie, and Sam, spent the entire time talking about work, while Brent played Super Mario Brothers on his Nintendo in the back of the van. That's what he had learned in life—stay out of people's way and things will go better for you. When they stopped at a church where his dad would speak, or a radio station he was trying to get his program on, they were expected to be perfectly dressed and perfectly mannered. Yes ma'am, no sir, and don't you forget it. The marvelous Christian evangelist with his marvelous family.

When they got home, his father pronounced the vacation a success. He never referred to vacations as a "good family time" or a "bad family time," only successful or unsuccessful.

His sandwich now finished, Brent put the scrapbook back inside the duffel bag and washed up his few things using water from a jerrican he'd filled up the last place he got gas. The water was cold on his hands, and he had no dish soap, but he got them reasonably clean, clean enough to use again in any case.

27

When Teri arrived back at Marnie's, the kitchen was filled with the aroma of vanilla and ginger, ham and seasonings, with a slightly burned smell adding a bottom note to the chorus of all the other smells. Plus, every inch of space was laid with gingerbread men and chocolate chip and sugar cookies. In one corner Marnie was decorating a rather lopsided pink-and-blue cake.

"I see you've been baking," Teri said.

"Oh yes. Got so much done."

"I brought something for supper, too," Teri said.

"Oh, Teri, I've got enough for an army. You didn't need to."

"I wanted to contribute. You've been so kind to me, opening your home in the middle of winter, introducing me to people, taking me down on the beach the way you did. Sure smells good in here. The soup…"

"The soup!" Marnie dropped her icing spatula and raced to the cauldron of watery green liquid boiling on the stove. She stirred, pulled the wooden spoon out, examined it and wiped it on her apron. "Oh dear, I'm afraid the bottom is burned a little. I think it'll be okay. We'll just have to eat the soup closest to the top."

Teri plunked her bakery bag full of buns on the counter next to a disorganized mountain of cookies.

"Those cookies, Teri? Those cookies are for us, for tonight. I always end up with burned cookies, and I thought we'd eat the burned ones while we watch our video."

"Great."

"I want to save the good ones for my boyfriend."

"Great."

"Oh, Teri, would you mind terribly making the coffee? I'm up to my elbows here. The coffee's in that canister."

"I would be absolutely delighted to make the coffee," Teri said. She had even bought a small container of cream to go with it.

Marnie ladled soup into bowls and placed them on TV trays in the living room where they watched the news. The pea soup very definitely tasted scorched, but if Marnie noticed, she didn't say anything. Teri told Marnie about visiting the wharf, about visiting the library. Then she asked, "Marnie, is Garda Green related to Flynn Green?"

"Oh my goodness, Teri, I'm certain that she is. Most everyone around here's related in one way or the other. I think Flynn is a second or third cousin or something."

"That's interesting."

Marnie put down her spoon and looked over at her. "I've been doing some thinking about Garda on my own. I've been thinking of talking to Will. A lot of what you're saying makes me think about Will and Garda a lot. And poor Jerome. If Garda was unfaithful to him, like everyone says, it would've really hurt him. He was that sort of person. I thought Will might know."

They finished their soup and cleared their bowls, and Marnie brought back cups of coffee and a plate heaped with burned cookies. "Tomorrow we'll be with our men, so I thought we'd have one last girlfriends' night together."

She popped a bag of popcorn into the microwave and dumped the smoky, blackened kernels into a ceramic bowl that read *Popcorn is for Sharing* on the side.

Steel Magnolias was Marnie's favorite video of all time. She had watched it at least a hundred times, she told Teri, and from the time the first titles came up until the rolling of the credits at the end, Marnie gave a running commentary on every hairstyle, every line of dialogue, every item of makeup and clothing. She'd love to live in the South, she told Teri, where women were gracious and paid attention to things like hairstyle and makeup. When the credits rolled, Marnie was crying.

"Look at me. I'm ruining my mascara. I do this every time I watch this movie, every single time I watch Julia Roberts die like that. No one should have to die like that, should they, Teri?"

Teri agreed, no they shouldn't.

"Movies about people dying, they always make me cry," Marnie said.

Teri said they did that to a lot of people.

Marnie was quiet for a few seconds, then she said, "Teri, if you don't mind, would you tell me about your mother? I bet she was beautiful. Like Julia Roberts."

Teri said yes, she was.

Marnie looked down and clucked her tongue. "Oh, Teri, how horrible that must've been for you. When your mother died. Like those poor little children in the movie. What a sad thing, to have a mother die like that."

"I was mad at God for a whole lot of years because of it."

"I don't blame you. I'd probably feel the same. You know, I used to go to church." She examined a fingernail. "I was a charter member of the Baptists, the one you see when you drive up here? The white building? Do you know which one I'm talking about, Teri?"

Teri said yes, she did.

"But I haven't been back in a long while. Boy, wouldn't they be surprised if I showed up there all of a sudden!"

"I saw Liz Caruthers today. She says hello."

"You saw Liz? She's a nice lady, Liz is, but the rest of them..." She made a face. "I've sort of gone off church for a while." She patted her curlers, tightened her scarf.

"When my mother died, I was so hurt and angry that I quit church, too. I pushed everyone away. I got into a lot of trouble."

"You, Teri? I don't believe it. Not you." Marnie was sorting through the cookies, putting the really burned ones to one side.

"Yes, me. Drugs, drinking. I barely graduated from high school. Then I bummed around a while, pretty much flunked out of college, finally pulled up my socks and went back, improved my grades and got into the police academy. But I was still running. It wasn't until I realized that God loved me just the way I was that I was able to really connect with people. It was a long road. I'm still working on it."

Marnie ate half of a burned cookie and then put it down. "The reason I haven't been back in a while is that some of the people there, I don't exactly see eye to eye with them. Clara Potter told me it was my makeup. Can you imagine that? Can you, Teri? I mean, if Clara Potter would use a little bit of makeup, she'd look a darn sight better, don't you think?"

"Well, I don't know about that."

Marnie waved her hand. "Well, of course you don't. You don't know Clara Potter. But isn't that a stupid reason to keep a person away from church? That they wear too much makeup?"

She looked at Teri expectantly until Teri agreed that was a stupid reason.

"That was a while ago now. People wear more makeup now, but maybe I'm just a little too fashionable for the rest of them. That's what I think."

"I can't imagine people being that petty," Teri said.

"Oh, you don't know the half of it. The stories I could tell. But what I think it is is this—way back when, I was a regular wild child. And now I go, and I know they're all remembering. You know. The whispers. About me then. Even though that was ages and ages ago. People around here don't forget. I don't like to go and have people whisper about me."

"I didn't go back to church until I realized that it was a safe place for me to be."

"A safe place?" Marnie grunted. "Not with the way *they* talk about me."

"But you have to remember, Marnie, that not everyone feels that way about you. And besides, the most important thing is that God doesn't feel that way about you."

"Really, Teri? You think that's true?"

"I know it's true."

They talked more then, about death, about life, about grace and redemption. It was late when Teri finally made her way up to bed, after declining an invitation to watch *Steel Magnolias* a second time.

Even though it was late, she wanted to call Jack. But when she did, her light mood was soon deflated. Patsy Mellon had called to tell her they had found someone else to do the Sunday school class.

"What?" She sat very still on the edge of the bed. Downstairs she could hear the opening strains of the movie.

"They've asked Marta Ramone to do it."

Teri got up and went to the window. "Why? Did she say?"

"Just something about the fact that you're gone a lot."

"I'm not gone a lot."

"Well, there was the thinking that sometimes you travel."

"I'm usually home on weekends. I can be home on weekends. I can plan on it. I was planning for it."

"I tried to press her, but that's all she said. I wouldn't take it personally, though. I really wouldn't, Teri. You know what they say..."

"I know. 'Never attribute to malice what can better be explained by stupidity.'"

"I wouldn't call them stupid, exactly, but I don't think they knew how much this meant to you. I just think it was an oversight."

"It's okay. Hey, it leaves me more time to work."

"As I said, I wouldn't take it personally."

After the phone call, Teri stood at the window for a long time and looked out into the blackness.

28

By midafternoon of the following day, Teri was home and unpacking, doing laundry and packing up again for a trip down to Philadelphia. Maybe it was time to pay the Pellermans a visit. And Daisy. And if she planned her trip to coincide with Sunday, she could visit Carl Houseman's church, plus miss her own church and having to deal with Verna Plant and Patsy Mellon. She was trying very hard not to "go off church" like Marnie had, but sometimes people's stupidity made that difficult.

"This should be my last trip," she said to Jack when he got home. "I've just got to check out a few things down there. It really shouldn't take me all that long." She had filled up her plastic watering pot and was watering her plants. Two of them were flowering. "Won't be long now before I'm fertilizing these babies again," she said. "Now if I can keep Tiger and Gilligan out of them..."

Jack stood in the doorway. He was very still.

"Teri, come here," he said. She put down the watering pot and went to him. He pushed her hair away from her eyes and looked at her. "I talked with Frank Plant this morning. I happened to run into him at the Irving."

"Frank Plant?"

"Sunday school board chairman."

"Okay, so?"

"I happened to mention about you being disappointed about the Sunday school class."

"Oh, you didn't need to do that." Teri backed away. "You really didn't need to. I prayed about it. We prayed about it in Bible study; maybe this is my answer. Maybe I'm really not ready. Maybe I should give it another year. I'm okay with it."

Jack wasn't saying anything.

Teri waited. She finally said, "What?"

"I asked him, 'Why was my wife passed over for this?' And he gave the answer that you weren't home a lot, which I pointed out wasn't true. He was sort of looking at me strangely, obviously wanting to get in his car and be on his way, but I blocked his entrance. I said, 'Frank, we've known each other a long time. What's the real reason?' And after hemming and hawing he said that the board decided that you weren't a good role model for young girls."

Teri put her hand on the dresser. She stood very still.

"That *really* got my back up, as you can imagine. I said, 'Frank, why?' He kept talking about role models and police officers and detectives, and did they really want their young girls growing up and going into such a violent profession. He also said they weren't sure about Christian women being private detectives, or some other equally nonsensical thing like that. But as I stood there and listened to him, I knew that wasn't the real reason. I was still blocking his way. I kept shaking my head, saying, 'Frank, that's not the real reason. What is it?' He advised me to go to the minister then, and I said that he was the board chairman, and I wanted the answer from him. I was really in his face. I'm usually so meek and mild."

"Yes, you are." She smiled.

"Finally, he said that some people in the church had been upset because of the number of times your car was overnight in my driveway before we were married."

Teri's eyes went wide.

"At first I didn't know what he was talking about. I kept looking at him, saying, Frank, what are you talking about? And then I remembered."

"Remembered what? When was I ever overnight at your place? When was my car ever—" But then she remembered, too. A year ago, before they were married, she had flown out to visit her father, who was sick. She was going to leave her car in long-term parking. Jack said nonsense. He would drive her and take her car in to the shop to find out why the brakes were squealing. It was a simple problem, a slight adjustment, and the car was ready the next day.

"I told him," he said. "I told him all of that."

"And 'number of times'? What's this 'number of times' all about? It was there two nights, and it was in the shop one of those nights, wasn't it? One night is not a number of times."

"We—or I—should've been more aware of how it looked."

"Why do we always have to be so *aware* of how things look? Why can't people just mind their own business? What business is it of theirs in the first place, anyway?"

Teri was walking around now, fingering things on the counter, touching the leaves of her plants, squaring the edges of books on the coffee table. "Oh, and another thing... Why am I the one blamed here and not you?"

"Oh, I think I'm blamed, too. Nobody's been clamoring for me to get back on the deacon board lately."

"So what do we do now? Maybe I should photocopy the plane tickets. They could photocopy them and put them in the bulletin. Would that satisfy their nosy little minds?"

"Teri..."

"No, Jack, I'm mad."

"I apologized to Frank. It just never in a million years crossed my mind as to how it would look. I wasn't thinking. A lapse there in judgment. Especially since I thought everyone knew you were visiting your father, since we were praying for him as a church."

Teri picked up her watering pot and began dousing her grapefruit tree until water slopped out and drenched the carpet underneath. "And that's part of it, too, isn't it? The people in that church would rather nitpick than pray for you. No wonder Marnie went 'off church' as she puts it."

As Teri mopped up the water with a towel, she fought tears. Why did everything have to be so hard?

The evening of the following day, Saturday, Teri arrived in Downingtown, Pennsylvania, and followed an Internet map to Pellermans house on Sugarloaf Lane. She and Jack had called their pastor the previous evening and met with him, along with the chairman of the Sunday school board, which Teri thought was a big to-do about nothing. ("This idiocy is part of why I left the church in the first place," Teri said to Jack before the meeting.) They straightened things out as far as the pastor and the board chairman were concerned. In the end, however, Marta Ramone was still teaching the class. She had had the lesson book for almost a month now and had spent a lot of time preparing.

On the daylong drive to Pennsylvania, Teri had plenty of time to think. And pray. And try to figure out where she fit into things. Halfway down she left a curt message on Carl Houseman's voice mail saying that she was on her way down and expected to see him.

Take it easy, Teri, she told herself. Don't take it out on Carl.

The thing that hurt her the most was that no one had come to them earlier. Not even their pastor.

"I've known these guys forever," normally sanguine Jack had said to her after the two men left. "I've been on the board with them. I know them personally. I've had dinner in their homes. Our families have taken vacations together."

They hadn't gotten to sleep until quarter after one, and then she was up at six to head south, keeping herself fueled with coffee and anger.

As much as she tried to turn her thoughts toward Carl and Ellen and her impending surprise visit to the Pellermans, her thoughts went uncontrollably back to the church.

The ghost of Jenny was everywhere: in the church, in the Sunday school, on the back of bulletins, even in Teri's own house. And that's what she was really angry about. That no one thought she was good enough to fill Jenny's shoes.

Every once in a while Teri came across something of Jenny's: a birthday card, a recipe hastily jotted on a piece of paper and stuck in a book. The last one had been a week before she had taken on the Carl Houseman case. She had been going through some old books and magazines in the basement, tying them up for the recycle box. On the top of the metal bookshelf she found a tattered poetry anthology. She picked it up, and it opened to a photograph, yellowed and crinkled with age. It was a younger Jack and Jenny. Teri sat down on the cold cement floor and studied it. How young they both looked there; Jack with a headful of thick brown hair was a different person to her. Jenny looked like all the pictures she had ever seen of her: tall, blond, waiflike, delicate. The church people had given Jenny Addison baby showers in the church lounge, they had stood by her when she was sick, had brought casseroles to the house when she died.

It was an odd sensation, looking down at them. She couldn't call it jealousy. It was more intense curiosity. What was Jack like then, this Jack from another lifetime? This thinner Jack with his thick brown hair and heavy horn-rimmed glasses and smooth face? She had never seen Jack without a beard. She threw the picture into the recycling box.

It was dusk when Teri reached Peg and Paul's estate. For that's what it was, a huge rambling white house tucked away among trees and standing majestic and cathedral-like behind a professionally landscaped lawn that featured shrubs surrounded by a lot of little white stones. She drove up the circular driveway and parked in front of it. She had visions of her arrival being watched from attic windows by whole fleets of maids and butlers.

But Peg Pellerman herself answered her knock. She was casually clad in gray corduroy slacks and a blue turtleneck sweater and looked like she had stepped out of one of Marnie's Coldwater Creek catalogs. She was a very tall woman. Teri hadn't expected Peg to tower over her the way she did. Her wavy dark hair was expertly cut and she wore gold earrings. If Teri wasn't mistaken, in the center of each earring was the Houseman Ministries logo, a stylized cross with a sheaf of grain. Peg was frowning.

"Mrs. Pellerman?"

"I am she. And you are?"

"I'm Teri Blake-Addison, Carl's private investigator."

"Teri! You're here? Did we know you were coming?"

"I was in the neighborhood."

"Come in, come in. Paul's out for a quick dinner meeting. What do you have?"

"What do you mean, what do I have?" asked Teri entering.

"A report for me? Anything new? Is that why you've come all this way?"

"Actually, I came to ask you a few questions." Teri followed her down a hallway of gleaming hardwood floors.

"I'm so sorry Paul's out. An emergency meeting. You know how it is with ministry—if it isn't one thing, it's another."

"Hmm."

"He will want to meet the girl we hired."

The girl we hired? Teri followed Peg into an immense country kitchen in the back of the house. French doors opened onto a deck, and beyond that a garden, brown now, but looking well weeded, well organized, professionally cared for.

"Would you care for some iced tea?"

Peg poured two glasses without waiting for an answer. The glasses were frosted and had the Houseman Ministries logo along the sides. "I would be happy to hear an update," she was saying. She motioned Teri to sit at the table across from her. Teri did.

Peg put her hands on the table, and Teri looked at her face, at the deep frown lines between her eyes. "So, tell me how the investigation is going."

"I came to talk with you about Ellen."

"Ellen was my closest friend on this earth. I still grieve the loss of such a close friend. We shared everything."

"I've spent some time talking with her Maine friends, her sailing friends."

Peg leaned back in her chair, flicked at something on the sleeve of her sweater, one hand still on the table. "Once a year she went home. It was expected of her. She knew it and she did it."

"Home? But her parents were both dead. She had no family in Maine."

Peg reached for her tea, took a long drink. Her face had that earnest expression that Teri had seen so often on Jack's students, that look that they alone are the holders of life's grand secrets and serious truths.

"I don't know how to say this without coming across as commercial or crass," Peg said, "but Ellen realized that she had to hold on to those childhood ties, the people there. It was of benefit to the ministry and she knew that."

"Benefit? How? You mean financial benefit?"

"I wasn't thinking in money terms so much but generally of the ministry. She went home to make it known that she was a woman of the people. She was devoted to her work here, and there were so many times when we knew she didn't want to go back to Maine. She was working hard and wanted to stay. Still she went."

Teri opened up her notebook. "So, Ellen went to Maine every summer so she would come across as a small-town New Englander, one of the common people."

"You make it sound so crass."

Teri looked up at her. "Were you ever on her sailboat?"

"Oh no, not me. Of course not. No, that was Ellen's avenue of ministry. Carl went overseas, Paul and I were involved in the home office here, and Ellen's sphere was in Maine. Her mission field and ministry was in Maine. It was something we prayed over before she left every summer. Ellen needed that prayer. It's so easy to get overwhelmed by the demands of the ministry. I was that friend that Ellen could come to in safety, and she confided in me and I in her. I miss her." Peg looked away, and Teri saw real tears there.

"Did she ever talk about her sailing when she came back? Did she ever show you any pictures?"

Peg shook her head. "It really didn't mean that much to her. You may not believe that, but it's true. When she got back she would barge into the office and say something like, 'Well, I'm back!' and then she would be back. We never thought to ask for pictures."

"Do you know Jane Jarvis?"

"I'm sorry; that name isn't familiar to me." Peg looked wistful when she said, "The four of us, she and Carl and Paul and I, there was a time we had so much fun together. We made it a point to get together once a week for dinner. Our kids were both in youth group at the time, and since the youth met on Friday nights, that was our time for each other. We live a bit of a distance from Philadelphia where Carl and Ellen lived, and where Carl lives now, and there were times they just stayed over. Spur-of-the-moment times. We'd pull down sleeping bags and foam pads and spread them out in front of the fireplace over there and...well, we just had your basic, old-fashioned sleepover. That's how it was with us."

"Fun," Teri said.

"Oh, it was fun. We had some good times, the four of us."

"And you four never talked about Maine?"

"It actually, honestly never came up. It just wasn't a part of the things we talked about. We four were the backbone of the ministry. Carl was the visionary of the group. He always was. Paul was the doer. He would take Carl's visions and put money and wheels to them. Ellen was the writer, and I was the prayer. God has gifted me with discernment, and I just—"

"Ellen was the writer?"

"She was a good writer. Yes, she was."

"Did Ellen write Carl's books? I notice he hasn't had one out since Ellen died."

Peg looked down at her hands. "Well, I guess it's no secret now. I guess with Ellen gone. She was certainly a part of his writing projects. Her editing skills were sound."

"So, she ghostwrote his books, then?"

"Ghostwrote? Well, I wouldn't go that far."

"How far would you go then?"

"Ghostwrote..." She splayed her hands, put the tops of her fingers together. "We don't like to use that term. The reading public would expect them to come from Carl."

"But there were two with her name on them, two they wrote together."

"Yes, her name appears on the two books they wrote about family ministry. But it was felt that the theological books should come from his pen."

"Do you know where she kept her scrapbooks?"

"Her what?"

"She kept scrapbooks, according to the Fergusons."

"I'm sorry. That name isn't familiar to me."

"The Fergusons. Ted and Alma. And you should know them, they've contributed plenty to this ministry."

"It's certainly difficult to keep tabs on everyone who sends in a few dollars."

Teri shook her head, then said more quietly, "One of the things Carl wants me to do is to look at Ellen's state of mind before the accident. Carl thinks there may have been something troubling her before she took that last trip. You, being one of her closest friends, would have known that. That's why I'm here."

Peg was quiet for a while, frowning, before she said, "It could've been Brent, their youngest."

"Brent?"

She leaned forward. "Carl Jr. is a godsend, especially now that Carl Sr. has gotten so…how shall I put it, distracted with all of this. Carl Jr. is there day in and day out making sure things run smoothly. He and Paul both. Charlie and Sam are in ministry, serving God. But Brent…well, Brent marches to a different drummer, I'm afraid."

"How so?"

"He's not serving the Lord. He's always been a bit of a strange duck. Stealing from us was the last straw. We never told Carl. We didn't need to add even more misery to his misfortune, but when Brent left he took our car—mind you, it was an old one and we never used it anyway—plus he stole one of Paul's guns."

"And you reported that to the police, of course."

She shook her head and frowned. "We thought it best not to. Well, Brent had been a problem all along. Very much a loner. Ellen and Carl both were always worried about him. Paul and I tried to befriend the boy. Carl was away so much…well he had to be. We were as much Brent's parents as Ellen and Carl."

The front door opened and a hearty hello was heard. Peg jumped up. "Paul, I'm in the kitchen. You'll never guess who's here."

Paul stood in the doorway, sleek, elegant in his expensive suit. And he grinned. He more than made up for Peg's permanently serious face.

Teri stood. "Mr. Pellerman, I'm Teri Blake-Addison."

"Well, hello. It's nice to finally meet this person, in person." He shook her hand, grinned some more.

"Teri came to give us the latest on the investigation."

"And to find out about Ellen's state of mind prior to her death," Teri added.

The smile never left his mouth, but his eyes sobered. Peg rose and poured him an iced tea. Teri could hear her quietly ask him, "How was the meeting?"

His voice was meant to be a whisper, but Teri heard every word. "Most of the board is really having difficulty with the name change."

"Name change?" Teri asked.

"Paul!" Peg said.

He waved his hand. "It's okay, Peg. It's no secret. It's going to get out soon anyway. Plus it has nothing to do with the investigation. Well, here's the story: the board wants to change the name from Houseman Ministries to something else, something more encompassing—Family Christian Ministries, Christian Home Ministries, something like that. It's been in the works for a long time now. It's no secret."

"Interesting," Teri said.

"We don't need to bore our guest with these details," Peg said.

"I'm not bored," Teri said. "What does Carl think about this name change?"

"Carl? He generally approves."

"Generally approves."

"That's what I said, yes."

"So, he was at the meeting then?"

"Carl wasn't there tonight. He was unable to make it."

Teri accepted Paul's refill of tea. Then asked him what he could tell her about Ellen's state of mind.

29

Teri found her way to Carl's church, which was on the outskirts of Philadelphia. It was an impressive building with a cross that was visible for blocks. There was a light on and several cars in the large, paved lot. The large sanctuary, however, looked dark. She pulled up beside a white van and got out.

The door closest to the cars was unlocked, and she walked inside. She heard music and followed it down a hallway and into a large room with a stage at one end. The door said *Youth Lounge.* A worship band with drums, a couple guitars, a bass, flute, and a stringed instrument Teri didn't recognize, was practicing. She stood at the back and listened for several minutes.

"They're good, aren't they?" A young man with a New Jersey Devils sweatshirt was standing beside her.

"Oh, um, yes, quite."

"And they're not even the regular church band. That's only the youth worship band."

"Nice."

"Is there something I can help you with?"

"I was sort of looking for Carl."

"Dr. Houseman?"

She nodded.

"You won't find him here. I'm Matt Brodwizen," he said putting out his hand."

"Teri Blake-Addison."

"TBA. To Be Announced." He flashed her a grin.

"Most people don't pick up on that."

"You a visitor?"

"I'm doing some business for Carl. I'll be here tomorrow morning."

"Oh, you're in for a treat."

She looked at him, guessed his age to be midtwenties. "Do you know Brent Houseman?"

"Brent? He doesn't work here anymore."

"Did you know him when he was here."

"Yeah. We were in youth group together. Quiet guy. Was a hotshot soundman, though. Could make any group sound good. Didn't matter if you couldn't sing a note. You looking for him? I don't know where he is these days. You might check with the church office, they might know."

Teri said, "His mother's death affected him, didn't it?"

"I guess. I don't know much about that."

Back outside, Teri passed the main office door and noted the hours: *M–F, 9–4:30.* Underneath was a sign: *Emergencies call,* and there was a number. Teri wrote it down—although for what reason, she really didn't know—then headed back to her car.

She found a decent enough looking motel a couple blocks from the church and took a room. She never booked motel rooms ahead, which Jack could never understand. She always waited until she got to a place and then drove around until she found a room. Not Jack; he always booked well in advance. Every trip he planned was meticulously organized down to the last restaurant.

The motel she chose now was a two-story one attached to a restaurant and next to a shopping mall. She unpacked a few things and got a pot of coffee going in the little coffeepot on the desk. (They actually had one!) She made herself comfortable on the bed, clicked on the TV, and opened her iBook. She was tired, blitzed, still upset about the Sunday school class, but she'd force herself to get all of her notes into her iBook before she went to sleep. The TV was always the first thing she turned on when she entered a room. It came from her "alone years," she called them—the years when she lived alone and liked the sound of a human voice. It usually didn't matter what they were talking about, but Diane Sawyer or Larry King were like comforting friends who chatted with her in her living room.

She got comfortable with her computer on the bed and transferred her notes about Peg and Paul into it. She added them to her people folder, highlighted in blue.

Teri still held to her theory that Ellen needed a place to kick back, and that for a time each summer she needed not to be reminded of her responsibilities. She would see Carl tomorrow and talk with him if she could. In the meantime, she had some phone calls to make.

Her home phone was answered with, "Dr. James Addison's home."

"Hey, I'm looking for Jack."

"Hi, Teri; this is Stephan."

"I didn't recognize your voice."

"I'm not sure Jack's here." She heard noise in the background. "He was here a minute ago. He might've gone to drive someone home."

"Can you have him call me on my cell when he gets in?"

That was one of the things she had to get used to living with Jack, the number of young people that were always around the house. Her next call was to Brent Houseman again. Amanda Mast told her that Brent was still not back and that she didn't know where he was or when he'd be home. And not only that, she was sick of him taking off like this.

"He's done this before? Left?"

"A few times."

"Do you know where he goes?"

"No."

"So you have no idea?"

"He's mental."

"Mental?"

"He's like pure mental."

"What do you mean?"

"In the way he is. I mean he can be this really great guy, but there's this weird part about him. You know like when you hear on the news that there's been this serial killing, and when they find the guy and talk to the neighbors, they're all, 'He was such a quiet person, kept to himself.' Well, that's how Brent is."

Teri sat up. "Are you saying that you believe Brent is capable of murder?"

"No, of course not. Brent wouldn't hurt a fly. He's just sorta pent up, ya know? Are you that detective?"

"I am."

"Well, maybe I shouldn't say this, but I'm sorta glad you called. I was wondering, could you sorta look out for him? I think he might be in trouble."

"Why do you say that?"

"Like maybe drugs or something. I don't know."

"Does he take drugs?"

"I've never seen him using. I gotta say that much for him. But he's got this duffel bag in the back of his closet and there's all this money in it. And books. And a gun. He'd freak if he knew I was telling you about this. I'm just worried about him, because yesterday? I looked in the back of his closet and the bag was gone. And I can't go to the police. What if he's into drugs or something, like dealing? So, could you sorta keep an eye on him? If you happen to run across him?"

"I'll keep that in mind."

Teri's next call was to Molly Cedars at Pizza Hut. Molly surprised Teri by saying that she knew exactly who Brent Houseman was when she hired him.

"He doesn't know I know, but I know who he is. He came to me needing a job, and so I hired him with no references. I knew about his mother's death, and I figured this youngest son just needed some time on his own. He's turned out to be a good worker. Quiet, keeps to himself, but good, on time. The things that matter."

"Quiet. Keeps to himself."

"What?"

"Nothing. Do you have any idea where he might have gone?"

"I assume he's in Philadelphia. He said it was a family emergency. I'm sorry I can't be more helpful. I wish you the best on your investigation."

Teri was just slipping off to sleep when Jack phoned.

"Miss you," he said.

"Hey," she said, rubbing her eyes.

"Did I wake you?"

"No. I had to get up to answer the phone anyway."

"I was worried about you. You okay?"

"I'm fine, Jack."

"I've got some information for you."

"Some information?"

"I've done some research of my own that I think you might be interested in."

"Research? About what?" Teri wiped her sleepy face with the palm of her hand.

"I learned that Archibald Ryder worked for Carl for seven years and then left suddenly six years ago, a year before Ellen died."

"How did you find this out?"

"My own methods. You're not the only hotshot researcher in the family."

"I know. When it comes to researching Jane Eyre, you can knock the socks off me. So, how'd you find this out?"

"When I heard the name Archibald Ryder, it sort of triggered something that I had read once. So I looked him up on the Web, and after going from link to link, like I've seen you do, I found that out."

"Wow, I *am* impressed."

"I thought you would be. You also got a phone message. A private investigator named Buck Jonas from Boston called. He wants you to call him."

"Did he say what he wanted?"

"No, just to call him." After he gave her Jonas's phone number, he said, "I love you. Don't forget that."

"I won't."

"We'll get through this, I promise."

"I know."

30

She overslept and arrived ten minutes late to Carl's church. She was handed a bulletin and ushered into the overflow area by a smiling, wrinkle-faced man wearing a name tag that read *Usher Milt.* She soon discovered that not only was she in the overflow area, but she was in the overflow area of the overflow area and seated on a folding chair. Through a wide window with the blinds pulled back she could see into the cavernous sanctuary. In the far distance down a long aisle was the platform lined with white poinsettias. A robed choir sat in a high loft behind. A worship band consisting of drums, a variety of guitars, and five well-dressed singers was already leading the congregation in worship choruses projected on screens throughout the place by unseen projectors. The man Teri was seated beside was singing with vigor.

From where she stood, she had her choice of three views of the platform: through the window or on two wide-screen monitors bolted on either side of the overflow area.

The "real" service didn't start until eleven, and this fifteen minutes prior was a time for announcements and worship choruses. In the center aisle the television crew was ready for when the "live on air" service began. Near the front she saw Matt Brodwizen talking to two of the camera crew. She looked through the bulletin and noted that today's speaker was Rev. Paul Pellerman. Reverend?

A few minutes before eleven, Paul, a younger man who was probably Carl Jr., and a woman in a blue dress that needed a good spraying of Static Guard made their way across the platform. Behind the woman walked Carl Sr., and next to him Daisy Best. As befitting her name, Daisy wore a pale yellow suit that looked expensive. Even from this distance, gold earrings glinted in the overhead lights. For some reason it made Teri think of Ellen.

There was a note at the bottom of the bulletin that CDs of the worship team and choir—featuring many new choruses and traditional hymns; plus original music by our own songwriting duo of Rebecca Rainsbury and Jonathan Wire; the outstanding vocals of Claudia Apple, Matt Brodwizen, and Sarah Smith; plus two songs by the youth worship band—could be purchased in the Fellowship Room following the service. She also noted that visitors were invited to the Fellowship Room for coffee, and first-time visitors would be given a copy of the CD.

Carl rose and stood silently behind the pulpit for a few moments. Then it was eleven, and the live service began with a welcome from Carl. He sat down and Carl Jr. rose and led choruses. She didn't know Carl Jr. was musical. Well, maybe one didn't have to be. Maybe all you needed to be was related.

The choir sang, and if Jack were here, he would have been able to tell her what they were singing. It was beautiful, though. More singing, more prayer, and all through the service, black-clad stagehands moved mikes and instruments practically unseen. The soloist in the blue dress rose and sang a song that began quietly enough, but was soon in danger of breaking fine china.

There was so much glitz here, Teri reflected. This is what happens when you get humans to invent beauty. You get plastic glitz and shiny things and gold earrings with ministry logos in the center and microphones for perfect sound. When you get God to invent beauty, you get Grand Manan Island with its majestic cliffs and a sunrise on the bay and the sound of the ocean.

Carl and Daisy were together now at the pulpit, Daisy talking about a new women's prayer ministry she was inviting all ladies everywhere to be involved in, and here was how. All this from a romance writer.

More singing, another choir number, and Paul rose to speak. His passage was from Nehemiah, and he spoke about building walls.

Teri was disappointed that Carl wasn't speaking. She had heard him a few times since she began the investigation, and he spoke with a power and a refreshing honesty about grace, about pain, about forgiveness and redemption. The underlying theme of Paul's message seemed to be God's judgment on murderers, homosexuals, and fornicators, and how the church needed to build walls against such things.

If she had heard a message like this three years ago, she would have been counted among the people he was condemning. She would have heard this message and bolted out of there.

Teri tried to study Carl's face while Paul spoke, which was difficult because he was miles away from where she sat, and the television screens focused on Paul only. To see Carl she had to lean her head sideways and squint through the window. Carl was looking down at his hands folded on top of his open Bible. Once when the television camera shifted to his face, Teri thought she saw his left eye twitching. Ever so slightly.

"I will spew you out of my mouth," Paul was saying. Loudly. The camera was immediately square on his face. She looked down at her Bible, and tears welled up in her eyes. She found a Kleenex in her pocket and wiped them.

For her, being confronted with absolute love made her want to come back to God. Not this. Not condemnation. It had taken her a very long time to realize that even during her lost years, God had not spewed her out of His mouth. Never once. Even if the Sunday school board was rejecting her, God wasn't. And never would. She wiped her eyes again with a Kleenex. The man next to her smiled. He, too, was wiping his eyes.

When it was over, the man turned to her. "He's a powerful speaker, isn't he?"

Teri nodded.

After church she followed the press of people into the Fellowship Room, a huge carpeted reception room with a lit fireplace at one end. Coffee urns were set up throughout on little tables covered with white tablecloths. Teenage girls in black skirts and white blouses carried around trays of coffee cake and muffins. It wasn't five minutes before a gray-haired woman with a name tag that read *Welcomer Helen* asked Teri if she was new or visiting.

"Visiting," Teri said.

"First time?"

"Yes."

She grinned, took Teri's arm, and led her to a table where she signed the guest register and was given her free CD. She plunked it into her satchel.

"Would you like a coffee?" Helen asked.

"That would be nice."

"What do you take?"

"Lots of cream and a bit of sugar."

"Visiting from where?" the woman asked when she returned with Teri's coffee.

"Maine."

"Maine. It must be nice up there."

"It is."

"Visiting family?"

"Business actually. Have you been going to this church a long time?"

"Oh, just about forever. More than thirty years now. Now, I'm really showing my age. This is such a friendly church. We pride ourselves on our friendliness. It's what we're known for."

"You must've known Dr. Houseman's first wife then."

"Ellen? Such a tragedy. Why do you ask?"

Teri shrugged. "Just curious, I guess."

"Her death came as such a shock. Most of us didn't even know she was out on a boat. I thought she was at a women's prayer retreat."

"Does Rev. Pellerman preach very often?"

"More and more. Some of the people like Pastor Carl—he's such a gentle soul—but Pastor Paul, now he's a powerful preacher. He preaches the messages that we in America need to hear. That's for sure. He preaches the truth."

"Do they like take turns preaching, first one and then the other?"

Helen moved closer to her. "It's getting to be mostly Paul. But then Carl Jr. does his fair share, too."

"And everyone's happy with that?"

Helen moved even closer. "I was thinking, was telling my husband just the other day that if this were any other church, and if these men weren't so godly, this could be a problem. I just thank the Lord that there are no divisions here."

"Good thing," Teri said.

Further conversation with Helen was concluded as Paul and Peg Pellerman found her.

Helen looked on with raised eyebrows and an open mouth when Paul said, "We're so glad you could make it, Teri. Did you get your free CD?"

"Yes, thank you."

"We hope you enjoyed our service."

"Very much. Thank you."

Carl Houseman and Daisy Best strode toward her, arm in arm. Up close, Teri could see that Daisy's suit was indeed expertly cut and made of some expensive material. Teri suddenly felt out of place in her straight black skirt, turtleneck sweater, and boots.

"Teri," Carl said, "I'd like you to meet my fiancée, Daisy Best."

"Hello," Teri said extending her hand.

"It's so nice to meet you finally," Daisy said. "I've heard so much about you." Teri watched her, the fluttering of the false eyelashes, the nervous smile, the way her manicured fingers held on to Carl's arm a little too tightly. Daisy asked her to lunch the following day.

"Thank you. I would enjoy that."

Teri also made an appointment to meet with Carl Sr. in the morning. Then Carl called his son over and introduced her to him and his wife, Mariana. Carl Jr. had a pinched, painful look about him. And his wife looked pale and malnourished, and Teri wondered if she was sick.

"It's nice to meet you." Carl Jr. was all business, from his purposeful stride to his firm handshake.

"Why don't you give Teri a tour of the facility, son?"

Carl Jr. looked toward his wife, who said, "Go ahead Carl. Do what needs to be done. I'll take the kids home in my car."

Carl Jr. twirled on his heels. "I could do that. Come with me."

His wide-legged stride was practically a run for Teri. In about half an hour she was shown the offices, the Sunday school rooms, the sound room, the various production rooms, the bookstore, the counseling center.

"Do you preach much?" she asked him.

"I'm on the roster a good four months of the year," he said.

"Does Paul preach often?"

"Yes, he does."

"How about your father?"

They were in the middle of one of their production studios. Teri had lost track of what this one was for; maybe they made their CDs here?

"My father is choosing to hand the reins more and more over to others," he said.

"Is he retiring then? He's pretty young to retire, isn't he?"

"No, he's not retiring."

She followed him out of one studio and into another where they recorded their CDs.

"So, when your dad does retire, who's going to take over? You or Paul Pellerman?"

"We're a ministry team here."

And if I hear those words one more time I'm going to scream, she felt like saying. They were walking side by side when Teri said, "Tell me about your brother."

"I have three."

"Brent."

He stopped and looked at her. "What about him?"

"I've heard that your mother may have been worried about him. There's some thought that she may have had something on her mind before the accident, and that it had something to do with Brent."

"Let me tell you something about my little brother. When Charlie and Sam and I were little, we didn't have much. We were just starting out, and as you may or may not know, your average, everyday minister isn't one of the richest members of society. We struggled. But by the time Brent came along, we were doing much better. Brent never had to struggle. He doesn't know the meaning of the word. Both of my parents doted on him, and he never appreciated it, never realized how much my father had to work to get to the place he was. And Brent just kept demanding. More and more. Nothing was ever enough."

"I take it your father wasn't home a lot when you were growing up."

He was walking again, and she struggled to keep up. "He did what had to be done."

"Perish the thought of anyone being just your average, everyday minister."

They were back in the Fellowship Room, which was practically empty now. Teri went back to her motel and ate lunch in the coffee shop. For all their self-proclaimed friendliness, no one had invited her to lunch.

31

It was pretty smart of him, Brent thought, making friends with Tracie. Being a waitress, she would know a lot of people. And even though she hadn't been here at the time, she seemed to know a lot about the accident. She might even know where his mother was.

Funny he should put it like that. But he had known this ever since the boating accident, that somehow, some way, his mother had not died. Or at least not died in that accident. Brent was sitting in the back of his van and looking at an old bulletin that had fallen out of one of his mother's scrapbooks. On the front was a picture of the church in Philadelphia, the whole thing, from the high cross to all the office buildings. The bulletin was brittle with age, and unconsciously he was tearing away at the edges of it.

His mother had not died in that accident. He had tried to tell his father at the time. He had tried to tell them all, his brothers, the Pellermans, all of them. But no one had understood that it wasn't Brent just trying to make trouble again, that this time he had something to say. It was something he felt, something he knew.

"The other two bodies were found—doesn't that tell you something?" he had yelled at his father on the morning of the memorial service, but all his father did was tell him to make sure his suit was clean for the afternoon. They were all supposed to be on best behavior, in suits. Little soldiers of the cross. Brent didn't own a suit, and the day before the memorial, Peg Pellerman brought him one to wear. She carried it in a plastic bag from the cleaners and hung it on the hook on the inside of his bedroom door. That she had gone into his room, had hung clothes there, like a *mother,* had bothered him. That she would know his exact size bothered him.

He didn't even try it on. He had put on a nice pair of slacks and a sports jacket and tie and gone down to lunch where the extended family all sat, along with the Pellermans. (How they were always in on family things!) His oldest brother had scowled at him, told him to go up and change. He said I'm fine the way I am.

"Look at the rest of us and look at you," Charlie said. "We've all tried to make the effort. Why can't you just—"

"Leave him be," said their father.

Finally Paul Pellerman rose from his seat, put his hand on Brent's shoulder with that phony smile he always wore, and said, "Brent, son, come with me. Let's have a talk."

Brent shrugged away from him. "I'm not your son."

"All of us are finding it hard. This is a difficult time," Peg said.

It was then that Brent had yelled, "She's not dead. Just no one's looking in the right place."

"Go change, Brent," his father said.

"I'm not going," Brent said simply. "I'm not going to a funeral for a person who's not dead."

His brothers looked at him in wonder. The errant younger brother all of a sudden with this psychic connection to their mother?

As the years passed, that feeling that his mother was still alive faded. It still lurked in the back of his brain every so often. Every time he looked at the duffel bag, and thought about the money he had stolen, it came back to him. Not that she was alive, so much, but that she *had* lived. And that once upon a time she had tried to reach them.

And now as he sat in the back of the van tearing the edges of the church bulletin, he remembered the startled look in his father's eyes, the realization that his father felt it too, and like him, was being railroaded by the Pellermans.

Perfectly straight little pieces of bulletin were scattered around him on the hard metal floor of the van. He was surprised at how easy it tore. It tore better up and down than sideways. He wondered why that was. The mystery of paper. He looked down at the cross, in pieces now.

He hadn't gone to the memorial service. Instead, he walked over to the mall and sat on a bench, Eddie Bauer in front of him and the Gap behind him. Lots of people in and out all afternoon. No one paying attention to him, everyone oblivious that in the other end of the city, a big memorial service was going on. He sat there and sat there, until Peg Pellerman came and drove him home.

Rapidly, he tore the bulletin, the little strips into littler strips, over and over again until the entire Houseman Ministries had been turned to confetti, all around him and covering him in the back of his van.

32

The following morning at nine-thirty, Peg greeted Teri in the outer office and told her to sit in a chair along the wall.

"He'll just be a minute," she said.

In the twenty minutes that Teri waited, Peg was on the phone or the computer or into the filing cabinet and barely said a word to her. It seemed to Teri that Peg wasn't busy as much as wanting to look like she was busy. The few times Teri tried to engage her in conversation, Peg answered quickly without looking up.

At ten to ten Peg said, "You're just about finished now, aren't you?"

"Finished?"

"With the investigation. I could write you a check right now for the balance; then you can be on your way."

"Pardon me?"

"Your investigation. I can write you check for the balance. There's no need for you to stay."

"I'm meeting Carl."

"Daisy agrees with us. So does Carl Jr. This whole investigation was a mistake. It's just something Carl needs to get out of his system."

So let him get it out of his system then, she thought.

Five minutes later, Carl emerged from his office and looked at Teri. "How long have you been here?"

Teri looked at her watch. "Around twenty-five minutes, I guess."

Carl looked at Peg. "I thought you were going to let me know when she arrived."

"I've been nonstop on the phone, Carl," Peg said. "I thought you were equally busy."

"Peg, you should've buzzed me. No need to have made Teri wait. I'm sorry, Teri."

"It's okay," Teri said.

Carl's office was massive, bigger than Teri's entire Bangor apartment. His desk was pale wood, enormous; the carpets plush; and on the walls were what looked like original oils. Behind his desk were a few framed photographs, among them, one of himself and President Bush. When he saw Teri looking at it he said, "I was involved in a prayer circle with him just after September eleventh."

"Oh."

"It's big, isn't it?"

"Big?"

"This space. All of this. I've raised a lot of money in my lifetime. I've built up this whole organization. Everything you see here. From the ground up, because I thought it was important. I thought it was work I was doing for the Lord. And Carl, my son?"

"Yes?"

"I was just as intense as he is, just as zealous. I was afflicted with a disease just as debilitating, just as insidious as alcoholism or gambling, and I believe I've passed it on to my sons. Unfortunately, I don't think the WA is a group. Maybe I need to start one."

"WA?"

"Workaholics anonymous. Hi, my name is Carl and I'm a workaholic." He laughed and then frowned. "I was a workaholic. And it cost me my family. I have three sons who are just like me. They learned the pattern well, that your family is window dressing, something to make you look good. I'm especially concerned with Carl Jr. Do you know he already has high blood pressure?"

"He's so thin, though."

"He is. And his wife Mariana has suffered with anorexia. He's going to destroy her life as I destroyed my Ellen's. Charlie and Sam the same. I taught them all well. Then there's my other son, my youngest." He made a tent with his hands on his desk, seemed to study his fingernails.

"Brent."

"The child of my heart." He blinked, turned away for a moment, and then back again. "You have something specific you want to talk to me about? Have you found out something about Ellen?"

"Archibald Ryder."

"Archibald Ryder." He said the name thoughtfully.

"He worked for you for seven years?"

"Yes."

"Was he fired?"

Carl relaxed, shifted in his chair. "No. He left. The story I got was that he wanted to devote more time to his Boston business."

"The story you got?"

"Paul told me. I was out of the country at the time building up the UK office. Do you know we have Carl Houseman ministries in seven countries?"

"Mmm," Teri said.

There was muffled conversation on the other side of the door, and Carl turned toward it. Finally, he said, "This isn't fair to you, Teri. You've done an admirable job. Your weekly reports have been thorough. And interesting reading, too." He opened his mouth to say more, then paused. "I'm not stupid. I know what the Pellermans are up to. They want you to quit. That I know. They picked you pretty much out of a hat, but I think you've done an admirable job, and I have no compunction about referring others to you."

"Thank you."

"There is something I need to tell you." He cleared his throat, looked away and then back again. "Did you know that Daisy and I have been engaged for two years?"

"I didn't, no."

"I need you to find my wife."

"I thought that's what I was doing."

"No. You've been looking for a dead woman. I don't believe she's dead."

Teri stared at him.

"I know what the reports say. In my head I know she must have died in that accident, but I've never quite believed it. If she had died in that accident, I think there would've been a part of me that would have known it, that somehow would have felt it. That would have died, too."

"But—"

"Brent knew. He tried to tell me on the day of the memorial service. And as soon as he voiced his concerns, something hit me. I knew immediately that what he was saying was the truth. That she was alive and trying to reach us."

"I've studied the accident reports. There's no way—"

"Yes, there is. There must have been something overlooked." He looked at her. "When I was alone, I would study those reports, over and over, until I could go mad with them. There has to be something that was missed. I told Pellermans I was hiring you to find out what happened to her, find out *how* she died. But that was never why I hired you."

"Why didn't you hire me without telling them?"

"They would've found out. Paul and Peg, they want control of this ministry."

"You told me Paul was your right-hand man, that they were your friends, that you trusted them."

"I'm ready to give them what they want. I would resign tomorrow were it not for my sons. I feel I need to watch out for their interests. It's long and very complicated. I just feel she's alive. Will you look for her?"

Were these the ravings of a grief-addled old man, or was there any truth to what he was saying?

"Okay, I know I'm going to regret this, but okay. I'll do it. Under certain conditions."

"Name them."

"No weekly reports to Pellermans or Daisy."

He laughed. "That's understood. I won't even be telling them of this. As far as they know, this is our last meeting."

"Fine with me." She got up to leave. "I just have one more question. Does the name Buck Jonas mean anything to you?"

He shook his head. "No."

"It's probably something else then."

33

Daisy Best arrived at the restaurant moments after Teri pulled up and ran toward her from across the parking lot, out of breath. "Teri, hey!"

"Hi."

"I was afraid I was late. Have you been waiting long?" She was breathless and fluttery.

"I just got here myself, actually."

"This is one of my favorite restaurants. I phoned ahead to get a table by the window, looking out on the garden. Not that there's much of one this time of year."

Teri followed her in the front door of the Garden Inn Restaurant. Baskets of flowers were hung against every wall and in every corner and lined the window ledges. On one wall a mural of a huge garden featured cement birdbaths and southern women in long dresses and big hats having tea underneath mossy bowers. No wonder Daisy likes this place. Teri thought of Marnie's favorite movie.

When they were seated, Teri asked Daisy where she was from.

"Georgia," she answered. "I live in this little town just outside of Atlanta. It's beautiful. I have a huge back deck with bird feeders. And shade. Even in the summer I sit out there and write. It's just lovely."

Their waitress brought them waters and menus.

"You must miss it."

"I have an apartment here in Philadelphia. Peg got it for me. I'm supposed to get more and more involved in the ministry. But I miss it there."

"I've never been to the south," Teri said.

"Well, honey, then I formally invite you to visit me. You'd love it there. I met Carl when I came to Philadelphia to do research on a novel. And of course, I would love it if we could move to Atlanta once we're married."

Daisy was full of flounce and scarves and jewelry and talked with her hands, waving her fingers as if drying her nails. Teri watched those fingers, nails a shimmery peach, waving, waving in the lights, but a little too exuberant, the fingers straight, the knuckles locked, her eyes blinking rapidly.

"Oh my, well, no sense going on about that! I guess we better order." She picked up her menu and adjusted her reading glasses.

"What's good?" Teri asked.

"Oh, just about everything. I often come here alone for lunch. I get this exact table, order my lunch and spend the next few hours eating and writing. I like this table because there's a plug underneath for my little computer."

Daisy ordered something called a California blue cheese salad, and Teri ordered a burger with fries.

After their waitress left, Daisy looked seriously at Teri and said, "I'm so glad you agreed to have lunch with me."

She laid her hands on the table, palms down, and Teri's gaze was drawn to the engagement ring, a huge diamond surrounded by small ones. She saw Teri looking at it, and began playing with it self-consciously.

"I was so hoping for a Christmas wedding," she said. "Of course, this followed on the heels of a September wedding, and then a summer wedding, which was supposed to occur last August. August seven to be exact. The restaurant was booked. We'd invited guests. We all but announced it on the air…" She looked away and blinked her eyes rapidly a few times. She ran a pinky under each eye, turned back, smiled, and said, "You're married, Teri?"

Teri said yes she was, and she told her about Jack.

"And he was a widower, and not too hung up about his first wife?"

"Didn't seem to be."

"Well, you're fortunate then." Her hands were trembling ever so slightly. She put them in her lap. Daisy wasn't all breeze and confidence and hair and jewelry; there was a genuineness underneath it all that was appealing. Teri could see why Carl was drawn to her.

After their waitress brought their meals, Daisy said. "Will you forgive me? I had no reason to ask the favor of you the way I did. Phoning you the way I did. I was probably..." She was picking pieces of radish out of her salad with her fork and laying them on her side plate. "There's a word for women like me." She stirred dressing into her salad. "Desperate. Maybe I'll write all about this one day. It would make for a tragic romance, now wouldn't it?"

Teri did something very uncharacteristic for her—she reached out and touched Daisy's hand.

"I want to thank you, Teri, for not saying anything to Carl about my appalling phone call to you."

They ate in silence for a few minutes, and then Teri asked her about her writing. "I'm sorry," she said, "I know you're very popular, because I certainly see your books all over the place, but I have to admit that I'm not much a reader of romance."

"That's okay certainly; don't apologize for that. I know Christian romances sound frivolous and fluffy, but I take this calling of mine very seriously. I get letters and e-mails from women who've been helped, or so they tell me, by what I write. Yet my own life seems to be falling..." She paused, dabbed her eyes, ate more of her salad, and asked Teri what she read.

Teri told her she mostly read true crime, with some mysteries thrown in.

"My romances always have a bit of mystery to them. It's what my readers like. Stories set in exotic places featuring beautiful people. And everything working out by the end of the book. Thin, beautiful people. Thin, beautiful people who don't wear glasses and always get the guy in the end. Did you ever notice that none of these romantic heroes wear glasses, when the majority of people in the world *do* wear glasses?"

Teri didn't know why she did it, but she burst out laughing. "I wouldn't be a very good romantic heroine then, would I?"

"Well, neither would I, honey, neither would I."

An hour later, when Teri was on the road north to Maine and to home, she thought about Daisy Best, the breezy, confident novelist who specialized in romance, and was about to lose her own. And she knew it. Deep down she knew it. And there was nothing in heaven or on earth she could do about it.

34

Her pharmacist had wanted more. By the end of that second summer he had wanted more of her. Well, of course he would. He wanted to marry her. He wanted her to leave her husband and marry him. By the end of their time together, he kept at her and kept at her about this until she began making up excuses not to go to him. And on those occasions when she did, she would ask Why can't it be like it was? She would sit on the blue couch in the apartment where he lived above the pharmacy, having hidden her hair in a scarf, because this was daylight after all. And he would demand, Is this what you want? To disguise yourself so you can be with your lover? And he would pout and pout until she would leave the way she had come, down three flights of stairs and through a series of alleys and back roads back to the wharf.

She had to make him understand that if she left her husband to marry him, her husband and everything he stood for would be destroyed. Couldn't he see that? It's not that she didn't want to—she wanted to, oh how she wanted to—but she couldn't. Couldn't he see that?

She remembered the very end, that last day when he had grabbed her arm rather gruffly, so unlike him (or unlike the him he used to be), and had spun her around. Either you tell your husband, he said, or I will. He was holding her letters by bunches in his other hand, raising them above her head like a weapon.

You told me you loved me, in these! But you don't! Or you would leave him!

I'm leaving you, she said backing away. I'm leaving now. I won't see you again.

So you've made up your mind?

Yes, she said, I have. I'm going back to my husband.

Well, I hope he takes you back.

He will, she said. He will.

And then he had called her a name, and she had turned and walked out of his apartment and down the three flights of stairs and around to the back where no one would see her, and down through the alley until she came to the wharf where she had parked her car. She was crying, could barely see her way for the tears.

She was remembering her husband. She was remembering the way he was before the crazy things started happening and he became involved with a mistress. Work was his mistress, his office the lover's boudoir. But she was remembering before that. She was remembering the way he would sit beside her on the rock, their fingers intertwined while she told him the secrets of the ocean. She was remembering the way he used to wave to her from the shore, the funny straw hat he sometimes wore.

Why can't it be like it was? She had just said these words to her pharmacist, but weren't they words she really wanted to say to her husband?

Driving home, the full realization of what she had done came to her. This was not some casual thing, easily forgiven, easily forgotten. She had committed that most unpardonable of sins, the ultimate of betrayals. And she had lost both of them, both her lover and her husband. And she had lost herself. There would be no forgiveness for her. By the time she pulled her car into the driveway, she knew she would never tell him.

When she found out she was pregnant, there was nothing to be done but to seduce her husband into her bed.

The woman in the phony lighthouse was writing all of this down while outside the January wind blew against her stone cottage, threatening its very foundation. So, she had raised the child as his.

35

Ellen disappeared when she was fifty-two. Teri's own mother was fifty when she walked out on a summer evening in 1981 to buy groceries and never returned. Brent would have been—Teri did a quick calculation—nineteen when his mother died. Teri had been fourteen when she lost hers. In both cases, no body had ever been found. Despite a massive ground and air search that took in the whole county and neighboring vicinities, her mother, Barbara Ann Blake, was never found. They found her car where she had parked it, two spaces from the grocery store in the well-lit parking lot. Her purse was on the ground beside the driver's door along with a plastic bag containing tin roof sundae ice cream, a carton of milk, and a container of orange juice. Her keys hung from the driver's side door, and the ice cream had melted all over the asphalt.

The case was still on the books, technically, but Teri knew that little if any hope was left for a missing person's case from twenty years ago. Someday, maybe twenty years from now, maybe more, some hunter will stumble upon a pile of bones. They might sit on some police officer's desk until a forensic anthropologist could be summoned away from more pressing duties. When they were determined to be human, the police would declare the site a crime scene and string up yellow tape on trees, and the forensics people would sift through the soil for bits of bone, clothing fibers, fragments of a life. If a skull was found, the dental records would prove conclusively whether it was her mother.

Then there would be a new surge of interest in the case, the story written up in the paper, the old facts reexamined. But by this time, the murderer could be long gone, maybe dead. She gripped her steering wheel tightly as the countryside sped past her. Her mother's story would be written up in the paper—of course it would be—but as a human interest story. Not on the crime page.

She also knew on some deep level what it was like to experience the kind of loss that made Carl Houseman believe that his wife was still alive. A year ago when her father was sick, he had said to her, "There's a part of me that hopes your mother will walk through that door."

"Dad."

"I'm serious. I wonder what she'd look like now. Twenty years older."

"Dad, she's gone."

"But we can't know. We can't know for certain. She could have just left. Decided she needed a break from all of us."

"Mom was happy."

"How does anyone know what a person is really feeling on the inside? Sometimes I think about that, Teresa."

"Dad, don't do this."

But he could not be convinced.

It was snowing lightly, a skiff of confectioners' sugar. She prayed it would let up. She so wanted to be home.

About two hours after leaving Philadelphia, she stopped for a coffee fill-up. She tried Buck Jonas again.

"Buck Jonas here." His voice was deep, gravelly.

"Mr. Jonas, this is Teri Blake-Addison."

"Buck."

"Buck."

"I have some information for you."

"Information?"

"You're working on Carl and Ellen Houseman, right?"

"What have you got?"

"Something you might be interested in."

"Mr. Jonas…Buck, I really don't know who you are or what this is all about."

"Where are you?"

"Right now I'm on I-84 heading north to get home."

"Get on the turnpike, take exit 12, the Framingham exit. There's a rest stop on the right. I'll be there."

"How will I recognize you?"

"You will."

And she did. He stood beside a rack of paperback books near the entrance holding a Styrofoam coffee. He looked as if he had stepped out of the pages of *The Maltese Falcon*, from his grizzled, worn face right down to his trench coat and bloodshot eyes and the battered brown briefcase with the lockable flap over the top.

She approached him. "Are you Buck Jonas?"

He nodded, crunched the coffee cup in one hand and threw it into a trash can. He smelled of old cigarettes.

"I'm Teri."

"Let's go over there." And he led her to a booth against the wall, somewhat away from patrons lining up for fast food. "Sit down," he said.

She did.

He opened his briefcase and removed a thick file folder and laid it on the table. He moved it toward her with tobacco-stained fingers.

"Open it," he said.

At the top of the first page was his name. *Buck Jonas, Private Investigations, Looking into the life of Carl and Ellen Houseman, hired by Archibald and Laura Ryder.* The date at the top of the report was 1997. A year prior to Ellen's death.

She raised her eyebrows and looked at him.

"Read it."

> After pursuing the life of Carl Houseman for a period of approximately seven months, and looking into his assets and with some surveillance, it is my opinion that Carl Houseman has conducted all of his proceedings with due care and attention and that he hasn't been engaged in, nor involved himself in, any untoward business proceedings or activities, AKA affairs or adultery or money laundering or any kind of embezzlement.

Teri tried to get its meaning. She looked up at him, "The Ryders hired you to dig up dirt on Carl?"

He nodded. "Keep reading."

> Pursuant to this, I commenced an investigation into said person's spouse, Ellen Houseman. Whereas the life of Carl was without fault as I could ascertain, my investigation into the life of Ellen Houseman revealed quite a different story.

According to Jonas, Ellen had had an affair with someone named Jimmy Jarvis of Belfast, Maine, in 1979. Teri found herself leafing through a series of letters from Ellen to Jimmy, declarations of love. "Where did you get these?" she asked.

He grinned rather lopsidedly. "Let's just say they came into my possession in the course of my investigation."

"I'm not sure I believe you. I did a search on Ellen, and I thought it was thorough. I never found even a hint of anything like this. How do I know these aren't forged?"

"Oh, these are real all right. If you have anything with Ellen's handwriting on it, you'll find that this matches exactly. No, our little white princess minister's wife was not as clean and pure as the driven snow, shall we say."

"You went to New Brunswick and spoke with the proprietors of a guest home there, right?"

"Right. I talked with lots of people."

"Did you talk to the guy, this Jimmy Jarvis?"

He nodded his head. "I did. He verified it. I recorded my conversation with him on tape. There's a transcript of it at the bottom."

"You are thorough."

"He was quite insistent that I not tell his family, that none of this come out."

"I'll talk to him."

Buck shook his head. "You can't."

"Why not?"

"He's dead. Died a couple months after I handed this report to the Ryders. Suicide. Out hunting by himself. Remorse. That's what they said." He grinned. "But the timing's just a little too coincidental to me."

Teri leafed through the letters. "Why didn't you go public with this?"

"I was going to; don't think I hadn't thought of it. But the Ryder–Pellerman machinery would be too much. They would discredit me. I'm not that stupid. Especially after what happened to this Jarvis character."

She looked at him, then down at the report. "But why would the Ryders want to dig up dirt on the Housemans?"

"All of these people are cut from the same clerical cloth. It's my guess that Archibald Ryder wanted a bigger piece of the Carl Houseman television preacher pie, and when it wasn't forthcoming, he decided to see if he could do something about it."

"Archibald Ryder left or was fired from Houseman Ministries a year before Ellen died," Teri said.

"Very coincidental. I handed this report over to Archibald Ryder July 14, 1997. By September of that same year, Jimmy Jarvis was dead and good old Archie was history."

"Does Carl know about this alleged affair?"

Buck leaned forward, his elbows on the table. A baby was wailing in a neighboring booth, and Teri had to lean forward to hear. "It was not an *alleged* affair. It was a real affair. And no, I don't know if Carl knows. In any case, I never told him."

"He doesn't know," Teri said. "If he did, he would never have hired me." She paused. "But why are you sharing this with me?"

"Ryders can ride right off this planet, far as I'm concerned. Bloodsucking sharks that they are. They still owe me money. It took a lot for me to get this. I could've lost my license. But they never paid me the final amount they owed me. The way I figure it, the report didn't have the desired effect, so they figured they didn't owe me anything."

"You couldn't find anything on Carl."

"Everyone has skeletons. I could've found something on Carl if

I'd dug long enough. I'm convinced of it. Just as I could find stuff on you if I dug."

She leveled her eyes at him. "Well, I'm sure of that, Mr. Jonas, and you wouldn't have to dig too far, either."

He grunted. "You mind if I smoke?"

He took a pack out of his pocket and was shaking down a Marlboro when Teri said, "I don't mind, but I think the establishment might. Can I have this file?"

He shrugged. "It's yours. Like all good PIs, I have copies. Lots of them."

"One more question," Teri said. "How did you know about me?"

"I'm a PI. And a good one. I figure it's about payback time."

After Buck Jonas left, Teri sat for a while at her booth, mind whirling as she read letter after letter from Ellen to Jimmy Jarvis. She began to feel more and more sick. Even her coffee tasted sour. She liked finding people. That's what she liked. Making people happy. She hated it when things got ugly and rotten and she had to deal with it. She got her cell phone out of her satchel and dialed Jack's number, knowing full well that he was in class. Still, she needed to talk to someone. She left a message on his office machine to call her right away.

She would have to tell Carl. That's what he hired her to do. But this information would destroy him. So devoted was he to his wife's memory that he couldn't even marry again.

Should she go to the police with this? Was the death of Jimmy Jarvis really a suicide? What do you do when you're holding documents that may prove that the late wife of America's best-known television preacher and foremost Christian apologist had an affair twenty years previous?

God, what do I do? She took off her glasses and massaged her eyes. What she needed was prayer. And wisdom and strength.

She managed to dig her Palm Handheld out of her satchel and scroll down the names and numbers. There was a woman in their Bible study, a nice woman, a seamstress, a person she occasionally had coffee with, and someone who seemed genuine when she had said, "Teri, I know in your job sometimes you encounter dangerous situations, difficult things. If you ever need anyone to pray for you, I want you to call me at any time. I'm always home. I'm always sitting in front of my sewing machine. I want you to know you can call me. I don't even have to know what it is." Andrea Silver. Teri punched in her number.

Then she pressed End.

This was something she needed to deal with on her own. She put her head in her hands. *If you don't believe Jonas's report has merit, then find out for yourself. Prove it wrong. Find out the truth before you tell Carl.*

She sat for a few more minutes, and then she looked up another number on her Palm Pilot and punched it in. A secretary put her immediately through. When he answered she said, "Hello Mr. Ryder. This is Teri Blake-Addison. I'm sorry I missed you the last time I was through. I'm in Boston, and I'd like a moment to speak with you if I may."

"I'm afraid that's impossible. I have appointments all day."

"Oh, that's too bad. I'm in over my head here. I'm getting the royal runaround from Carl and his crew. I could use your expertise on this one."

There was a pause. Teri waited.

"Help with what?"

"From what I gather, you knew Carl, at least a little bit. And you seem to be respected in your field, and as I said, I'm getting the runaround from the Pellermans and their ilk." She could picture him grinning, nodding. "I'd like to meet with you. I've got a few personal documents of Carl's I'd like you to have a look at."

He told her that if she could get there right away, he'd meet with her. "Ten minutes," he said. "And then I've got to head downtown."

"I'm on my way."

36

She hung up, consulted her map, got back on the highway to Boston, and took the third exit. But as soon as she was on the exit ramp, she stopped. Along with every other car on the ramp. A tie-up on the bridge. An accident? This could take hours. She craned her neck, but couldn't see what the hold up was. She looked to a few of the cars beside her, but no one looked her way. It was past rush hour. Had to be an accident. She tapped the steering wheel, turned on the radio. Turned it off again. She called Archibald Ryder and was told that he could wait only five minutes more max.

She hung up, uttered a small prayer, and miraculously traffic began clearing. God was smiling down on her. Twenty minutes later Teri parked in front of Ryder Real Estate, a long glass-fronted office building at the end of a strip mall in one of Boston's better sections, if the make of cars parked in the front was any indication.

She raced inside only to be told that Mr. Ryder had just left.

"I missed him?"

"I'm afraid you did. He said you can call him on his cell."

"What rotten luck." She turned to face the doorway.

"There he is!" The woman pointed. "Just getting into his car. If you hurry you can still catch him."

Teri was breathless by the time she reached the man climbing into the driver's seat of a Volvo.

"Mr. Ryder!"

He looked up. He was a large man who looked as if he'd enjoyed a few too many all-you-can-eat buffets. His face, when he turned it toward her, was fleshy and pockmarked, and small red veins railroaded across his nose.

"I'd like to help," he said. "I could certainly tell you things about Carl, but I can't stay. I'm going to be half an hour in traffic as it is."

"Good. Half an hour is all I need." Teri hiked her satchel over her shoulder "I'll come with you."

"What?"

"I'll ride with you. We can talk while we ride. I'll get a cab back to my car."

She opened the passenger door and slid in beside him.

"Nice car," she said. "New?"

"New. Yes."

"Business must be good."

"I do all right."

"Well, good for you."

"I think it's important to take clients out in a comfortable car. This car's my office. You said you had documents?"

"You worked for Carl for seven years?"

He shrugged. "If you can call the occasional consultation 'work.'"

"I heard it was more than that. You even lived in Philadelphia, right? Had your own office space at Houseman Ministries?"

"I worked for Carl in a consultancy capacity."

Traffic was clogged on the bridge, and ahead of them the highway was full of slow moving cars like one of those jointed colorful plastic snakes.

Teri looked over her notes. "I have it here that you were the finance manager. I also heard that you were all grand friends."

"Friends?"

"Yes. You and the Pellermans and the Housemans. Grand friends. Shared everything."

"What's this about?"

"You had left Carl's employ, let's see, a year before the sailboat accident. Who fired you, the Pellermans?"

"I don't like the things you're implying."

"I'm not implying anything. I'm stating."

"I can't believe he hired you."

They had left the highway now and were making their way into Boston's downtown core.

"I was hired to look into Ellen's state of mind prior to the accident."

"No, I mean I can't believe he hired a private detective." He was shaking his head.

"I guess he learned a thing or two from his former finance administrator."

He looked over at her sharply.

"Hey, you're going to want to pull ahead now. The light's green."

He drove into the intersection, turned right.

"Does the name Buck Jonas mean anything to you?"

"I don't know what you're talking about."

Teri pulled out the forms with his signature on them and laid them on her lap.

"I'd forgotten about that."

"I'm sure you had. We private investigators look out for each other. If one of us gets stiffed out of our money, well, there's this unwritten blacklist among PIs. You probably didn't realize this when you decided to stiff one PI out of his final payment."

"It was never supposed to be about Ellen." He paused, looked as if he was about to say something else, then closed his mouth.

"Go ahead," Teri said. "What were you going to say? I've got the letters; I've got Jonas's transcript of his conversation with the now conveniently dead Jimmy Jarvis."

"I can't expect you to understand."

"Try me."

"These issues are so very convoluted. But Carl was taking the ministry in a direction that the board was dead set against. We had to find a way to stop him. Yes, it was foolish. And we made some wrong choices. I admit it." He looked at her. "But it was never supposed to be about Ellen. Jonas knew that."

"I just have one question for you," she said as they neared downtown. "Did you kill Jimmy Jarvis?"

"Of course not." He said it too quickly. "He shot himself, and if you were such a hotshot detective, you would check the police reports."

"Oh, I shall, Mr. Ryder. I shall."

37

Brent was going to Tracie's for supper. That was the good news. The bad news was that she lived with her parents, and her father—get this—was a minister! (Had he known that about her, would he have been so quick to seek her out? It was certainly something to think about.)

He was sitting on a flat rock behind his van, parked in his secret place near the airport, and cleaning Paul Pellerman's gun with a dish towel. When he stole it from Pellerman's house, on his way out of the kitchen, he had wrapped it in a dish towel hanging beside the stove. There was a food stain in the corner of it—gravy, it looked like. After all these years it was still there, darkened now and dried into the pattern of the towel. He had taken the bullets out today—no sense being stupid—while he ran an edge of the rag down through the barrel, cleaning it the way he had seen Paul do. Next, he shined up the outside.

Good thing no one had noticed it at the Canadian border. They'd even gone through his van but hadn't seen the duffel bag underneath the rug in an indentation in the floor. Good for contraband, the previous owners of the van had told him. Meaning drugs.

Since arriving on this island, Brent had a feeling that the answers he was looking for were here. He just needed someone to tell him. Tracie maybe. Or Tracie's mother who worked in the library. Like ministers, librarians knew a lot of things. His mother had died here. Maybe it was from here that she had tried to reach them. The Pellermans had kept them all from finding her. He knew that idea sounded crazy, but the more he thought about it, the more he knew it was true. And the more he was glad he had brought the gun with him.

Maybe it was a good thing that Tracie's dad was a minister.

Ministers were in cahoots with each other. All of them were. Tracie's dad could even be involved in the cover-up! Anything was possible.

He was meeting Tracie at the Coffee Perk at six when she got off, and then they would drive together in his van. It was 5:30 now. He reloaded the gun and shoved it to the very bottom of the duffel bag and placed the duffel bag in the indentation in the floor. He then placed the piece of rug carefully on top of it. He started the van and drove into town.

He'd made the happy discovery that there was a shower at the Laundromat. It was even free. Well, you were supposed to pay the manager a couple of bucks or something—that's what the sign said—but he found that at certain times, like now, the manager wasn't always there. He'd have a shower and then go by and pick up Tracie.

Tonight at supper, he'd casually steer the conversation around to the accident, see what they knew, watch their reactions. Figure out what his next move would be.

38

Before she was married, Garda wrote things down: journal entries, stories, articles for magazines, whole books. Ghostwriter. She smiled at that one. That's what she was. A ghost. A writer. "We are both ghosts," she said to Audrey. "Just look at the two of us."

It was a calm and lovely afternoon. The woodstove made the room cozy, the smell of apples filled the small kitchen, and Will was on the mainland. At the table Audrey was intently forming a rolled coil of clay into a bowl, the tip of her pink tongue peeking out the side of her mouth. The bowl was a beautiful thing, and Garda commented on it, smiling down at the girl. Every now and then she marveled at this child who would not finish a bowl until every coil perfectly aligned with the one underneath it. When a clay worm sagged, refusing to obey her patient ministrations, she smashed it down and started over.

Garda picked up her pen and turned back to her notebook. Maybe it was a day like this when the four of them had hatched their plans. She wondered, was it one person that came up with the idea, and the others agreed? Or was it one of those brainstorming sessions where ideas flow back and forth like water, and no one really knows who had the idea in the first place? Was it late at night that they talked about this, sitting around a kitchen table drinking cups of coffee? Or was it in a morning meeting that the idea was first presented? She didn't know any of that. She would probably never know the very beginnings of the plan. She just knew that on that spring day, her world changed.

The day of the beginning of the betrayal was a day when the trees were in flower and the grass was a soft, pale green, the kind you can walk on with bare feet and not have it hurt. Her friend had walked into her office, closed the door, and sat down. "Can we talk?"

The two of them had gone for a walk then, and when they were seated on a bench in a park, her friend had turned to her and said, "God told me in a dream that you're troubled about something that happened a long time ago. God wants you to let it go."

The sound of her indrawn breath was her only reply.

Her friend persisted. "Is there something you need to let go of?"

She felt chilled, despite the sun, and wrapped her arms around herself. They were friends. Of course, God would want the best for her. Her friend would want that, too. She allowed her friend to touch her, to enclose her hands in hers and say, "It was an affair, wasn't it? And it happened a long time ago."

How would she know this? Who had told her? Does God *really* tell people things like this in dreams?

So she had nodded, bent her head, and cried into her friend's arms while crab apple trees blossomed behind them, and skateboarders rocketed in front of them.

"Tell me," her friend said softly, soothingly, touching her hair. "Sometimes it's better to get these things out."

She nodded. She was David. Her spiritual sister was Nathan.

"Tell me about him," her friend had said. "Tell me."

And so she had told her. She told her everything.

Except the part about her son.

39

When Teri arrived home, she was exhausted. It was late at night; she'd driven all day, discovered information that she really didn't want to know, and uncovered a possible murder, or at least a good reason for a suicide. More than anything she just wanted to talk to Jack. In his typical solid Jack way, he would be able to make sense of things.

Stephan's beat-up old truck was in the driveway, and Teri groaned. She wanted Jack all to herself tonight. And then after that, all she wanted to do was lie on the couch and watch the back-to-back episodes of *Law and Order* that she'd taped for the last couple weeks. Her neck hurt, and she rubbed it as she pushed open the kitchen door.

In the living room, Peter was gently playing the congas with the heels of his hands while Stephan lay on the couch, Gilligan on his stomach, reading *The Modern Anthology of Poetry* that Teri had found some weeks ago in the basement. There was some sort of jazz in the CD player that Peter was drumming to.

"Hi guys. Where's Jack?"

Between beats, conga poet pointed upstairs.

Teri carried up her duffel bag and found Jack sitting on their bed, hunched into the phone. She walked over and put her hand on his head, smoothed back his hair, touched his beard with her fingers. He smiled up at her, took her hand with his free one and mouthed, "Cooper."

"How is he?" Teri mouthed.

"The same."

"That's too bad."

Cooper was Jack's son and Cooper was always the same. He was twenty-two and lived with an aunt in Pennsylvania and was studying computer science in college. Jack always referred to Cooper as your classic Eeyore. Everything was a downer with Cooper. A month ago he had phoned, sure that when he graduated, the high-tech industry would have totally bottomed out and there would be no jobs for him anywhere. He was absolutely sure of it. He should have gone into poetry like his dad. Jack was on the phone with him for half an hour that time, trying to soothe his fear. Tonight, the problem seemed to be about a girl. As Teri threw her dirty clothes into the hamper and hung up her clean ones, Jack was saying, "This isn't the end of the world, Cooper. I know it hurts now." And then later, "No, you're not a useless person."

Teri got her makeup case out and readied it for her next trip, ran a comb through her hair, bundled her receipts, watered all of the upstairs plants, and Jack was still on the phone. Poor Cooper. He was a good-looking kid, and Teri thought he must look how Jack looked when he was younger: tall, rangy, long nose, high cheekbones.

He was still on the phone when Teri went back downstairs and into the kitchen to scrounge something to eat. She found a pizza box on the counter and ate a few bites of a cold, cardboardy deluxe supreme. But putting it in the microwave would have made it worse.

Stephan came in while she was leaning against the counter eating her pizza.

"Have a good trip?" he asked.

"Okay. It was, you know, business."

He grabbed the last piece of pizza. "Did you get a chance to read my book yet?" he asked.

Book? Oh, yeah, his book. "Not yet. But I plan to. I've been so busy on this case."

"I think it's so cool what you do," he said. "Very Sherlockian."

She smiled.

"You better look at it now," Peter said entering. "He's making everybody read his book."

Peter was getting the coffee down from the cupboard and spooning it into the Mr. Coffee. Teri yawned, looked at the clock on the stove. Eleven-thirty.

"Isn't this kind of late for coffee?"

"Decaf," he said.

Teri picked up *submerged* from the kitchen table. The cover was striking, with an enormous school of blue stripy fish with yellow eyes.

She sat at the kitchen table and flipped through it, yawning. His poetry was sparse, but the photography was stunning. Schools of golden fish, schools of red fish, and in one a round, puffed-out white fish with a yellow snout.

"These are really good," she said. "Did you take these?"

He nodded. "Do you like the poetry?"

"Some of these pictures should be in posters."

"I told Stephan that," Peter said. "That he should do photography with poetry rather than making the poetry the main thing."

"Where is this?" Teri asked.

"The ones near the front were taken in Mexico. The ones near the back, of the rocks, are right here."

"We've got stuff like this in Maine?"

"That's off Deer Island. Canada."

At the end of the book there were a few photos of Stephan standing on a rocky shore in his black scuba suit, "U.S. Divers" in yellow along the left sleeve. He was surrounded by mounds of equipment whose function she could only guess at.

"So, how do you write this poetry underwater?"

He pointed to a little white board with a pencil strapped to it leaning against a tank.

"You can actually write underwater? I thought when you said write, it sort of meant that you thought about what you were going to write, but actually wrote it when you got to dry land."

"No, I really write it underwater. Those little white boards? It's the way divers communicate with each other. They have these underwater pencils."

"Wow." Teri continued leafing through the book. She had never done more than snorkeling. She'd never trusted her entire air supply, which meant her entire life, to anything as small as a mouthpiece and tank.

"There's something so cosmic about being underwater," Stephan was saying. "The only sound you hear is the sound of your own breathing. Very meditative. Very Zen." He was in his element then, telling her about tanks and regulators, buoyancy compensators and weight belts, and the tiny computers they wear on their wrists to tell them how deep they are.

"So, can you take me diving sometime?" Teri asked.

"Sure. Anytime. You have to get certified, but I could do that. There's nothing like it, underwater. The first time I dove I realized that from now on, all my poetry would have to be written underwater."

"Maybe things under the water are less crazy than things on land."

"They are."

"I should probably move there, then. Maybe we all should."

40

After Stephan and Peter finally left, Jack was still on the phone. Despite the hour, despite her exhaustion, she sat at the table and drank several cups of decaf, which seemed to revive her. She sat in the quiet and in the darkness and recorded her entire day into Cut Throat, transcribing every conversation, every nuance of speech as clearly as she could remember. Then she looked at her spreadsheet, studying first the blue notations, then the yellow. Then she called up the pink ones.

Patterns. She was looking for patterns. If her years, short as they were, on the police force had taught her anything, it was to look for patterns. Sometimes the most obvious thing can be lost in the muddle. Sometimes you just have to ask the right questions. And sometimes you just have to take the whole case and turn it upside down and inside out for it to make sense.

She began jotting notes into her iBook:

1. Ellen had an affair more than twenty years ago. But in those twenty years she coauthored books, was interviewed in countless women's magazines, and stood by her husband on the stage. Did her husband know? It appears not. Did this slowly eat away at her, causing her to be less than careful on that last expedition?
2. Was Jimmy Jarvis murdered? Or was it a suicide?
3. Is Jane Jarvis, the woman who sailed with Ellen, related to Jimmy? Wife?
4. Carl believes Ellen is alive. Is he delusional? Could she be alive?

Her eyes were tired and her head hurt and still Jack was on the phone. She took off her glasses and massaged her face. Then she dragged herself into the living room where she wrapped herself in an afghan and lay on the couch and rewound her video. Kelly climbed in with her, and she stroked her ears. Detectives Briscoe and Green had just been called to the construction site where the body was found when Jack came downstairs. Without a word he came over to where she lay, gently lifted Kelly off, and lay down beside her.

She clicked off the video. "Is Cooper all right?" she asked.

"I'm worried about him. I always put his moods off as childishness, but he seemed almost suicidal tonight."

She raised herself on one elbow. "Really?"

"I have finally persuaded him to phone his minister first thing in the morning. And I'm going to phone him, too. It seems the girl he was going to spend the rest of his life with, his eternal soul mate, has dumped him." He sighed.

"Doesn't sound like much of a soul mate."

"I'm sorry. I should've been here for you when you got home." He was smoothing strands of hair between his fingers. "I know this whole Sunday school class thing has you down, and here I was upstairs talking on the phone."

"Believe it or not, Jack, in the past twenty-four hours the Sunday school class has been the furthest thing from my mind."

She disentangled herself from him, got up off the couch, and showed him the Buck Jonas file. He looked through it while she told him about her trip.

"I don't know what to do with this information," she said. "I don't know what's appropriate. And then, aside from this, I have Carl Houseman telling me he's sure his wife is alive somewhere."

"Maybe Jimmy only faked his death. Maybe the two of them ran off together and are living in the Caribbean. No, I shouldn't have said that. It's not funny."

"Jimmy's suicide. Doesn't it seem fishy to you? The timing's just a bit too coincidental. And Ellen having an affair so many years ago and no one knowing."

"Is this something we go to the police with?" Jack asked.

"It's not against the law to have an affair."

Jack frowned and put the papers on the coffee table. "Here's what I think. I think that the two of us go to Carl with this. Privately and quietly, without Pellermans being there or Daisy or anyone."

"But does that matter at this point, Jack? What if someone came to you and said they had proof that Jenny had had an affair before she died. Even though she was dead, how would that make you feel?"

He rubbed his beard thoughtfully. After a while he said, "Other people know. It's bound to get out. Secrets have a way of getting out. No matter how tightly you try to hold them in."

"And then to top everything off, I told Carl I'd take on this new challenge, of coming up with a *live* Ellen. What was I thinking?"

"What I'm thinking is that you need some sleep. A good night's sleep. I'll try not to wake you when I leave tomorrow."

On the way up to bed, he told her that the video from Carl had arrived. Teri made a mental note to look at it first thing in the morning. She was asleep practically before she hit the sheets.

41

The guilt of it had clung to Garda like dust all these years. After her confession, she had expected her guilt to lift. Had counted on it. Her friend told her it would. It hadn't. It had only deepened, especially when her spiritual sister smiled at her and touched her. A finger on the wrist and "I'm praying for you." And little "Smile, Jesus loves you" notes taped to her coffee cup, her computer, her office door, her window.

Her friend would peek her head around the office door and say, "Hey!" and then give her a Bible verse to look up. Instead of sharing her burden, it had given her spiritual sister something to lord over her, and Garda had grown wary. The notes were too gushy. Something in them felt wrong.

"You have my word," her spiritual sister had said to her after that day in the park. "I will tell no one about any of this. This is between you and me. God told it to me in confidence, and I will keep it there."

"Thank you," she said.

A month later, however, she learned the true extent of her betrayal. She had been walking past her friend's office. The door was ajar, and she paused when she heard her name. The four of them were in there. She stood outside and heard words like "damage control" and "affair," and "private detective." She stopped. She listened. She heard her friend say, "She's no threat to us. She's so consumed with guilt she will pose no threat. He'll be like putty in our hands."

She made her way into her office, closed the door, and sat at her desk, breathing hard. All of them knew. Her friend had told them her dream. But what was this about a private detective?

And then the news later—was it that day or weeks later?—that she learned that the pharmacist was dead.

Garda looked up from her writing and watched Audrey dancing to classical music from the radio. It was odd, but she was finding God here in this place. At the place where she thought she had lost God forever, she was beginning to find Him, like rays of light through the clouds. She was finding redemption in small things: Audrey twirling to the music, round and round, her fingers moving expressively to the melody. The way her cheeks brightened when Garda told her a Bible story or read a Psalm from an old King James. The words were strange and odd sounding, as if from another language, but beautiful like the music Audrey danced to.

She would stare out at the sea from the front room or from the place at the top of her cliff, and God would whisper to her that He loved her, loved her, loved her, loved her.

On that day so long ago she had sat in her office, the side of her face against her desk, and her friend had knocked and poked her face in. "Hey," she had said cheerfully.

When her greeting wasn't acknowledged, her spiritual sister came in and closed the door. "Hey, why the long face? God's in His heaven, all's right with the world.

"You lied to me."

Her spiritual sister stood there, saying nothing.

"You told me no one else would know. Ever."

And her spiritual sister had looked at her with that sad, serious expression before saying, "You are my closest friend. And I knew, I knew you were troubled about something. I just didn't know what it was. We had to find out. So we hired a private investigator. It was nothing against you, personally. Think about it."

And then her spiritual sister had taken her hand, but Garda jerked it away.

"I will tell him to get rid of you and your husband both."

"No, my friend, no you won't."

"Yes, I will."

"If you had wanted to tell him, you would've told him long before this."

"I'll tell him what you've done."

"No, because it would destroy him if he knew. And you don't want to do that. You love him too much to tell him."

And she stared at her friend, because that part was true.

And so finally she fled to this place, where she hoped to die. Where she prayed, *Just let me die. God, just let me die.*

Instead, through the years, she was finding redemption in small things.

42

Teri slept until ten-thirty the following morning. She hadn't moved so much as an eyelid when Jack got up and showered, and Jack wasn't noted for his quietness in the morning. He loved doing his Pavarotti imitations in the shower. He left her a note on her dresser, "I love you and I'll be home late tomorrow night. In Augusta for the conference." Then he left the number for his hotel. His cell phone, the one she'd gotten him for Christmas, was lying serenely on his highboy.

Drat. She'd forgotten about his literary symposium in Augusta. She showered, grabbed the video package, and went downstairs. She had the animals fed and was drinking coffee and eating a toasted bagel with blueberry jam by eleven-fifteen.

No Stephan. No Peter. No Jack. No phone calls. A nice quiet day. It was odd having a full day spread out before her like this. It was sort of like the old days when her time was totally her own. Since marrying Jack, she strove to be home by supper time, and evenings often included joint activities: Bible studies or walks or just sitting together reading or watching TV. In eight months she had grown used to that. She wasn't altogether sure she wanted a whole day with no one there.

The package from Carl held two videos. One was labeled "Ellen's Memorial Service," and the other "Holiday Trips and Candid Family Shots." A note taped to the top video said, "Sorry these took so long to get to you. I had my staff compile some vacation shots for the second one and it took longer than I anticipated. I hope they help. Blessings," and then *Carl* in his big scrawly handwriting.

She ran her fingers through her still wet hair and plunked the first tape, the memorial service, into the VCR. There was a note at the beginning of the video. *The following is dedicated to Ellen Marie Houseman 1947–1998.*

The video began with a pan of the front of the church, which was covered with white flowers. On a white-clothed table at the front was the picture of Ellen, the publicity picture of her, the sad smile, the blond hair, the blue suit, the scarf tied just so around her neck. Teri recognized the church and even remembered individual members of the choir.

She would force herself not to fast forward through the choir singing and special numbers. One picked up things in the most obscure places.

Teri watched Peg Pellerman in a dark blue suit walk up to the pulpit. She stood there for several seconds, knuckles gripping the sides of it before she began to speak. Her eyes were red, and while she spoke she dabbed at them a few times with a handkerchief.

Then she began. "My friend Ellen Marie Houseman...my best friend Ellen was a true friend, a true godly woman. She personified Proverbs 31. She stood by her husband in everything." Peg's eyes brightened, and a smile crossed her face when she talked about Ellen and her working closely on a project, about the jokes Ellen would make. "She was an intelligent woman, a woman without guile, my best friend, and my spiritual sister."

Her voice broke at the end, and she had to be escorted by her husband, literally sobbing, back to her seat. Organ music played while the camera panned the front of the church, while Paul, head down, made his way slowly back to the pulpit. His shoulders were heaving while he stood there. The organ played on.

It was an odd sort of memorial, and Teri rewound the video several times to study Peg's performance. Teri had been to a few Christian funerals since she had come back to God, and while it wasn't a happy time, they were always filled with a hope. Not this sobbing, not this despair. Even Carl seemed startled by it. The camera panned where he sat in the front row, looking up at Paul, his brow furrowed ever so slightly, that twitch in his eye.

When Paul regained his composure, he led the congregation in singing "Be Still, My Soul." Several others came forward to read eulogies.

During a choir number, the camera panned the front rows again. Carl was flanked by his three sons, their wives and children. There was Carl Jr. sitting next to his father, his thin face red, the bones more prominent. Poor Carl Jr. seemed to have inherited the worst features of both parents. Ellen had been a beautiful woman, but with a nose that some might say was a bit too long and thin. Carl Jr. had a long, thin nose. Carl Sr. was strikingly good-looking, but his forehead might have been a bit too wide and too high. Carl Jr. had a high forehead and receding hairline. His wife, Mariana, looked just as thin and tired as her husband. She was wearing a dark print dress in some flimsy material that seemed too big for her narrow shoulders. They had two children at the time of the funeral, and they sat primly beside them on the front pew.

On the other side of Carl was second son, Charlie, who looked like Ellen with his blond hair and narrow nose. Next to him was his wife, Michelle, a very pretty, slightly round woman, with curly dark hair. Teri knew they had two children now, but had none at the time of the funeral.

The third son, Sam, sat at the end of the row. His then fiancée, Cathie, was next to him, her arm entwining his. She was the most stylish of the group, with high tousled hair and heavily made-up eyes and lips. She was some sort of Christian pop singer. Jack had found that out. She was really making her mark in contemporary Christian music, he said.

Brent was not there.

Nor were the Ryders. Although, Teri thought, they would have had their own funeral to prepare for.

Paul Pellerman gave the funeral message, and he spoke mostly about what Ellen's life could teach us. It could teach us patience, because Ellen had patience. It could teach us love, because Ellen loved her family and her children almost more than her own life. It could teach us faith in God, because right up to the end, Ellen's faith was the most important element in her life.

Maybe Teri was still tired from yesterday, but the whole thing seemed somehow staged and false. Teri thought that Ellen would want her funeral to be more about Ellen than platitudes of the Christian life. Also, none of her Maine friends were there—Jane or Fred or the people in the café, the people that took care of her boat when she wasn't there. And none of the eulogizers mentioned sailing.

During Paul's sermon, the camera shifted to still pictures: Ellen and Carl on their wedding day thirty-six years before, Ellen with straight blond bangs, long hair, and a veil entwined with flowers. And Carl, handsome and tall beside her, looking down into her eyes. He had loved her. He loved her still. Why had she been unfaithful? How would Ellen answer this if she were alive? What explanation would she give?

After the service the packed church filed out to quiet organ strains of "I Surrender All."

The second video was clips of various family trips along with still shots of Ellen and the family. The first clip was obviously from 8mm film. It was Christmas, and a younger Houseman family of five was gathered around a Christmas tree. A young Carl Jr., still in pajamas, flew a model airplane with one hand, Ellen beside him on the floor. Then the camera must have been handed to Ellen, because Carl was helping baby Sam open a gift. The camera went back and forth between Ellen and Carl. Teri watched Ellen scurry between her sons, bend down to talk to Charlie, ruffle the head of Carl Jr., help Sam open a present, clear up the wrappings and shove them in a cardboard box. She was smiling. She was full of smiles then. She had a pretty smile that lit up her face, eyes crinkling above it.

There were other video clips then: birthday parties; family trips; baby Brent home from the hospital, and the older sons, Carl Jr. a teenager already, peering down at their little brother, trying to get him to laugh, grabbing his fingers, scooching him under the chin, smiling for the camera. More Christmases, more birthdays. Always Ellen with her children, never alone. After that wedding photo in the other video, there was never a picture of Ellen and Carl alone. It was always with the children.

But her smile was fading. She hardly smiled in the cross-country trip. And there she was again bending down to ruffle her youngest son's hair and straighten his baseball cap. But without the smile.

There was something troubling about the video. Something Teri couldn't name. She got dressed, filled up her travel mug with coffee, and headed into Bangor.

Her first stop was the public library where she looked through the microfiche for articles about Jimmy Jarvis. She scanned the newspaper published the day after he died, and there it was: "Man Killed in Hunting Accident." It was on the third page and took up a quarter of the page. Jimmy Jarvis was out alone in the woods northwest of Coffins Reach, Maine, when he apparently stumbled and was killed when his gun went off. He is survived by his wife, Beth, and three children, James, Kirsten, and Kea. He is also survived, Teri read, by one sister, Jane, from Belfast, Maine. The newspaper was kind. It didn't even hint at the possibility of suicide.

Teri ran down through the article. He had grown up in Coffins Reach, Maine, attended school there, and graduated from the Massachusetts College of Pharmacy and Health Sciences in Boston. He then came back to Coffins Reach, where he worked as a pharmacist. He was an avid hunter and sailor. He married Beth in 1983 and they had three children. Teri printed off the article and left.

An hour later she was in Belfast, Maine. She knocked on Jane Jarvis's door, and as soon as she answered, Teri said, "Tell me about Jimmy. Tell me about Jimmy and Ellen."

Over the top of her glasses, the wrinkles on Jane's forehead deepened. She stared at Teri for a few minutes, then said quietly, "Come in, then. Come inside."

Teri followed her down the same hall: the same clocks, the museum chairs. But in today's light it was not just dark; it felt oppressive, as if the walls themselves were sliding closer. Teri followed her into the same solarium where she sat on the same wicker chair she had been in a week ago. Teri opened her folder, got out Ellen's letters, and spread them out on top of the coffee table.

Jane picked up one and studied it. "Where did you get these?"

"A private eye named Buck Jonas."

"Buck Jonas." She put the letter down. "Buck Jonas. I remember him. I always wondered what happened to these letters. Jimmy gave them to me years ago, for safekeeping. He knew he could trust me. I never read any of them. A couple of years ago I looked for them, and they were gone."

"Do you think your brother was murdered?"

She leaned back in her chair. "Leave it alone, Teri."

"Why should I leave it alone?"

"There was a whole group of us. Ellen was part of that group. We went to school together. We sailed together. Ellen was probably my closest friend growing up."

"And was Jimmy a part of that group? They knew each other from school?"

She shook her head. "No, Jimmy was older. Ellen didn't know him then. She would have known of him, but he was older."

"Was Jimmy murdered?"

"Teri, for your own safety, for your own sake, don't even ask that question."

"Why not?"

"You don't know these people."

"What people?"

"You have no idea what they're capable of."

"Who are *they?*"

"The Pellermans and the Ryders." Jane was rubbing her knuckles as if they were arthritic and said quietly, "She never loved my brother. This was the one sadness of her life. She truly loved Carl, and all that she did was out of love for Carl. She wanted attention from her husband. She wanted her husband to notice her, so she had the affair with my brother." She paused. "Ellen never felt good enough for the ministry. She used to tell me that Carl would have been better off if he had married one of the girls from Bible school instead of her. We shared a lot in those early days. But later not so much. She just drew into herself. Later on, after she left Jimmy, she spent the next twenty years trying to be worthy of Carl. She sought forgiveness. The years went by and we didn't talk about it. It was as if it never happened. But I kept those letters."

"Does Jimmy's widow know about Ellen?"

Jane shook her head. Somewhere a clock ticked. "Jimmy wouldn't have told her that."

"Can you tell me where she lives?"

Jane stared at her. "You wouldn't see her? You wouldn't go and tell her all of this, would you?"

"I won't mention Ellen, but if your brother was murdered, if his death was not a suicide, then we have to find out. You owe it to him, Jane."

"People are going to get hurt."

"People are hurt already."

Beth Jarvis and her three children lived in a gray Cape Cod on the top of a rise in Coffins Reach. A red van was in the driveway. Teri's knock was answered by a beautiful boy in his early teens with unruly black hair and large brown eyes. He looked familiar to her, but she didn't know from where.

"Hi, is your mom at home?"

The boy turned. "Mom! Someone's here!"

"Who is it?"

"I don't know. A lady!"

"You should be in bed, Jamey," said the woman emerging from a side room. "You're home sick. What're you doing up?" Beth Jarvis was wearing a pair of jogging pants so old and faded that whatever color they had started life in was uncertain. A pair of dark-rimmed glasses were atop her head. "Can I help you?" She was carrying a stack of file folders.

"My name is Teri Blake-Addison. I'm a private investigator. I'd like to talk to you about your husband."

The woman turned to the boy. "Go to your room now, Jamey." Then to Teri, "My husband is dead."

"Mom?"

"Go to your room, Jamey. Now."

Beth stepped outside and closed the door, still holding on to her file folders. Despite the cold, she didn't invite Teri in.

"What's this about?" Her eyes were wary.

"I'm a private investigator looking into a case that may involve the death of your husband."

"What's this 'a case that may involve the death of my husband'? You're going to have to be a little more specific than that."

"It's about the alleged suicide."

"First of all, it wasn't a suicide, and second, I'd really rather not talk about it. If you'll excuse me..." She turned to go back inside.

"I believe you," Teri said.

She turned back to Teri. "Who are you?"

"My name is Teri Blake-Addison, and I've been hired to find a missing person. The course of my investigation has led me here. To the death of your husband. And I agree with you. I don't think your husband killed himself."

"I'm listening."

"I believe your husband's death may have been the result of a huge cover-up. I'd like to know why you feel so strongly that his death was not a suicide?"

"I told this to the police, but I'll tell it to you, for all the good it will do. Before his death, my husband told me about a relationship he had with a married woman some time before we were married. I was only mildly interested, but a few months before he died, he said a man had come to him offering him a lot of money if he kept quiet about the affair—if he never made it public. He was confused by the offer, he said. He told the man he had no intention of making it public; why would he want to destroy his marriage? He was a perfectly happy man. He refused the money. About a month after this, he was dead."

"Did this man have a name?"

She shook her head.

"Did he tell you who the woman was?"

"No. I know nothing more than what I've told you."

"Thank you for letting me intrude on your day, Mrs. Jarvis."

43

Brent woke cold and shivering in his van at eight-thirty, his feet uncovered. The window on the passenger side had come down a few inches. That window was always coming down on its own. To get it to stay up, you had to press against the glass while you rolled it up. And sometimes even that didn't work. It drove Amanda crazy.

He got up, pressed against the window, wound it up, and, miracle of miracles, it stayed. He turned on the engine and the heater, though he didn't really want to. His van was a gas guzzler, and the heater wasn't all that great. He grabbed a couple of extra blankets, then lay back down on his mattress, his fingers intertwined behind his head. Gray metal ribs ran lengthwise along the roof of his van. There were five of them in all. There were rusted spots, too. He hadn't noticed those when he bought the van.

In the week since he'd come here, he'd been to Tracie's house once for supper and then to church once. Actually to church! The dinner he'd been to had been useless. It wasn't just him and Tracie's family; they'd invited this other couple, too. The guy reminded him of his brother Sam, sort of thick and muscular, and his wife had short red hair. They also had a baby, which Tracie immediately went to and picked up. They were introduced as a new couple in town. He didn't pay attention to the name, but he caught that the guy was in the RCMP. He knew that stood for Royal Canadian Mounted Police. He thought of his van without the license plate, just out there at the front of the house, and of the gun and the money, and he felt a ripple of fear.

"So, you're Tracie's friend?" the man had said.

Brent nodded.

"You here for a visit?" The guy looked like a cop with his cop's mustache.

Brent nodded and looked down at his hands folded in his lap. What was this, an interrogation? Should he have a lawyer present?

"Brent's traveling through Canada," Tracie said. "He's on an extended break from his job at Pizza Hut, and he's decided to visit every corner of Canada."

This was a variation on the "looking for a job in Grand Manan" that he originally came up with. Laughing, he had told her that no, he wasn't really looking for a job; he had just said that to get a reaction. Actually, he was on vacation and wanted to visit all the places in Canada that he'd never been to before.

The cop looked at him and raised his eyebrows, and suddenly Brent wanted to leave. So much for his plan of getting information out of Tracie and her family. Of finding out about the witch and her elf daughter. He would be spending the evening fielding questions from a cop!

Even though there were three extra people, it was a regular family dinner, Tracie's mom said. Tracie and her parents and her two younger brothers and the guests all had their special places at the table. The only time Brent's family ever sat together for a meal was for show. When some magazine was coming to interview them, they'd all have to dress up and sit around the table as if this were something they did all the time.

He thought it was funny that his parents wrote books about family devotions. He used to wonder, didn't they notice that the Houseman family didn't do any of those things? Didn't they notice that his father was never home? That he even slept at his office sometimes? Didn't they notice his bed there and wonder about that?

The turkey dinner was really good, and there was lots of conversation. No one talked about the accident, and no one talked about the witch in the lighthouse. Brent just mostly sat there trying to figure out a way to leave. He had to get out of here before the cop left so he wouldn't notice the license-plate-less van.

Sunday had been stranger still. Actually going to church without having to, without it being a part of his paying job. At the church he was handed a bulletin by a very old man whose face looked as though it was made up of spare parts from a rubber mask factory.

"Glad to have you. Welcome. Welcome. Welcome," he told him, nose bobbing.

Brent nodded his head ever so slightly.

The church was an old-fashioned one with wooden pews going up each side and an aisle in the middle and windows along the sides. Awful for acoustics. There was a place for hanging coats in the foyer, and along the back of the church was a table with brochures and Sunday school papers and bulletins. Tracie was waiting for him beside the coat rack. She wore a short beige skirt and green sweater. She looked pretty with her brownish-blond hair curled up at her shoulders. He felt shy around her.

A musical group up at the front with piano, guitar, and bass led the church in choruses. A couple of the choruses came straight from Brent's father's church, written on commission for the church, another one of his father's ministries.

Brent followed Tracie along the back of the church past a man bent over a very old six-channel soundboard. Brent wondered that the group up front got any sound at all. The guy running the booth looked half dead as he sat there with earphones on. Earphones! Brent glanced at the soundboard. Okay, he thought, it's a pretty old operation, but all you'd have to do to get better sound out of the vocals is to take the smiley face out of the EQ and boost up the gain a bit. Maybe tweak the treble, knock out some of the bass. He'd like a few minutes with it; he knew he could get a better sound out of it. But all the controls were set almost the same way, and the guy was only raising and lowering the mains. Plus the way the vocalists were singing into the mikes, the way they held them under their chins like Popsicles? All wrong.

The man looked up. "Does this sort of thing interest you?"

"I used to work sound for...ah...for some bands."

"So you're familiar with this stuff?"

"Yeah."

"We just got this board. We're pretty proud of it."

"Oh yeah?"

"Got it used. Good price, too."

Tracie took Brent's arm and introduced him to three girls, friends of hers. One of them, very tall with black hair, gave him a start the way she reminded him of Amanda, and like Amanda she wore multiple earrings up the sides of her ears.

When they sat down, he found himself between Tracie and Tracie's little brother, and for a moment, looking down at the photocopied bulletin, he wondered again how he had gotten to a church on Grand Manan Island with an innocent, nice girl named Tracie who worked at the Coffee Perk and wanted to be a nurse.

He listened again to the badly mixed music from the front and pretended not to know the lyrics. He watched the vocalists standing stiffly, without any stage presence. His brother would have a fit. But with all its obvious flaws, there was something about this place that soothed him. It was like Tracie, all innocent and open, no one worrying about camera crews and satellite feeds to Australia and someone missing their cue. There were maybe fifty people who ranged in age from old to what looked like newborn.

The church followed the regular format: announcements, some choruses, hymns, a special music piece, which was two children on saxophones playing "I Know Whom I Have Believed." There was a time for visitors to be welcomed, and Tracie introduced her friend Brent Smith from Toronto.

He had even paid attention to the sermon, something he hadn't done since...well, he couldn't remember ever paying attention to the sermon. Not really. Back when he did sound at his dad's church, he'd sit in the back listening for levels, making sure the sopranos did not overpower the basses in the choir. Making sure the bass guitar didn't overpower the vocalists in the worship team. Making sure the levels were set for the special music and that the accompaniment CDs were ready. And if there was ever an error, he heard about it. His brother would storm into the sound booth and call him an idiot.

And now, here was Tracie's dad, not even using a mike but walking right down into the congregation and leaning against the back of the front pew, his opened Bible on his knee. He was talking about Moses and the burning bush, but he was giving it a new twist, paying a lot of attention to the fact that Moses took his shoes off, and that this very ordinary place where he was working had become holy ground. And that God met him out there doing a very ordinary thing, taking care of sheep. Moses wasn't in church. He was expecting his life to go one way, and it ended up going quite the other.

As Brent lay on the mattress in his cold van, he couldn't remember much more of the sermon than that. But he remembered the *way* it was. He felt drawn to Tracie's dad in a way he had seldom felt drawn to Paul Pellerman or Archie Ryder. Tracie's father didn't know Brent from Adam. He could be anybody—an escaped serial killer, for all he knew—and here they'd invited him to supper and to church, and Tracie's mother even packed him up lots of turkey leftovers. No one knew that he was living in his van behind the airport. Not even Tracie. She thought he had a room in a hotel in Grand Harbour.

His van was beginning to warm up, so Brent got up and got dressed. He was meeting Tracie at her house at ten to go on a hike (his choice) until he had to drop her off at work at one. Brent knew exactly where he wanted to go. Ever since he had followed the PI down the path to the phony lighthouse a week ago and heard that girl scream bloody murder, he knew that the woman there knew something about his mother.

So that's how, two hours later, he came to be wearing a pair of Tracie's dad's gloves and Tracie's dad's hiking boots and Tracie's dad's rain jacket, hiking down the trail toward the lighthouse. Clearly, he hadn't brought the right clothes with him, Tracie's mother had said to him on her way to the library where she worked.

It was a misty and shivery kind of cold, and Brent was glad Tracie's mother had forced gloves on him. And a hat.

"So, tell me more about the lady who lives in that weirdo cottage," he said.

He learned from Tracie that the woman's husband had died and she came back to live here in disgrace with a baby who wasn't even her husband's. "And she's lived here ever since."

"I saw her once," Brent said. "Just the back of her. She was chopping wood. But the girl was strange."

"Some people think she's a witch, you know. That girl. The mother too. Both of them are supposed to be witches."

Sometimes the sound of the girl screaming at him still haunted his dreams. Those big dark eyes looking off into space, like she didn't fully live on this earth or in this dimension. She reminded him of a nymph, a forest fairy.

"A witch?" he asked.

"But I don't believe in witches."

He stole a sideways glance at her. Tracie with her wide, innocent smile, her smooth makeup-less face, could not be more unlike Amanda than if they'd come from separate planets. Today Tracie wore a red woolen hat and matching red mittens that looked as if they'd been knitted up by someone's grandmother.

"Why do people think she's a witch?" he said.

"Because of the rumors."

They had made their way down the cliff path and were walking along the beach below the little lighthouse, stepping from wet black rock to wet black rock.

"What kind of rumors?"

"That she could like morph herself into two people." Tracie said this with a flourish of her arms.

Brent stopped then, and an idea flitted sideways into his thinking. "What are you talking about?"

"I don't know much about it." Her teeth were chattering.

"You're cold."

"I'm okay."

"So, what about this two people thing?"

"Some people were saying that you'd see her in town at the same time the Save Easy guys would see her at her cottage, that sort of thing. But I think they just got their times wrong, and so naturally everybody makes it into something it's not. And because of this there were these rumors that she had caused the sailboat accident because of her powers. Like put a curse on it or something."

"Could we meet her?" he asked.

"No way. They say she has a gun. I'm not going anywhere near that place."

He didn't tell her that he, too, had a gun, stuffed in his pants pocket.

They hiked to the edge of the cottage property but didn't see anything except for a plume of smoke. Then they headed back to the van.

She had to be at the Coffee Perk at one, so he took her there and ordered coffee and a hamburger and fries and stared at the wall opposite where he was sitting until he had his idea fully worked out in his thinking.

Here was his theory: A bunch of stuff from the accident washes up on the very shore he and Tracie had walked on this morning. The crazy old lady finds the stuff, takes all of it—wallets, money, jewelry—but she tells the police she only found a few things. But the thing that she didn't count on was the fact that his mother swam to shore. So the crazy old lady finds her, kills her, throws her life jacket back into the water before his mother has a chance to tell anyone she's alive. The old lady isn't a witch, just an opportunist.

And those things belong to him—well, to his family—but he was here. He figured it out. So they belong to him.

44

Something was bothering her about the video, something Teri couldn't name, some connection right there at the edge of things that she couldn't quite make. As she drove home she wondered what she was missing. It had to do with the video. Something on the video. Look at the video.

At home she put the tape in the VCR—not the memorial service, but the other one, the one of the Houseman family. Whatever it was had to do with Ellen. It was Ellen she needed to see. She sat at the edge of her chair and studied Ellen, her long blond hair pulled back in a barrette at her neck, laughing with her sons as they opened presents, ruffling their hair, straightening it with her fingers. She rewound that part and watched Ellen bending forward, straightening the hair of Carl Jr., pushing it away from his eyes. She rewound it again and again and again. What was it about that gesture? What was it?

She stopped the machine. It couldn't be. She replayed the video again. Looked hard at Ellen.

Stephan. She needed to talk to Stephan. His phone number was sticky-taped to the fridge, and she called him, hoping, praying, that he was in. He was. After they talked for twenty minutes, Teri got all the answers that she needed and more.

Her next call was to Jack's hotel. She left a message, telling him where she was going, telling him it was urgent, and could he possibly drive up and meet her there? As he knew, she was kind of in over her head with this one.

Next she packed, gave the cats enough food and water for two days, changed the litter box, and packed up food and water for Kelly. In an hour she and Kelly were on the road heading east.

Snow was threatening. The clouds were heavy with it, and she could almost smell it. She was thinking ludicrous thoughts, but outrageous as they were, they were beginning to make sense. The more she worked it out in her thinking, the less absurd it seemed.

She had to see Garda, but she wanted to see Marnie first. She was unsure about Will. She hadn't worked out how he fit into the whole scenario, but Marnie would know. She had a copy of the ferry schedule with her, and a half-dozen times she tried calling Marnie from her cell, but her phone rang and rang. She should have e-mailed her. Marnie was always on her computer.

She didn't call Carl either, and wasn't going to until she knew for sure. If this new theory of hers had any elements of truth, it would have far-reaching effects, from Daisy, bless her heart, to the very foundations of Houseman Ministries, or whatever they were going to call themselves if the Pellermans had their way.

She also called Jack again and couldn't keep the urgency out of her voice as she left another message. Banks of clouds swirled on the horizon and Teri headed into them. Even Kelly picked up on her mood and whimpered quietly on the seat beside her.

She made the ferry with only moments to spare, left Kelly in the locked car with the windows opened a crack, and went upstairs. She bought herself a cup of coffee and settled into a chair beside the window. The sea was as calm as oil. A few people around her were talking about a coming storm.

Always like this, she heard them say, the calm before the storm. When she went to the rest room, a woman washing her hands asked her if she was ready for it.

"Ready for what?"

"Barometer's dropping so fast it'll go through the floor," she said pulling down a brown paper towel. "All I want is to get home safely on Grand Manan and then not go anywhere for a while."

"What kind of a storm?" Teri asked.

"A blizzard to end all blizzards. That's what they're saying. You see the movie *The Perfect Storm*?"

Back out in the cabin, she heard people saying that it would surely hit by tonight.

"How long do you think it'll last?" she asked.

"Oh, they usually blow themselves out in about twenty-four hours," said a man with a huge mustache.

"Will the ferry run? Will I be able to get home?"

"The ferry always runs," the man's wife said. "Maybe a bit uncomfortably, but it always runs."

She tried Jack's hotel again, and left yet another urgent message. She'd keep her cell phone on, she told him. "Call me, no matter what time it is. I've got this really insane idea I'm checking out. Plus there's this storm coming. I think I'm crazy for being here."

An hour and a half later she was knocking on Marnie's door. Neither Marnie nor her car seemed to be there, and like the thundery horizon, that unsettled her for reasons she couldn't explain. She tried the door. Locked, but she knew where the key was, and a few moments later, Teri and Kelly were safely inside.

It was ice cold in Marnie's small kitchen, and Teri hugged her arms around her and looked around. That pile of burned cookies was still on the counter beside the microwave. "Marnie?" she called, but her voice sounded hollow and empty. She went from room to room then. All were cold. All were dark.

Marnie was probably not too far, maybe just down at the Save Easy getting groceries or arguing with the manager of the drugstore about getting more romance novels in. She'd be back any minute.

"Well, Kel," she said, "I don't know where everyone is, but we might as well get comfortable." She carried her bags upstairs into the guest room that had been hers. The bed she had slept on was stripped. The other bed, the one under the window, was still made up. She laid her bag on the bed and placed her computer on the bird-watcher's table. Kelly wagged her tail.

"I don't know what we're doing here either, Kel. All I can say is I'm glad you're with me."

The phone started ringing then. She stood frozen for several seconds before she decided that she should answer it and raced downstairs.

"Hello?" she yelled into the phone. "Marnie's Bed-and-Breakfast," she added as an afterthought.

Just a click and a dial tone. She started shivering. She punched in *69 and a cheerful voice told her this calling feature was not available on this phone line.

She touched the black stove. Cold. She flicked the switch and the stove immediately lit up with flames of yellow around the artificial logs. She stood over it and warmed her hands.

On the range was a pot with a lid. She lifted it. It was the pea soup, topped now with little bubbles of blue mold. She decided to get a pot of coffee going and rummaged in the cupboards for the canister. Something warm on a day like today. When Marnie came home from wherever she was, a nice cup of Teri's strong coffee would be nice. Marnie was disorganized. Marnie was a lousy cook. Everyone knew that. It was just like her to leave a pot on the stove. Probably that boyfriend of hers came and whisked her away for a romantic weekend somewhere, and she forgot about everything else. Yes, that's where she was, on the mainland with her boyfriend.

While her coffee dripped through, she sat at the table and rubbed Kelly's ears. When it was ready she poured herself a cup. She opened the fridge for cream just as a gust of wind blew against the window, and she slammed the fridge shut. She let out a breath and opened it again and got the cream out and poured it into her coffee. It curdled.

She dumped her cup into the sink. She'd go shopping before the storm got too bad. She picked up one of the burned cookies and tossed it to Kelly, who lay down on the rug beside the stove and gnawed on it for a while. On top of the fridge she found the cookie tin and looked inside. Filled with unburned cookies. None eaten. That disturbed her more than anything she had seen so far.

Outside the window the sky was heavy. Little gusts blew here and there. What was she doing here? If her theory was correct, she never should have come back here by herself.

A knock on the kitchen door made her gasp. But it was Flynn

who stood there in his heavy wool coat, the flaps of his hat down over his ears.

When she opened the door, he stepped inside. "You're here," he said. "I saw the car, phoned a couple minutes ago. I was wondering who was here."

"I tried phoning Marnie, but I didn't get an answer," Teri said.

He snorted and pulled off his hat. "That's because she's not here."

"So she's okay then? You know where she is? With her boyfriend?"

He snorted again, louder this time. "Boyfriend."

"Well, she was getting all ready for him to come. Is she with him? Did they go to the mainland? But they didn't take the cookies. Marnie baked special cookies for him and they're all still here."

"Boyfriend!" He stamped his feet on the mat and unbuttoned his coat.

"Do you know where she is? Is it okay if I stay here?"

"I don't care if you stay here or not."

"Where's Marnie then?"

"That's what I want to ask you. No one's seen her for a while. That's what I been trying to say, if I could get a word in edgewise. You must be taking lessons from Marnie. Been around her too long."

"You don't know where she is?"

He looked at her. "Didn't you hear me? That's what I just said. I thought you knew where she was."

"How would I know where she is?"

"She was trying like the dickens to call you, that's why."

"I never got any message that she was trying to call me."

"That's because she didn't have your number. She called me, wanting to know did I have your number? I said, how would I know your number? But she was all fired up about something she had to tell you."

"I gave her my card. She had my number."

They both looked at the clutter that was the kitchen, books and papers piled everywhere. A small business card didn't have a chance.

He shrugged. "Well, I'll be going then." He started buttoning his coat.

"Wait. You can't go. What about Marnie?"

He turned. "What about her?"

"Where is she? Should we go to the police?"

"She'll turn up. She can take care of herself."

After he left, Teri went to the Save Easy and bought cream, milk, cereal, bread, some cheese. She unloaded the groceries back at Marnie's and wandered around the house. When she had been here before, she had only been in the kitchen, the dining room, the television room, and her own bedroom. But now she looked through each room, walking into the center and turning around slowly, observing things. Even the way a person arranges furniture speaks volumes.

Off the dining room were two rooms that were Marnie's quarters; one looked like her office and the other was her bedroom. Teri stood in the middle of the tiny office and turned around. Marnie's computer was a huge machine with a tower, an external modem, an external DVD player, scanner, printer, and other attachments and gadgets. Her office was the most cluttered room in the house, if that were possible. Against one wall, romance and bridal magazines were stacked three deep. Teri picked through them quickly; they appeared to go back to the 1970s. Against another wall were romance novels, four deep this time. *Marnie must own every romance novel known to humankind.* Her printer held several printed sheets.

The computer was still on. Teri pressed the space bar and the screen came to life. An error box said that the modem had disconnected itself. Behind the error message was the Website for a romance readers group. Teri picked up the sheets in the printer and found herself reading the latest installment in a continuing love story. She looked at the date—two days ago. She searched the monitor screen for a way to connect to the internet, found a little icon, clicked on it, and immediately heard the modem dialing. She reloaded the website. Nothing here that Marnie hadn't printed off.

On the floor next to the printer was a pile of three-ring binders. She opened the top one. It looked like Marnie printed the stories and collected them in the binders. There must have been a dozen of these. Each one held around a dozen stories separated by little colored tabbed sheets. Teri leafed through the binders. At the front of each, Marnie had written her own comments, and seemed to have rated the stories according to criteria she had laid out in an elaborate spreadsheet.

All very interesting. All very voyeuristic, but it wasn't telling her where Marnie was now. Teri put the sheets back into the printer tray.

Against the far wall were more three-ring binders. More romance story installments? Teri picked up one labeled "Makeovers" and found pages and pages of before and after pictures of hairstyle and makeup, clipped out of magazines and pasted onto lined notebook paper and dating back more than five years.

She put that binder away and picked up the next one. It was entirely devoted to "Skin Care" and featured articles and pictures about facials and skin creams. Another book featured hairstyles of movie stars, and yet another wedding cake decorating.

Teri put them all back and checked the computer again. It didn't look as though Marnie had bothered to password-protect it. Still connected, Teri checked Marnie's e-mail. There were at least a dozen e-mails from web companies with advertisements or information on various orders. Teri realized that without too much hassle, she could find out Marnie's credit card numbers. They were all there in her outgoing mail.

Marnie also had received a number of personal e-mails. *Where are you?* wrote one, and *Hey, get back to me.* Teri checked the e-mail addresses then opened one at random:

> Hey Marnie, I was trying to reach you, but you didn't answer. Where the heck are you? Did you read Time for Love? What did you think? I hated Diana, especially where she tried to poison Lady Sarah so that she could get Liam. That was SO contrived. Tell me what you thought. Am DYING to hear!

And another:

Where are you? Been dying to know what you think of my first chapter! E-mail me. Your critique partner.

And finally:

Been missing you, Marnie. Love, Johanna

That was all. No secret life. Nothing from a boyfriend. If need be, Teri could search through Marnie's hard drive for clues, but for now, there seemed to be no mystery here.

In Marnie's bedroom, Teri found the same clutter, only this time it was perfume and face cream bottles of every conceivable brand on her dressing table, which was antique and ornate. On a high dresser sat a plastic basket full of pink curlers.

Marnie's single bed was neatly made, and an opened romance novel rested facedown on her end table. Her closet was open and overflowed with silky pants and tops. Teri looked for luggage, but found none. Maybe she *had* gone somewhere. But then, Marnie said she never went anywhere, so why would she need luggage in the first place? Besides, this was a big house. She could keep luggage anywhere.

Next Teri went into the living room where they had shared a bowl of burned popcorn and talked about life while watching *Steel Magnolias.* She flipped through the clutter of bills and papers. No clues.

Before she thought too much about it, she and Kelly were in the car and heading for the RCMP detachment. The officer she had talked to before wasn't there. And the one she talked to now, a husky young man named Trevor, appeared to think it was strange that she would come to a police station because her bed-and-breakfast host wasn't in.

"Did she know you were coming?" he asked.

"Well, no."

"She's probably on the mainland."

"I don't think so. She never goes to the mainland."

Teri explained that she was looking again at the accident.

"I wasn't here when it happened," he said. "So I can't really add anything new to that."

"That's okay, because now it's Marnie I'm worried about."

"Do you know her well?"

"I stayed with her the last time I was here."

Trevor kept looking at her.

"I'm sorry," Teri said. "This must seem strange. I used to be a cop, and I have an instinct about this. I think there's something wrong."

He took the particulars and said he would have a look around the island. She never did tell him about the preposterous theory that had brought her here in the first place.

On her way back to Marnie's, she went down to the wharf and talked to a couple of fishermen. No one had seen Marnie. It was the same at the Save Easy. Everyone knew her, of course, but no one had seen her for a few days. Teri went to the library and was met with the same story.

"She comes in here all the time for her romance books, but she hasn't been in for a week. If you see her, tell her I've got in two new Danielle Steels for her."

"I'll tell her."

By the time Teri got back to Marnie's, it was dusk and the place was still dark, so she and Kelly headed off to the Coffee Perk for supper. She left Kelly in the car and promised to bring out the leftovers. A cute little waitress with *Tracie* on her name tag waited on her and told her that the day's special was meat loaf.

"Sure, anything," Teri said.

During supper, her cell phone rang. It was Jack. She told him she needed to talk to him, that she had some important things to say but couldn't say them in a public place. She couldn't trust anyone, she said.

"Do you know there's a storm brewing?" he said.

"I think it started."

"Are you sure you're okay?"

"I'm fine. I'm fine, Jack. I'm going to get my supper to go and then call you from the house. I need to talk to you."

"I'm worried about you. Carl called."

"You didn't tell him anything, did you?"

"No, I didn't."

"What did you tell him?"

"That you were gone, but that you'd call him. He said he had something important he wanted to tell *you.*"

"I don't want to call him yet."

By the time she got back to her car, wind was swirling new snow around like confetti, blurring the road on the way back to Marnie's. Driving through it was like driving through hyperspace. At Marnie's she phoned Jack, and they talked for twenty-five minutes. She told him everything. He tried to persuade her to get right back on the ferry and come home before the full force of the storm hit, and she said, no way José. She had to find out where Marnie was first. She owed her that much.

After the telephone call, she looked through Marnie's computer again. She discovered, much to her surprise, that Marnie was working on a romance novel! Teri read parts of it. Not bad, she thought, if you like that sort of thing. There were a few new e-mails, mostly of the *Hey, where are you* variety.

Teri sat in front of the television and turned on the weather channel. The forecast called for high winds and snow. Lots of it. Yes, the barometer was lower than it had been for a long, long time.

It was dark, and she walked around the place several times making sure all the doors and windows were locked. She thought about Garda and Will. About Jimmy Jarvis. Funny how these two cases, these two deaths, were intertwined. Might be intertwined, rather. Two murders, and the one common denominator—Ellen Houseman.

She fell asleep on Marnie's couch wrapped up in Marnie's orange blanket, the TV still on. When she woke it was still dark out, and the house was shuddering on its foundation. Literally. She could feel the wind coursing through the walls like a living thing. Glasses rattled in the kitchen cupboards, and she thought of Christ's greatest miracle. Peace, be still.

Kelly was whining. Teri heard a clanging but dismissed it as a dream. She heard it again. She got up and looked out the window at a fir tree bent double in the wind, bent so low that the branches clicked against Marnie's shed. She thought about Ellen and her two friends caught out in a wind like this. She turned off the television and went back to sleep on the couch.

The following morning, the wind was still strong and it was still snowing. She shoveled out the driveway with a scoop shovel she found leaning against Marnie's shed. Then she drove through the gusty wind to the Coffee Perk for breakfast. Trees were down, and her tires crunched on branches that had blown across the road.

After breakfast she and Kelly drove down to Southwest Head, where she parked and looked at the sea, at the powerful white crests, their tops blown off by the wind. Kelly whimpered in her seat, and Teri said, "You're not going to like it outside, girl, but okay."

They went for a walk then, barely making any headway. A few other cars were there, their occupants apparently watching the water as well. She took Kelly to the lee side of the lighthouse so both of them could catch their breath.

And then she saw it, a flickering of pink underneath the snow, caught in the bushes. She walked over and picked it up, squeezed it in her fingers, shook the snow from it. It was one of Marnie's pink foam curlers.

45

A spring tide came in this morning, high and fierce against the rocks. It's as if the wind were a hand moving across the land, bringing with it time and tides. The writing on the wall of Nebuchadnezzar's palace. The Medes and Persians are already at your door.

Garda felt the stone cottage tremble and pictured yet another rock dislodging itself from the foundation and tumbling down the cliff. Even though she worked hard, she could not keep up with it.

Audrey was dancing to silence today. There was no more music. The radio had run out of batteries and would be stilled until Will brought more. Audrey danced to music only she heard.

The woman sat on the rocking chair and read the old Bible while Audrey wound the gossamer-thin string of her body around the chairs and the back of the table, her hands animated, her long fingers reaching forward, reaching upward. Only her face remained expressionless. She needed bright colors, silver shawls, bells, and cloth sandals, and she would be a dancer from the Middle East. She needed a black leotard, her hair pulled back stiffly off her face, and she could dance on a darkened stage. But she was all in white. Wispy. A ghost. The only sound, the sound of cloth brushing past and bare feet on the stone floor and the wind outside.

Garda turned back to her Bible. *He maketh the storm a calm, so that the waves thereof are still. Then they are glad because they be quiet; so he bringeth them unto their desired haven.* Garda was finding comfort in the familiar words.

She had been betrayed. That's what she always said to herself, that was the excuse she gave. Her husband had no time for her. Her good friend had told her secrets to others. The excuses were plentiful. There was no end to the storm of them.

But like David, she was betrayer, not betrayed. No one had forced her to go back to her pharmacist. She had done that. And like David, her sin had caused the deaths of many: Jimmy, Moira, Cheryl. And now, it seemed, someone named Marnie.

There was almost a triumph in his voice when Will came and told her that another islander had died, someone named Marnie. She had been hiking along the cliff path with Will and then suddenly had slipped, and when he turned back, there she was tumbling down into the fog.

"Right out there," he pointed.

Garda knew it was true. Earlier she had seen Will and a woman walking along the path. Even from a distance she could see the woman's purple scarf ballooning out behind her. It was someone Will had known a long time ago, he told her. Someone who was trying to meddle in his affairs, he said. Someone who thought she knew it all. Someone who, if not stopped, would expose Garda for who she was.

"You can be happy to see the end of her," he told Garda.

Garda had stared and stared at him. When she finally spoke it was to say, "I thought you were on the mainland."

"I wasn't." Then he had walked around the stone kitchen, his boots clomping, demanding to know why there wasn't any fresh coffee.

When Garda didn't answer, he said, "She's dead. Poor thing. It happens all the time around here, you know. Hikers not paying attention, people nosing around where they shouldn't be nosing, people falling off cliffs, slipping off the edge. And you know, with the tides the way they've been, the body won't be discovered for months, if ever."

He was threatening her. She would be next off the cliff, she and Audrey both, or maybe he would just wait until the wind blew this whole place over.

She looked up from the Bible to where Audrey was dancing, her eyes vacant, yet the mouth so intent, as if she were carrying the weight of the world.

Another shudder, more snow against the windows, mixed with rain this time.

The woman closed the Bible and put her hands on top of it and thought about Garda, the real Garda, the gentle woman who had taken her in when she found her half-dead on the shoreline that August day five years ago. How Garda, the real Garda, had nursed her back to health, had been with her during the long time when she had no memory of the events. And when her memory did return and it was worse than having no memory, Garda sat up with her and rubbed her hands when the nightmares overwhelmed her.

And when she was well, Garda had told her all about her brother-in-law, Will, and her husband, Jerome. Garda, the real Garda, had told her in whispers that her brother-in-law had killed her husband. Brother killing brother. The similarity of their stories, even the sameness of the names—Jimmy, Jerome, both dead—had bound them together. That and the similarity of themselves—same height, same size, both born with blond hair, both now gray. Ellen, when she was better, could fit easily into Garda's clothes.

As the wind blew rain against the stone cottage, it came to her then that maybe Garda, the real Garda, had not fallen accidentally but had been pushed. Just as Marnie had been pushed. Just as anyone else would be who came to the lighthouse and learned the truth.

46

Through the snow, Teri drove immediately to the RCMP detachment. She held out the sponge curler to Constable Trevor.

"You sure this is hers?" he asked.

"Fairly sure," Teri said. "There's something wrong. I just feel it. First, she tries to get a hold of me, and then when I come here she's gone. Marnie never leaves this island. She hasn't for years. And there aren't that many places to go on this island. Even her friend Flynn is worried."

"And you said she tried to call you?"

"Yes.

The officer twirled the curler around in his fingers. "And you found this down by the lighthouse?"

Teri nodded.

"You drove down there this morning?"

She nodded.

"Aren't the roads pretty bad?"

"Fairly. I'm used to it."

He shrugged. "What would her curler be doing down by the lighthouse, I wonder?"

"It might've slipped out of her hair. They were always coming loose, and she was always tightening them and then tying her scarf tighter around them. I told you yesterday I have a feeling about this."

He was looking at the curler, then at her, then back at the curler again.

"I told you yesterday that Marnie called me. I have no idea why but I think it's important."

He promised that they'd have another look around and told her to stay off the roads.

She drove back to Marnie's, snowplowing her car through the drifts. In Marnie's kitchen she made coffee and opened her iBook on the kitchen table. There were still a few loose ends in the whole Jimmy Jarvis thing she needed to clear up.

She called the Maine State Police and asked to talk to her friend Bill from the old days when she was a cop. Bill told her the death of Jimmy Jarvis was indeed a suicide. There were no other prints on the gun, and the entry wound to the head, the way the gun was situated in his hand, all pointed to a suicide.

"He went into the bush that day with one thing on his mind. And that was to kill himself."

"How can you be so sure?"

"Teri, you were a cop once; let me give you the facts. Jimmy Jarvis was quite a gun collector. But a careful one. The only guns he ever took hunting were his rifles, a Remington and a Winchester. He didn't have his rifles with him that day."

"The wife is convinced it was murder."

"She told us about the affair he had before he was married. She also told us about the money offered to keep quiet about it, but after months of investigation we couldn't find any evidence of a threat, no witnesses, nothing. We believe it was remorse over his business that caused his suicide."

"Business?"

"One of his assistants misread a doctor's prescription and a patient nearly died. The family was suing."

"His wife didn't mention that."

"No, she wouldn't." She could hear him sigh. "She was convinced he was a happy man. Our sources tell us otherwise, including his fellow workers. He was an active member of the Lions, then dropped out suddenly. His friends described him as very depressed. There was some feeling, even, that the wife made up the bit about the affair and the money."

"What happened to the lawsuit?"

"It was settled out of his estate. But Jarvis Pharmacy is no more."

Teri hung up feeling slightly out of sorts. It was eleven-thirty. She poured herself another cup of coffee and sat at the kitchen table trying to drink it, but it was settling in her stomach all wrong. Everything about this case now was filling her with bile.

She decided to clean up Marnie's kitchen a bit. At least she could do that. She washed the moldy pea soup down the sink and scrubbed out the pot. She wiped the microwave oven and rinsed out the coffeepot, swept the floor and unloaded the dishwasher. Then she took Kelly for a walk. Not far, just around Marnie's backyard, up to where Marnie's old shed faced up against the woods.

It was still windy, but she could feel that the power had gone out of the storm. Snow had drifted against fence posts and trees, and it was really quite pretty, she thought. Kelly raced around the white yard, nosing at the shed until Teri had to call her sternly. Drifts had settled across the driveway, so Teri shoveled them out again. By two, she was shoveled out and exhausted, but she had also decided that she couldn't wait any longer. Marnie or no Marnie, she had to hike in and see Garda.

In Marnie's mudroom were several pairs of snowshoes. Teri tried on various sizes until she found some that fit over her boots. She dressed warmly in several layers, and also picked up one of Marnie's walking sticks.

She parked beside Southwest Head, put Kelly on a leash, and battled the deep snow to the path. At the edge of the cliff, she drew back and hugged the tree line. Ahead of her, she could see the water, fierce and dark.

When she smelled the fragrant aroma of wood burning, she knew they were near the cottage.

"Come on, Kel," she said. "We're here."

She clumped her way across deep snow to the back of the cottage, noting that a narrow path had already been carved through the drifts to the outhouse. She knocked loudly on the kitchen door.

When the woman answered, Teri looked at her for a long time and then said, "Hello, Ellen."

The woman put her hand to her mouth and stared. It was a

long time before either one of them said anything.

Finally the woman said, "Did he tell you? He'll kill you."

Who? Carl? "No one told me. I figured it out."

"How?"

They were still standing in the doorway, the snow blowing in at their feet.

"Can I come in? Can we talk?"

Inside, the room was comfortably warm. A woolen shawl lay across the rocking chair. And an old leather Bible, cracked on top, lay on the table. The girl with the unfocused eyes was wearing a slim, white cotton shift and dancing, although Teri heard no music.

"I had my suspicions early on," Teri said. "Not that you were Ellen, but that you were hiding something about Ellen, that you knew something. But it was the video your husband gave me."

"Video?"

"Your husband gave me two videos, one of your memorial service and another of family outings and Christmases."

"Memorial service," the woman said. There was a half-smile on her face. "'So good to be alive when the eulogy is read.'"

"Pardon me?"

"It's from a Phil Ochs song. 'Crucifixion.' Popular when I was young."

"You had a lovely memorial service."

"Who preached?"

"Paul Pellerman."

"Then it wasn't a lovely service." The woman, Ellen, turned away from her.

Kelly found herself a place beside the woodstove, and Audrey sat cross-legged on the floor in front of the dog.

"How did you figure it out?" said Ellen.

"I recognized you. When I was here the last time I saw the way you smoothed Audrey's hair. On the video I saw you do the same thing to your sons. But then the question became, how could you have survived? Those waters are ice-cold. I have a friend who's a scuba diver. He told me that a wet suit can keep a body warm enough to function, even in very cold water. They're also buoyant. I hadn't realized that. Without the weights you wear, it's even more buoyant than a life jacket. And then I looked back in my notes to discover you're a certified scuba diver."

Ellen's back was still to her, and her shoulders sagged. Her voice broke. "He's happier now, and with someone more suited to the ministry than I ever was."

"But he loves you!" Teri fairly screamed it. "In all these years he never quite believed you were dead."

Ellen reached around and undid the elastic at the bottom of the long braid that hung down her back. She turned around and finger-combed her hair until it hung in silver ringlets around her face. It picked up the lights from the lanterns. And in that ghostlike vision, Teri saw a younger Ellen, the Ellen in her wedding picture, the long blond hair, the bangs straight across her forehead, the flowers.

"What happened?" Teri asked softly. "How did you get here?"

Ellen sat down at the table. Teri sat across from her. Audrey and Kelly continued to sit on the floor and look at each other.

It never should have happened, Ellen said. It was one of those times when everything that could go wrong did. It was windy, but she'd certainly been out in worse. They had just rounded the bottom of Grand Manan, the three of them, and were in the process of taking down the sails and firing up the engine when the wave hit. It came out of nowhere and knocked them down.

"I've been in knock downs before," Ellen said. "It's never pleasant, but if you keep a cool head, when the boat rights itself, which it always does, you just clean up the mess and keep on going."

The three of them were wearing full foul-weather gear, but not the kind of survival suits fishermen wear. "If we'd had survival suits, Moira and Cheryl would be alive." As well, they were harnessed to the boat. When the boat righted, they were a bit shaken, but otherwise okay. "Cheryl was terribly frightened, I remember that."

The boat, however, had suffered some damage. One of the windows had been knocked out, so Moira went to stuff cushions into it. Ellen tried to start the engine, but it wouldn't turn over. Most likely they had hit a log or debris in their knock down. Ellen was fairly sure the prop had been fouled, so she gave the helm to Moira and went below to put on her wet suit. If she needed to, she would go over the side to clear it. Meanwhile, Cheryl sat huddled and shaking against the bulkhead and wouldn't move.

"I can still remember her, the way she sat there hugging her knees, unable to move. I tried to tell her everything was going to be okay..."

"Why didn't you call the Coast Guard? Why didn't you issue a Mayday?" Teri asked. "And didn't you have a life raft? My reports said that you were fully equipped, EPIRB, everything."

Ellen sighed. "The radio antenna came off in the knock down, and we were not in immediate danger of sinking. I thought we were handling it." Ellen was fidgeting with a piece of modeling clay. "Yes, obviously, we should have triggered the EPIRB. Sometimes you think you can handle things..."

Ellen's memory wasn't clear, she told Teri, about what happened next. She had tried many times in the past five years to piece it all together, to reconstruct the timeline, but whole sections were blurs of wind and water. They threw out a sea anchor to keep from being broadsided by the waves, and then with her wet suit on, she tethered herself to the boat and went over the side to free the prop.

Ellen was silent for a moment as she looked down at the clay. "I remember a bang, a lurch, and being thrown against the transom. I think I broke my wrist at that point." She held up her left arm. It was slightly misshapen. "Garda bandaged it, put a splint on it, told me later it had been broken." She bent it forward. "I almost have full movement."

"You could probably still have that properly set," Teri said.

"I'm used to it now."

"Then what happened?"

"I don't remember this part, but I remember bobbing up very quickly. I think I remember seeing Moira, the look on her face. Or maybe that was only in a dream. I don't know. I remember the wind, the sound of it, like an old lady screaming, screaming until the noise was all there was. I remember thinking that the boat was going to go down. I remember quickly cutting my tether with the knife on my belt. I must have cut Cheryl's tether, too. Or maybe Moira did. Moira would've known enough to cut her own. I don't remember that part.

"And then the boat was going down. So fast. I never thought a boat could go down that fast. It was just moments—no wavering, no bobbing on the surface. It just sank straight down. I remember seeing the top few inches of the mast. And then nothing. Our life raft was still in its metal container strapped to the boat. Everything happened so fast.

"There's a rock reef out there. That's what we hit. We were off course, and that's my fault for not paying attention. That rock must have ripped a huge hole in the bow.

"My next memory is waking up in this house. My wet suit was stripped off me. I was wearing a nightgown, not my own, and I was lying in bed. I thought I had died. I thought this was death." She pushed back her chair. "Come with me. Put your coat on."

Teri followed Ellen through the door to the front of the house. Then Ellen opened a door that was half-height, and ducked under. Teri followed. They ascended a narrow, miniature spiral staircase to the top of the turret, the little lighthouse. Up there was a tiny hexagonal room with one window and a table; on the table was a kerosene lamp and a book. Ellen pulled a wooden box from underneath the desk and opened it. Inside was a black wet suit. Ellen held it up. Part of the arm was tattered and there was a large rip along the side.

"This is what I was wearing. Garda showed me this. When I couldn't remember who I was or how I got here, Garda showed me this. Bits and pieces started coming back, then. She also showed me newspapers."

"Where's Garda now?" Teri asked. It was cold, she was shivering, and she knew it was more than the wind crawling through the rotten boards. A sound like bullets against the structure made her back away toward the stairs.

"It's raining now," Ellen said. "The snow has turned to rain.

That will make the path treacherous. Don't go back by the cliffs."

"I don't know any other way."

"I'll draw you a map when we get downstairs."

Down in the kitchen, Ellen gave Teri the rest of the story. Garda brought her up here after she found Ellen almost dead on the beach. It took many months of recuperation before Ellen regained all her memory. But Garda was kind to her, and Garda shared her own story of pain.

"When she died, I didn't know what to do."

"When she died?"

"When Garda died."

"How did she die?"

"She fell on the cliff path. It had rained and the path was slick." Ellen's hands were fists in her lap.

When Garda died, Ellen realized that she couldn't leave Audrey. And since she and Garda were a similar size, it just seemed easier to become her.

"I had no reason to go back to my life and every reason to stay. Audrey was here. She needed taking care of. Plus there were...things I'd done. Reasons I couldn't go back."

"Who's Will? Why are you afraid of him? Why do you keep looking around the room even now?"

Audrey and Kelly had snuggled together on the mattress and were asleep. Ellen looked at the two of them.

"She's usually not like that," Ellen said. "Normally she flinches when people touch her."

"Maybe it's different with animals."

"Maybe."

"You were going to tell me about Will." Teri looked at her, waited.

"It really didn't have anything to do with me. Or it shouldn't. It's all about Garda. She and Will were engaged once."

"I heard that."

"But then Will's brother, Jerome, came home from the mainland, and Garda fell in love with him. Will's a very hard man, she told me. And was always very jealous of Jerome, even when they were younger. She told me that Jerome was so different, so kind. So they ran off and got married. Because of Will, because of how angry he was, they thought it best that they leave the island. Jerome had a fairly successful business in Saint John, and they went back to it.

"When Jerome died, and Audrey was born with her…her problems, Garda felt it was punishment, for having this…affair with Will's brother while she was engaged to be married to Will. All these years up here, seeking but never finding forgiveness. Thinking forgiveness, thinking redemption would come by external acts. The more one suffers, the greater one's remorse…"

"You're talking about Jimmy Jarvis now, aren't you?"

She was quiet for a few minutes before she said, "I had betrayed the very person that I loved most in this life. I began to understand that like Garda, this was my sentence. This is my sentence." Ellen looked at her, eyes gleaming with unshed tears. "Our stories were so similar. And when I came here, it was Garda's first human contact in so many years. She became the sister to me that my sisters never were. And Will again felt threatened. He didn't want either one of us to be happy."

The story was convoluted. The story didn't make sense. Teri found it hard to believe that Will would hold a grudge for so long and told Ellen so.

Ellen merely shrugged. "You have to understand Will. He's very bitter. He keeps long accounts. And then Garda died and I was all alone."

"How could you take Garda's identity without anyone knowing? Surely when the body was taken to the coroner…"

"I buried her. I needed to let Carl start over without me. Carl is married now anyway."

"He's not married."

Her head shot up.

"He's not married. They've been engaged for two years. He keeps postponing."

Ellen had risen from the table and was clasping and unclasping her hands, staring wildly around her. She leaned against the door, her hands behind her back, and looked at Teri. When she had calmed down, she said, "I wonder why not. I wonder." Then she sat back down. "Have you seen my sons? My family?"

"I met Carl Jr. when I was down in Philadelphia. He gave me a tour of the facility."

"Carl Jr." She smiled. "So like his father, that one. So intense. Is he still that way? How are Mariana and their two children?"

"There are three of them now."

"Three, imagine that." Her eyes were eager and Teri noticed how blue they were. "Sam? Charlie? Did you see them?"

"I got e-mails from both of them, haven't met them. Charlie's in India and Sam's in Colorado."

"Sam's in Colorado?"

"He's a youth pastor in Colorado Springs. A big church, I hear."

"Imagine that! He and that singer were going to get married."

"They did. I think they have a child now, too. And his wife is making quite a name for herself in Christian pop music, I understand."

"I always thought she would, she had this—" Ellen motioned with her hands—"this determination, or something."

"I don't know for sure that they have any children. As I said, I haven't spoken to any of your sons, except for Carl."

"What about Brent?"

"He lives in New Jersey and works at a Pizza Hut."

She touched her face. "Such a lost child. Neither Carl nor I had time for him. Carl, so busy with his work, so much travel, so many nights away, and me, so consumed with guilt that I couldn't properly mother him. Didn't know how."

She blinked away tears and put her hands on the table. They were ringless and chapped.

"Are you going to tell Carl that you found me?"

"I don't know," Teri said. "I don't know."

47

By the time she got back to Marnie's, it was dusk and the house was dark. But when Teri stepped into the kitchen and turned on the light, something was wrong. Had she left the coffee pot on that side of the sink rather than back in the coffee machine? Hadn't she put her cup on the drain board? She blinked several times and turned around. Kelly was growling softly, and Teri kept a tight hold on her leash.

Teri wished she had her gun with her now.

It was seeing the granola bar wrapper in the garbage, however, that really chilled her. Someone had been here. Kelly was whimpering, growling, straining at her leash. With her free hand, Teri grabbed a boot from the mudroom, one of Marnie's, and held it over her head.

The hallway was quiet except for a flickering blue light from the television room. The television? Teri moved cautiously forward, still holding the boot and Kelly's leash, and turned on the light.

On the floor next to the couch was a quivering mass underneath a blanket, which Teri whipped off in one stroke.

Marnie!

"Teri!" she said rising, using the arms of the couch for support. "For goodness sake, I didn't know who you were! You scared me half to death! I was sitting in here watching television, and I hear this growling. I'm thinking, what in the name of heaven and earth is *that?*"

"Everyone's been so worried about you!"

"That's your dog?"

"This is Kelly, yes."

"She looks like a nice dog, Teri. I should get a dog." Marnie got up and sat down heavily on the couch. She was wearing a faded purple housecoat, and her freshly washed hair was in curlers. But her face was a mass of scars and scrapes, and one eye looked swollen shut. Teri could see where she had applied foundation in an attempt to make the abrasions invisible.

"Marnie, are you okay? Your face…"

She put her hand to it. "Don't look at me, Teri. I know I look a fright. Oh, just don't look at me. What I need to do is to get me some more makeup. What a cute doggie you have. Come here, sweet pea. He's a sweetie, Teri. What a cutie he is."

Teri sat down. "What happened? Where were you? I thought you were with your boyfriend."

"I should be asking you that question, Teri. I was trying to get a hold of you."

"But where were you?"

"Teri, come sit down. Get away from the window. Certain people think I'm dead, and I want to keep it like that. Turn off the big light."

Teri did and sat beside her, put her hand on Marnie's arm. "Everyone's been frantic! Me, Flynn. Where were you? I even went to the cops. Where have you been?"

"Hiding." She said it simply. "I had to, no choice."

"Hiding where?"

"Carpet cleaning," Marnie said.

"Carpet cleaning? You were hiding at a carpet cleaners?"

"No, no, of course not." She was waving her hands. "I wasn't hiding at a carpet cleaners. I said carpet cleaning because it all had to do with carpet cleaning. I was hiding in my shed."

"You were hiding in your shed? In your backyard?"

"I'm supposed to be dead, so don't talk so loud."

"You were out in your shed in all this snow and wind?"

"It all had to do with carpet cleaning. That was the whole thing." She was whispering. "I figured out something about Will. I was trying to call you, but I couldn't find your number. He used to be a nice man—that's when I knew him way back when I knew them all. And I used to take his side—I told you that, Teri—because he was so in love with Garda. And then she ran off with the brother, but I've changed my thinking about the whole thing, let me tell you. I used to blame Garda, but after talking with him, well, let me tell you, Teri, I've changed my tune." She shook her head as she said this, and Teri noticed scratches on her left ear. One looked especially deep.

"Marnie, you should go to the hospital. You should get that ear looked at."

She touched it tentatively. "Teri, forget that, just listen."

She smoothed her robe with her hands, and Teri could see she had applied a fresh coat of pink polish to the nails.

"After you left it got me thinking and I figured something out. But then I couldn't find your number. I should've had your e-mail. Teri, you should've given me your e-mail. Before you leave, write down your e-mail for me. So, when I couldn't get a hold of you, I decided to go and see Will for myself. Well, he wasn't at his place in Grand Harbour. So I figure, where else would he be but Garda's? So I decided I would walk down the path, you know, just to see if he was there. And so there I am parking my car at the lighthouse, and who do I bump into but Will! We talked a bit, and I found out everything. He told me everything. Jerome had this carpet cleaning business over in Saint John. It was a long time ago, but it explains everything." And then she nodded, satisfied.

Teri looked at her. "What explains everything?"

"Jerome's death? His will? The money they made? It explains it all. You know, I never quite believed that Jerome died in a car accident, or at least that he wasn't helped in the car accident. I knew Jerome, and he was always a careful driver. He was, Teri. There was talk at the time that Jerome made quite a bit of money in this little venture of theirs. Well, not a lot by some people's standards, but enough for a pretty nice life on Grand Manan. Jerome always had a head for business; he was the smart one, and to tell you the truth, Will was always jealous of his brother. Even when we were all kids, he was. It was sort of like Cain and Abel, you know the story of those brothers that killed each other? And then the last straw, Jerome steals Will's one true love, Garda. I always thought it only had to do with love, but it had to do with money."

"A powerful motivator."

"Well, after Garda and Jerome ran off to Saint John, Will ups and goes. He tells everyone here that Jerome's invited him to be partners." Marnie shook her head, said conspiratorially, "But that wasn't it. Will set out to destroy him. So he weaseled his way into the business, then killed Jerome—did something to the brakes of the car—so that he could inherit the business and take it away from Garda. But, unbeknownst to him, that Jerome is no dummy. Garda inherits the business, not Will. Some papers or other had never been signed. So here's Will, madder than a hatter and back where he started."

"Will told you all this?"

"Yes, and then he told me I was a busybody and pushed me off the cliff."

"He pushed you off the cliff?" Teri was incredulous.

"Yep. It was foggy. The storm was starting. There was no way for him to see that my fall was broken by a tree, which was sort of hanging out there. Thank the good Lord for the fog."

Teri thought of those cliffs and a shiver ran through her.

"I just held on to that tree for dear life. I think God—you remember when we were talking about God? I think He may have had something to do with it, because here I am clinging onto this tree and praying and praying, and the darn thing held. It held enough for me to get a foothold and stay there until I was sure Will had gone. Then I climbed up and waited some more. I'm surefooted as a deer, you know."

"I know."

"I'm one tough cookie. Will should have realized who he was tangling with. When the coast was clear, I hiked back here. I was glad for the storm. It erased my tracks."

Teri thought of the hundred-mile-an-hour winds they had just endured, the way it made the house shudder and driving difficult. The thought of anyone hiking through it made her blink and stare at this woman.

"But where was your car? The police couldn't find it."

"Yeah, I noticed it was gone, too. I had to hike all the way back here on foot. I wouldn't put it past Will to steal it. That old truck of his is on its last legs. Probably thought, what a good deal—kill the owner of the car and then steal it. So I had to hike cross-country. And then when I got here, I didn't want to go into the house. I thought Will might be guarding it. So I snuck in, got some blankets, and hightailed it to the shed. When I saw the car pull up, I thought for sure it was Will, so I peeked out and saw it was your car. But I still had to be careful. Will might be following you. But then tonight I thought, I've got to get back into my house. A lady can only go for so long without a bubble bath."

The doorbell rang. Teri looked at Marnie. "Are you expecting company?"

"Teri!" Her voice was frantic. "That's Will. I'm sure of it! I'm hiding behind the couch." And she pulled the blanket over her and slid behind it.

But it was Constable Trevor and another RCMP officer, a woman with short orange hair. They told Teri they had some bad news for her. They had found Marnie's car at the bottom of the cliff by Southwest Head. As soon as the storm cleared, they would be sending a boat and divers around.

And then Marnie was standing in front of them, making a fist. "That Will! Shoving my car off the cliff! Well, he's going to have to buy me a new one and that's all there is to it!"

"Marnie?" the woman said.

And then Marnie told them her story. Afterward, they offered to take her to the hospital.

"I'm fine," Marnie said with a dismissive wave of her hand.

"Those cuts and bruises should be looked at," the woman said.

"Don't be ridiculous. I'm fine. And besides, you'll never get me into one of those hospital gowns. Can you see me in one of those?"

"I really must insist."

"She won't go," Teri said. "You're wasting your time. I'll take care of her. If anything looks really bad, I'll drive her in."

"No you won't, Teri. I said I'm not going. And don't talk about me like I'm not here."

Teri put up her hands. "Okay, okay. Sorry."

"What I hate is when people talk about people like they aren't there. That's one of my pet peeves, Teri."

After the police left, Teri washed Marnie's cuts and bruises and bandaged them as best she could before putting the desperately tired woman to bed.

48

At midnight Teri woke to find Kelly's dog nose up to her face. When Teri lived in the apartment above the bagel shop, Kelly slept with her. She would start off at the foot of the bed, but by morning, Kelly was a warm lump against her back. When she and Jack got married, Kelly was relegated to the kitchen, where she spent her nights in whimpering indignation. Since coming to Grand Manan, Kelly decided that the old rules applied, and Teri had to admit that she didn't mind.

Teri lay in the single bed with covers up to her chin and thought about Ellen. She hadn't told the police about Ellen and about the real Garda being buried in the garden.

As she shifted under the blankets, something felt odd. And then it came to her. It was quiet. The wind, which had rattled the island for two days, canceling ferry rides and blowing parts of trees and buildings across roads, had stilled. She sat up in bed and looked out the window. The moon was full, and she stared at winter bones, the groping fingers of branches. And she prayed that Ellen and Audrey were safe, that the police had found Will. She fell back into a dreamless sleep.

When Teri woke again, the room was filled with sunlight, and Kelly was whimpering. Teri threw off the covers.

"Okay girl, me first though," she said as she padded into the bathroom with her toothbrush and towel.

Down in the kitchen she flicked on the gas fireplace. Just to make sure, Teri looked in on Marnie. She was sleeping, covers to her nose, pink curlers peeking out.

Outside, the morning fog was eerie, little dancing ghostly wisps that reminded her of Audrey.

She started a pot of coffee, and while the coffee dripped

through, Teri sat at the kitchen table with her computer. She opened Cut Throat and entered her conversation with Garda/Ellen, plus what happened to Marnie.

Midmorning, while Marnie slept on and after Teri had drunk the entire pot of coffee, there was a knock on the door. She looked up expecting the police. When she opened the door, there was her husband, smiling widely.

"Jack!" Her eyes went wide. "Jack!"

"Hey, Teri."

"Oh, I'm so glad to see you!" She rushed into his arms. Even Kelly was barking.

"Hey." He bent down. "Did you miss me, too?"

"She missed you, and I did, too. I can't believe you're here!"

"I wanted to get here yesterday, but the ferries weren't running. I got the first one over this morning."

"Oh, Jack, so much has happened."

"Tell me."

She made a fresh pot of coffee and they sat down and she told him.

After her story she said, "I have to tell Carl."

"Yes, you do."

"A part of me just wants to leave Ellen in peace."

"You think she's in peace right now?"

"If I don't tell him, though, he's bound to find out. I think when they arrest Will Stanton he will be only too happy to tell the world and CNN all about Ellen and Garda."

"So you better tell Carl first."

"I could wait until I get home, go see him."

"Will might talk before you get there."

"Right. I'll phone him today."

"You did a good job, Teri. You found his wife when no one else could."

"Then why don't I feel so good?"

And then Marnie was there, suitably made up and clothed in some flowing flowery pantsuit, her curler scarf the same color. She was noticeably impressed by Teri's handsome husband, and fluttered around the kitchen making scrambled eggs and toast for the three of them and giving him warm-ups of coffee.

Afterward, Teri went upstairs to her room and called Carl's office. Peg answered. "I'm looking for Carl," she said.

"Carl isn't in."

"Can you tell me when he'll be in?"

"He won't be. Can I take a message?"

"I need to talk to him."

"You can tell me. I'll make sure he gets it."

"It's personal."

Peg hung up on her. Peg actually hung up on her. She tried Carl's cell phone, and he answered on the second ring.

"Hello, Teri, I'm glad you called. I was going to call you today. There've been some changes here. I had an interesting talk with Archie Ryder. He called me, told me that you talked with him."

Teri paused. "Yes, I did."

"I wanted to call and tell you that just after talking with Archie, I resigned. I walked into Paul's office and told him I didn't want to be a part of this ministry. That would have been yesterday. I have to say that after I resigned, it was like a great burden had been lifted. Teri, can you hear me?"

"Yes." She held the phone tightly to her ear.

"When Archie Ryder quit those years ago, I never questioned it. I never questioned anything. I've done a lot of soul-searching since yesterday, and I realized that for years the four of them—the Ryders and the Pellermans—had been trying to undermine me, for reasons that aren't entirely clear to me, even now. There were so many rumors that I heard but denied. I had heard about some sort of falling-out between the Ryders and the Pellermans, and it concerned Ellen. At the time I didn't want to know—"

"What did Archie Ryder tell you?" Teri asked it cautiously.

"That he and his wife, along with the Pellermans, hired a private investigator to dig up something from my past, something they could hold over my head. They felt I was moving the ministry down questionable avenues, whatever that means. So they hired a private investigator. Archie told me that the fellow they hired found nothing. The falling-out occurred when Pellermans had a bout of conscience and decided that they shouldn't have done this. So they fired Archie, whose idea it was in the first place. They suddenly wanted nothing to do with him."

"So, that's what Archie told you?"

"Yes." He paused. "But I know it's not the truth."

Teri sat down on the bed. She could hear laughter from downstairs. She didn't trust herself to say anything.

"Teri?"

"Yes?"

"I thought I could trust the Pellermans. The Ryders were one thing, Ellen and I never knew the Ryders as well as the Pellermans. We were so close at one time, our families…" He paused. "I trusted them with my life." He was quiet for a while. Then, "I have known almost from the beginning that my youngest son…that Brent is not my son. My biological son."

Teri had no words.

"These things don't happen, do they? Not to famous Christian authors and preachers. Not to their families."

Then Teri said quietly into the phone, "Your wife loves you. She loves you very much."

"It occurred at a time when I had no use for anything but my own empire building. And Ellen was only good for how much she contributed to the empire. I thought I was doing this all for the Lord. That was my motivation. I'd wake up every morning and read my Bible and think that I really had it all together. When all around me everything was falling apart. My big office…I even had a pull-out couch, an en suite bathroom with a shower, and a change of clothes so that I didn't have to go home if a meeting went too late. And being at home distracted me from my real mission. At home there were the concerns of three young boys, taking them to Little League, music lessons, soccer; all of that fell onto my wife…"

"She's here, Carl. And she loves you."

"And if I stayed overnight, it gave me more time to read my Bible, to devote to the work of the Lord… What did you say?"

"She's alive."

He was silent for such a long time that Teri was afraid he had hung up.

"Dr. Houseman?"

"She's alive? She's really alive?"

"She's living here on Grand Manan Island."

"And she's okay?"

"Aside from a wrist which might need some work, she seems in perfect health."

His voice was a whisper. "I'm glad I hired you, Teri. I'm glad God led me to hire you. If I had wanted closure, to get over my grief, I would've gone to a counselor. But all along I wanted to find a living, breathing person. Thank you so much. I will pay you well."

"That's not important to me."

"Yes. Old habits die hard. Not everything can be rewarded with money. I've a lot to learn. I was so caught up in it for a while there."

He wanted to know all about her, every detail, and so Teri told him how she survived the wreck. It wasn't pirates. It wasn't terrorists. The boat had hit an unmarked underwater hazard known locally as Old Maid Rock and had sunk instantly. Teri also told him about Audrey and about Garda and Jerome. And she told him about Marnie, who had almost been murdered, and about the arrest of Will Stanton.

His last words were, "I'm coming. I'm coming up there."

49

Ellen was writing in her book, writing very fast this time. She had this keen sense that she needed to finish her story, not leave anything out, and that there wasn't much time. It was a kindness that Will hadn't come by lately. Maybe he really had gone to the mainland this time. Still, every time she heard a sound, she'd run to the window, look out, make sure she was alone. But it would only be the snow melting off the roof, falling onto the path she had shoveled.

She was writing about Brent. She hadn't written a lot about Brent, and she should have. It was, after all, Brent's story. The whole thing was Brent's story.

The reason I kept my silence was because of you, Brent. It's because of you that I cannot be forgiven. You are the constant reminder of my treachery, my betrayal.

She paused in her writing.

But instead of hating you, I grew to love you more. My love for you would choke me at times. Do you remember those Friday nights when you were little and we would play Sorry? I watched your hands, the way you moved them, your dark hair, so thick it was, and I would think, you are a beautiful child. There is a sensitivity in you. I would watch you and pray for you, then, that God would protect you, and what I really meant to ask was that God would protect you from the truth. That the man you thought was your father was not really your father.

He loves you, though. I know this. I would watch him

look at you, see the pain in his eyes when he thought no one saw. Pain, because he spent so little time with you.

Your real father never knew you, Brent. I never told him about you. Again, a treachery on my part, because he missed knowing such a good, gentle, and fine person as you. He was a good man, a pharmacist, a scientist, smart in math, which is probably where you get your love of things technical, and the way you love to figure things out.

You have a half-brother and two half-sisters living in Coffins Reach near your Aunt Jane, who really is your aunt after all. And I think she knew that all along, too. Although we never spoke of it. Not once. (I have seen a picture of your younger brother Jamey. You look very much alike.)

And what will happen now? I have no idea. But since the detective was here last week, and told me she knew who I was, things have been strangely silent. Will has been gone. No one's been here, not the police, not anyone. (I half expect the police to show up at any second.) But nothing has happened.

But I'm not foolish enough to think that nothing will happen. Something will. I had vowed that I would keep this secret to my grave, but did I expect that would happen? Old secrets have a way of working themselves loose, like bones making their way to the surface. I always thought it would come by way of a medical emergency where you would need a certain kind of blood, or a transplant—something like that. I don't know of these things, but these are the things I always feared. My own mother knew about you. She urged me to tell Carl, to tell your father, but I couldn't. I couldn't...

She heard a noise, a clomping of boots, and fear took hold of her again. Audrey heard it and went to the door, opened it, and let him in.

Will?

But it was Carl who stood there. Carl wearing a heavy jacket and with snow on his head. He stood there. And so did she. No words passed between them. Her pen dropped to the table, the pages of her book fluttered closed.

How many times had she dreamed of this? Him coming for her? How she would rush into his arms, how he would say that everything was all right. There is such a thing as repentance. As redemption. There is such a thing as a second chance.

But here they were, staring at each other. With Audrey between.

Five years had deepened the lines at the edges of his eyes. In five years his hair had gone completely gray. He seemed heavier around the jowls somehow, but no less handsome. And still he stood there.

And then he said one word. "Ellen."

She stood, awkwardly, hands trembling at her side. But when he held out his arms, she went to him, and they held each other for a long time, both of them crying, all of her dreams not matching the reality of being close to this man again. She could feel his hands through her hair, stroking out the tangles, the familiar feel of them against her head, the smell of him, unchanged in five years.

They were standing like this as another person looked on—a young man with a gun, heavy in his pocket, who had followed his father down the path and to this house.

He had seen his father earlier in the Coffee Perk. He was waiting for Tracie to get off work when he looked up and there he was. His father. His father! Brent turned his face to the wall, but listened to him. The cashier, someone named Shannon, was telling him how to get to Marnie's Bed-and-Breakfast. But he was asking about the witch woman who lives in the little lighthouse. After persuading Shannon that he really did want to do some hiking there, she told him how to get to that path and where to park.

Yesterday Tracie had told Brent that the news all over was that some guy named Will, who was somehow connected to the witch woman, had been arrested. She didn't know why. No one knew why yet. That wasn't in the news.

And now his father was here.

Two days ago he had figured out that the mountain woman had killed his mother. But maybe it was that man Will who had killed her. He was trying to find out, trying to get Tracie to tell him what she knew, when in had walked his father. His father had not seen him, and he turned his back to the man.

Now he was staring in through the window of the cottage where his father and the mountain woman were in an embrace. The sight confused him, but he could not stop looking, could not move his eyes away. And when the woman turned in profile, he gasped, a guttural sound, and backed away. He felt as if he would throw up. But he could not stop staring.

The girl saw him and pointed. He needed to be gone or she would start screaming. He needed to be away from here. To figure things out. Nothing was the way he had thought. His mother alive after all this time? But isn't that what he had known all along?

He turned, then, and lurched out of the woods, running down the path to his van.

50

It took Jack and Teri a half hour to drive here, following a little hand-drawn map on the back of a check stub.

"It's a surprise," was all he had told her.

"What kind of a surprise?"

"A surprise. Just something I want your opinion on."

"You want my opinion on a surprise?"

"Don't get all detectivish with me; just wait until we get there."

At the end of a series of gravel roads, he stopped the car and they got out. They were standing in a bit of Maine woods, fir trees and rocks, the Penobscot River down below.

"Well, here we are."

"Here we are, what?"

"This land. And of course, I haven't signed any papers. I wanted your opinion on it. I've been thinking that you and I really need to start somewhere new. This piece of property we're standing on? A colleague of mine has owned this forever and wants to get rid of it. I'm sure we could get a really good price for the house, plus we wouldn't need to build anything quite so massive as that. I've been talking to a builder. They say if they start now, they could have this whole thing finished this summer. But I wanted to see it. So, what do you think?"

"So, you want to build a house here?"

He nodded.

"For us?"

He nodded, frowning now. "If you don't like it, Teri, we don't have to do this. I haven't signed any papers or anything. It was just talk. I'm sorry if I did this without consulting—"

Teri threw her arms around Jack's neck. "I love it!"

"You love it?"

"I do. It's beautiful here. Maybe we could build a log house and there would be plenty of places for the animals. And the river's so pretty."

Arms around each other, they walked around it then, down to the river, around a little copse of trees, and by the time they got back to their car, they were already calling it, "our property."

"I was also thinking," Jack said on the way home, "that if we move to this distance, we'd have to look for a different church. You know, one a little closer. It would be only natural."

She looked sideways at him and grinned. He took her hand.

Since winding up the case and arriving home from Grand Manan a month ago, Teri had done little more than go for long walks with Kelly and try to avoid the media. She had kept in touch with Ellen and Carl, who were trying to put their life and marriage back together. It would take some time. They were also trying to reconnect with Brent, who they discovered had been on Grand Manan Island. It was going to be a long road, but they'd already made some progress. They were looking at purchasing a home beside the water near Eastport, Maine.

Teri had also started an e-mail correspondence with Daisy, who was trying, as she said, to keep a low profile while she attempted to get her life back together.

"Why don't you put this all in a book?' Teri asked her over the phone once.

"Honey, I don't need the grief."

The spin doctors were alive and well at Houseman Ministries, which had recently changed its name to Family Home Ministry, or something like that. Teri didn't remember. Paul Pellerman was trying to keep the ministry on its feet, but people were leaving in droves. Every so often Teri wondered if Welcomer Helen, Usher Milt, and Matt Brodwizen were still there, and what they thought of all the publicity that now surrounded the church. *Christianity Today* reported that Carl Houseman Jr. and his family had moved to

Colorado Springs. Carl would be taking over the youth ministry position his brother Sam had recently vacated so he could manage his wife's pop music career.

The police opened up the Jimmy Jarvis case again, but no new evidence had come to light, and so it looked as though the Ryders and the Pellermans were in the clear. But as Jack was fond of saying, "They will not go unpunished, not in the long run."

A lot of things became clear to Teri then, including the reason Ellen never talked in her interviews about Maine or sailing. She didn't want anyone to find out about Jimmy. She wanted to protect her son.

The most surprising visit she had was from a kindly old gentleman named Harold Meeker. It was her second day home, and she was sitting on the couch with Kelly when the doorbell rang. On the front porch stood a white-haired man wearing a hat and black greatcoat. When she said, "Can I help you?" he took off his hat and bowed his head stiffly. He wished to talk to her about Marnie Doane, he said.

She looked at him in surprise. "She's not here. She doesn't live here."

"Oh," and he chuckled, a deep chesty sound. "I know that. I know where she lives, but I wanted to pay you a visit before I was on my way. You're the detective. I feel that what happened to her is my fault. I am eminently to blame."

Teri looked at him. "I'm sorry?"

"You're confused. My fault." He put out his hand. "Harold Meeker. I was to meet Marnie a day before she was almost killed. If I had been there, this awful thing wouldn't have happened to her. But I was unfortunately delayed by a rail ticket that didn't correspond with the bus ticket I had purchased. I had to stay overnight in Springfield."

She was still confused.

"I don't fly, you see. Life would be so much easier if I flew."

"You're the…ah, the boyfriend?"

"Boyfriend seems an odd title for someone my age, don't you agree?"

She couldn't help but smile.

"I have a few hours here in Bangor before I catch my limousine ride to Grand Manan Island. I told my driver to come here. I don't drive either, you see."

So she made tea, and they chatted about Marnie and the island and Marnie's cooking or lack of it, and of course, about how the two of them met. Which was on the Internet, of course. He was a romance writer, and Marnie one of his biggest fans. He wrote under the name Johanna Hawthorne.

"Surprising, isn't it?" he said wiggling his nose.

The doorbell rang. It was his limousine.

"Good day, Teri," he said, tipping his hat. "Thank you for being there for my Marnie."

Discussion Guide

1. When have you felt you wanted to "steal away," to leave your present life and run away?
2. What were the circumstances?
3. What did you do? Did you run? If you ran, where did you go? If you stayed, what did you do instead?
4. Did you feel that God met you at this time? Explain why or why not.
5. Which character in *Steal Away* could you most identify with? Which character could you least identify with? Why or why not?
6. Teri felt condemnation from her new church. Have you ever felt this? Would you have responded as Teri did? What did you do when you felt condemned?
7. *Steal Away* is about choices. Ellen made a wrong choice and lived a lie for more than twenty years. Have you ever had to "live a lie"? What did this do to you as a person?
8. *Steal Away* is about wrong choices, but it is also about forgiveness. If you were Carl, would you have forgiven Ellen? Describe a time when you had trouble forgiving someone for something very hard. At what point did you, like Carl, find peace? If you have not yet forgiven and found peace, why not?
9. Matthew 6:14–15 says that if we don't forgive others' sins against us, God will not forgive us our sins. What does this mean to you? Who does forgiveness benefit, the one being forgiven or the one doing the forgiving? Explain.

10. Second Corinthians 1:3–4 says, "Praise be to the God and Father of our Lord Jesus Christ, the Father of compassion and the God of all comfort, who comforts us in all our troubles, so that we can comfort those in any trouble with the comfort we ourselves have received from God." When have you found that because you have been comforted in an area of crisis, you have been better able to comfort someone else?
11. Compare *Steal Away* to two recent Hollywood movies, *Fatal Attraction* and *Unfaithful*. How is *Steal Away* the same? What makes it different?
12. What situation or scene in *Steal Away* do you most identify with? What do you think God is trying to tell you through this story?

A MYSTERIOUS DISAPPEARANCE...
A FAMILY IN TUMULT...
VOLATILE SURROUNDINGS...
CAN ONE WOMAN CONNECT THE PIECES IN TIME?

When nine-year-old Ally Buckley turns up missing, fear spreads throughout the New England fishing village where Sadie and her family live and worship. But when Sadie discovers one of Ally's drawings among her husband's possessions, she suspects danger may be closer to home than she had ever known.

ISBN 1-57673-659-8

DISCOVER THE SECRET OF THE SEASHORE

While investigating a long-unsolved murder, mystery writer Sharon Colebrook and her husband, Jeff, find unexpected secrets, startling revelations, and dangerous truth within their own family tree.

ISBN 1-57673-614-8

MYSTERY AND INTRIGUE IN THE ISLANDS...

Naomi and Zoe are distraught as police begin an extensive investigation of a friend's death. In a different state, Margot begins her own investigation. What she discovers shatters her to the core and intertwines the lives of the island-dwellers as they seek to make peace with themselves, each other, and God.

ISBN 1-57673-397-1

He grinned some more. "Ellen was Ellen. Always a bit quieter than most, but we loved her."

"Do you think she had something on her mind before she left on that last sailing trip?"

Peg said rather quickly, "I suggested it might be Brent. You know how worried we all were about him."

"It could've been Brent. It could well have been Brent."

Teri said, "I understand he was working here at the time? For his father?"

"For the ministry, yes," Paul said.

"What was there to be concerned about if he was working in the church?"

"Brent was very much his own person," Peg said. "I wasn't altogether sure that he was ministry team material. Paul tried to counsel him that he might be better off at the community college."

"And did Carl and Ellen know about your career counseling for their son?"

"No," Peg said. "I thought it best not. Both of them had a blind spot when it came to Brent. Being their last child, he may have been a bit spoiled. Carl was away a lot on ministry business, and so Ellen doted on Brent, and then when Carl came home, he doted on the boy as well. I could see the signs. He didn't have a lot of discipline."

"I think you're overstating it a bit," Paul said. He had removed his jacket and hung it on the back of a kitchen chair. "She's asking about Ellen's state of mind, not about Brent."

"I'm just thinking that this might be it, Paul."

"And there would've been nothing else on her mind? Just Brent?"

Peg flashed Paul a look and then said, "I knew Ellen better than probably anyone. We told each other everything. Yes, that was the only thing."